Here's what critics are saying about *Mayhem in High Heels:*

"I love how Gemma Halliday intertwines laughter and romance with grit, suspense, and murder. Her characters have incredible depth, which makes you feel like you know them on a personal level. Her story, *MAYHEM IN HIGH HEELS*, sparkles with charm unlike any other murder mystery."
—Romance Junkies

"Funny and appealing, Halliday's hapless detective is a pleasure to watch as she somehow manages to solve another mystery."
—Booklist

"Do not wait—rush right out and get *MAYHEM IN HIGH HEELS* and join Maddie and her gang for a thrilling mystery adventure!"
—Romance Reviews Today

BOOKS BY GEMMA HALLIDAY

High Heels Mysteries:
Spying in High Heels
Killer in High Heels
Undercover in High
Heels
Christmas in High
Heels (short story)
Alibi in High Heels
Mayhem in High Heels
Honeymoon in High
Heels (novella)
Sweetheart in High
Heels (short story)
Fearless in High Heels
Danger in High Heels
Homicide in High
Heels
Deadly in High Heels
(coming Feb 2015)

*Hollywood Headlines
Mysteries:*
Hollywood Scandals
Hollywood Secrets
Hollywood Confessions
Twelve's Drummer
Dying (short story)

Jamie Bond Mysteries
Unbreakable Bond
Secret Bond
Bond Bombshell (short
story)
Lethal Bond

Tahoe Tessie Mysteries
Luck Be A Lady

Young Adult Books
Deadly Cool
Social Suicide

Other Works
Play Nice
Viva Las Vegas
A High Heels Haunting
(novella)
Watching You (short
story)
Confessions of a
Bombshell Bandit
(short story)

MAYHEM IN HIGH HEELS

a High Heels mystery

GEMMA HALLIDAY

For my personal dream team, without whom this book would
not have happened—my lovely agent,
Nephele Tempest; my
amazingly talented critique partner, Eden
Bradley; and my
incomparable editor, Leah Hultenschmidt.
You ladies rock!

CHAPTER ONE

———

There's just something about weddings. Something about tulle and lace being spun into fairy tales. Something about friends and family gathering to welcome a new member. Something about gaudy bridesmaid dresses, embossed invitations, and five dozen lilies in strategically placed crystal vases that make grown women turn into squealy second-graders, men have nightmares of chains wrapped around their ankles, and mothers get misty-eyed at the slightest provocation.

"Mom, you're crying again," I said, pulling a tissue from my purse and handing it to my mother, lest her caked-on black mascara streak down her cheeks for the third time in as many minutes.

"I can't help it, Maddie. They're all just so beautiful."

I looked down at the array of place cards on the slick, black conference table at L'Amore Wedding Planners.

"They're place cards."

Mom nodded, her eyes shining. "I know. Aren't they lovely?"

I looked down again, chewing on a piece of Doublemint as I narrowed my eyes at the squares of paper. Personally, I was having a hard time telling the difference between the white, linen, embossed cards and the snow, woven, stamped cards.

"They are…nice."

"Oh, Maddie, they're breathtaking!" Mom squeaked out, holding the tissue to her face.

"Honestly, I don't know that we even need place cards, Mom. Jack and I want to keep things small. Intimate."

"And what's more intimate than hand-stamped place cards at each guest's spot?" asked Gigi Van Doren, the proprietor of L'Amore and grand dame of all things wedding. Her pen hovered just above her ever-present clipboard, eagerly awaiting the go-ahead to order several dozen.

I put Gigi anywhere from her early forties to late fifties—one of those women who seemed to defy time and age altogether. Pale blonde hair pulled back from her face in an artful French twist, cool blue eyes steady beneath a pair of rimless glasses, tailored suit fitting a body that spoke of regular pilgrimages to the gym. Or the plastic surgeon. But what had endeared me to her right from the first were the pointy toed, four-inch, black leather pumps on her feet. Prada. The woman knew style.

Still…

"What do you think, Dana?" I asked my best friend.

Dana pinched her strawberry blonde brows together, staring at the array as if she were taking a calculus test. "They *are* nice. Can I see the ivory-edged ones again?"

"But of course." Gigi signaled to her assistant, Allie, a blonde, blue-eyed twenty-something, who produced another indistinguishably whitish square of paper from her case, sliding it across the table.

Dana picked it up and let out a wistful sigh. "Oh, these are so romantic." She held the square up to the light, gazing at it like it might turn into Prince Charming on the spot.

"That one's my faveorite," Allie agreed.

"We can watermark it with anything you like—the date, hearts, even your photograph. Very intimate," Gigi assured me.

Hmmm.

"Exactly how much are these intimate water-marked cards going to cost?" I asked, narrowing my eyes at Gigi as I snapped my gum between my teeth.

She shrugged. "Inconsequential. Hardly anything. Besides, how can you put a price on a beautiful occasion like your wedding day?"

"She's right, Maddie," Mom chimed in, dabbing at her eyes. "It's your wedding day. You can't put a price on that."

Maybe I couldn't. But I was pretty sure my groom would have something to say about it.

Six months ago Jack Ramirez, L.A.P.D. detective and the last person in the world I expected to believe in happily ever after, proposed to me atop the Eiffel Tower in Paris. It was the single most romantic thing that had ever happened to me. Or, I ventured to guess, anyone outside of a Meg Ryan movie. He'd picked out the most gorgeous ring on the planet, and, once I'd given him my tearful "yes," we'd spent three days of bliss in Paris, wrapped up in each other's arms, floating down the Seine, feeding each other chocolate éclairs, holding hands under the most romantic sunsets in the world.

But, like all good Meg Ryan movies, it had to come to an end sometime. Once we'd gotten home the reality of being engaged had started to sink in.

Ramirez works homicide, carries a very big gun, has a very big tattoo, and a very big…well, let's just say I'm *really* looking forward to the honeymoon. He's not your typical family man, and the whole commitment thing is a new gig for him. For that matter, it was a pretty foreign concept for me, too. So far the biggest commitment I'd jumped into was a ficus tree. And that was plastic.

But when I'd shown my newly adorned left ring finger to Mom and Faux Dad, as I affectionately called my stepfather, reality didn't so much sink in as hit me like a cheap pair of loafers to the gut. Saying the word "wedding" to my mother was like saying "Häagen-Dazs" to a Weight Watcher. She was foaming at the mouth within seconds, planning a ceremony to top all ceremonies, appropriately scheduled for this coming Valentine's Day. Suddenly the romantic moments Ramirez and I had stolen in Paris were turned into a whirlwind of reception halls, bridesmaid dresses, honeymoon packages to Tahiti, gardens versus churches, lilies versus roses, prime rib versus Chicken Kiev. And currently, white, snow, or ivory watermarked place cards.

"I don't know…" I hedged, looking down again at the squares. "Exactly what is the dollar amount of inconsequential?"

Gigi shot me an annoyed look, her mouth puckering up like she was sucking on a lemon drop. "Well, that all depends on how many people are coming."

"Just friends and close family," I said. Then repeated my wedding mantra, "Small and intimate."

"Right," Mom agreed, bobbing her coiffed hair up and down. "Just four hundred."

I swallowed my gum with a hiccup. "Four hundred? As in people?"

Mom gave me a blank stare. Then nodded. "Didn't you look at the guest list? I emailed the final version to you last night."

I shook my head. "I didn't have time to print it out before I left. But I didn't realize it went on for fifty pages. What happened to small and intimate?"

Mom blinked her heavily lined eyes at me. "Honey, I did the best I could to pare it down."

"We can easily accommodate four hundred," Gigi told me, her annoyance being replaced by what I could only interpret as glee.

"Exactly, that's why we chose an outdoor venue. The Beverly Garden Hotel said they could seat four-fifty, so I figured we were fine." Mom gave me an innocent look that I didn't buy for a minute.

"Wait." I held up a hand. "Hold the phone. I don't even know four hundred people."

"Yes, you do. Honey, don't you want people to come to your wedding?"

"People, yes. Strangers, no."

"These are not strangers."

"Four hundred, Mom? I have four hundred close friends and family?"

"Oh, honey, we simply couldn't leave anyone out."

Was I not enunciating clearly enough? "Smaaall. In-ti-mate."

Mom cocked her head to the side. "But, honey, it's your *wedding*. It's your special day."

I clenched down so hard I bit my tongue. "Yes, my wedding *day*. One day. There is no way I can feel good about spending a mint on one day. It can be special without declaring bankruptcy over it."

Dana's eyes ping-ponged back and forth between us. Mom puckered her forehead. Gigi narrowed her eyes at me like I'd just spoken blasphemy.

"Well," Mom hedged, "not everyone has RSVPed yet…" She reached into her gargantuan purse and pulled out a leather-bound book, laying it out on the conference table.

"What's that?" I asked.

"The guest list."

I took a deep meditative breath. Then opened the book and started scanning names.

"Who is Amber White?"

"Oh, honey," Mom said, smacking my arm. "You remember Amber. She's that woman who did your hair that time for the recital."

"Recital?"

"You know, when you were Little Red Riding Hood?"

I blinked at her. "Mom, I was six."

"And you looked adorable."

"You did not invite a woman I haven't seen since I was six to my wedding." I hiccupped again, that gum lodging in my throat.

"Well, she took such an interest in you."

"Mom!"

She pursed her lips, an argument on the tip of her tongue. But, lucky for me, she bit it back. "Okay. Fine. Amber's out."

"Thank you." Now we were getting somewhere. "What about her?" I asked, stabbing my finger at a name halfway down the page.

"Dolly Schlottskowitz?"

"Yeah. Who is she?"

"Oh, surely you remember Dolly Schlottskowitz? You know, Megan Schlottskowitz's mom?"

"Seriously? Megan the cheerleader from high school? Mom, I haven't seen her in ten years. And we weren't even friends then!" I grabbed Gigi's pen and crossed Mrs. Schlottskowitz's name off the list.

"I remember Megan," Dana piped up. "I heard she got really fat after high school."

I raised an eyebrow. "Really?"

Dana nodded, her blonde shag bouncing up and down. "Oh, yeah. I ran into Karen Olsen at Starbucks one day, and she said she saw Megan going into the Lane Bryant at the Burbank mall. And," she said, leaning in with a pseudo whisper, "she's been divorced." Dana held up two fingers. "Twice."

"Reeeeally?" I said, drawing out the word. I put Mrs. Schlottskowitz back on. So I wanted to show off for the former cheerleader. So sue me.

"This looks like it may take some time," Gigi said, eyeing the list. She glanced down at the gold watch adorning her slim wrist.

"Why don't we adjourn for now? You can get back to me with a headcount tomorrow when we do the final cake tasting at…" Gigi looked to Allie who whipped out an electronic organizer thingie, quickly consulting it.

"One," she said.

"One," Gigi repeated. "Sound good?"

Mom clapped her hands together. "Perfect. Maddie, we'll go over it this afternoon, yes?"

I nodded reluctantly. I'd hoped to meet Ramirez for lunch, but unless I wanted my mom's neighbor's second cousin's milkman attending my *special* day, it looked like an afternoon with The List was in order.

"But let's at least decide on the place card design," Mom insisted.

I sighed. "Do we really need them?" I looked to Dana for help.

She shrugged. "They *are* nice, Maddie."

Three against one. I didn't stand a chance. "Okay, fine. Let's do the ivory linen one."

Mom clapped her hands with delight. Gigi's eyes lit up with that dollar sign look again.

I sincerely hoped Ramirez didn't mind working overtime.

* * *

Five hours—and a mere thirty-five pages worth of people I barely knew—later, I pulled my little red Jeep up to my studio apartment in Santa Monica. Just blocks from the ocean and sandwiched in between rows of eclectic buildings that conformed to L.A.'s hodge-podge school of architecture, it was my little slice of heaven. *Little* being the operative word here. A fold-out futon and a sketch table, and I was at max capacity. Which is why Ramirez and I had decided that I would move into his place after the wedding. Unlike me, he had an actual house. With an actual bedroom. And closets. Oh man, did he have closets. Little did he know they'd all soon be filled with shoes.

But I had to admit, a part of me was going to miss my little studio. It might be small, but it was cozy, quaint, and I'd come to love it.

I fit my key into the lock and shoved the door open.

"Hey, honey, I'm home," Ramirez said, grinning at me as he flipped channels on my TV.

I couldn't help it. My hormones did that little happy "squee!" they always did when I saw him. He had that tall, dark, and handsome thing down to a science, his broad shoulders tapering to a compact frame. Black hair, just a little too long, curled around his ears. Dark eyes, a square jaw, and a paper-thin white scar cutting through his left eyebrow all gave him a slightly dangerous air that made women swoon and men lock up their daughters.

Luckily, my father lived two hundred miles away.

"What are you doing here?" I asked, dropping my purse on the kitchen counter and leaning in for a hello kiss.

"Mmmm…hello," he murmured against my lips, wrapping both arms around me.

I swear it was almost enough to make my afternoon with The List melt away.

"My cable was out," he said, when we finally came up for air. "Thought I'd come watch the game here. I ordered pizza, too. Should be here any minute."

"Pepperoni?"

He grinned. "With extra cheese."

The man was a god.

"So, how was your day?" he asked, settling himself on the futon as tall guys in expensive sneakers filled the TV screen.

"Ugh!" I plopped down next to him. "Don't ask. Did you know that my fourth-grade teacher is coming to our wedding?"

"Okay. Cool."

"No, not cool. I haven't seen her since I was ten! And then there's my uncle Charlie's first wife who lives in Belize, my grandmother's third cousin from Oklahoma, and the guy who sold Mom her minivan!"

Ramirez raised an eyebrow at me. "Sounds like a lot of people."

"Four hundred."

"Damn. What happened to small and intimate?"

"That's what I'd like to know," I mumbled, grabbing for the remote as a Budweiser commercial flickered across the screen. "And we're getting ivory linen place cards."

"I'm watching that."

I flipped to the news, checking the weather for tomorrow. I had this new pair of suede boots I was dying to wear, but not if there was even the slightest chance of rain. "Just a sec."

"Darlin', if I miss tip-off, I'm gonna cry."

I gave him a playful smack. But gave in, flipping back once I saw we were all sunshine for the next week. Gotta love L.A.

"So," I said, relinquishing the remote and leaning my head against Ramirez's chest, "we're doing the final cake tasting tomorrow. One o'clock."

Ramirez threw an arm around me. "We?"

"As in, you and me."

A groan rumbled beneath my ear.

"What?"

"Didn't we already pick a cake months ago?"

"Yes, but this is the final sampling to make sure everything if perfect."

Another groan. "Do I really have to be there?"

I felt a frown settle between my brows. "You should *want* to be there."

He leaned back, narrowing his eyes at me. "What exactly does that mean?"

"It means, this is our wedding."

"I know. I'm just not a real wedding-y kind of guy. Can't you just taste it?"

"Alone? Come on, don't you want to have a say in the cake? Don't you want to have any input into the most memorable day of our lives? Don't you care what color the flowers are or what kind of place cards we have?"

He cocked his head to the side. "Is this a trick question?"

I threw my hands up. "This is *our* wedding, Jack. Not just mine. I want it to be special for you, too."

"And I'm sure the flavor of cake will make all the difference."

"Now you're just being sarcastic, aren't you?"

"A little."

I crossed my arms over my chest. "Not the way to win points, pal."

He sighed. A big, full bodied thing that said he was wondering if he shouldn't have just stayed at home and listened to the game on the radio instead.

"Okay, if it will make you happy, I'll go sample cake tomorrow."

"Really?"

"Really."

"Thank you. I'll pick you up at 12:30. But—" I held up one finger. "—you're not doing it to make me happy. You're doing it because you want to. Right?"

He shook his head at me, a hint of a smile playing at his lips. "Sure. I want to spend my afternoon stuffing my face with buttercream icing."

The sarcasm was thicker than my mom's mascara, but I decided to let it go, instead nestling back into the crook of his arm.

"So…" Ramirez's fingers began kneading the nape of my neck. "If we're previewing the cake, does that mean we get to preview other things, too?"

I leaned my head back and met a pair of dark eyes, simmering with that bad boy look that had me smitten from the start.

"What did you have in mind?" I asked, as his fingers kneaded lower, slipping inside my blouse and toying with my bra strap.

"The honeymoon."

I grinned, going instantly warm in all the right places.

"What about the game?" I asked, gesturing to the TV.

A wicked smile slid across his face, his lips leaning in toward mine as his eyes went from hunger to pure lust.

"What game?"

CHAPTER TWO

———

I took one step up, my thighs burning in protest, my breath coming out in short, quick puffs. Then I stepped back down. Then back up again as sweat trailed in unattractive beads down the sides of my face.

"That's it, you're doing great!" Dana shouted from the front of the room. Twenty-odd stepping, sweating, groaning people (including yours truly) filled the studio, following her lead, marching to her every command like a bunch of boot-campers. Of course, Dana's was the only sweat-free forehead. Not even a ladylike glisten, every hair on her pretty blonde head in place, her cute little red work-out tank (and I do mean *little*—Dana subscribes to the 'less is more' school of fashion), not the slightest bit damp under the arms even though my actress-slash-aerobics instructor best friend had been leading the Step and Burn class for the last forty-five minutes. Me—I was sweating and grunting like a linebacker as I went up, then back down the two bright orange plastic steps in front of me.

"Three more to go. You can do it!"

I glared at my cheerleader-esque friend. I'd swear that's what she said three step routines ago.

I did the up and down thing again, my Nikes squeaking on the freshly polished gym floor as I tried (in vain) to keep up.

I'm not exactly what you'd call a health nut. I'm more of a chocolate toffee-covered-macadamia nut. On top of a mound of ice cream. Served with a brownie. While Dana was the reigning Aerobics Queen of the West Side, the only times I ever actually used my membership to the Sunset Gym were on those ninety-plus-degree days of summer when the lure of the two Olympic-sized swimming pools won out over my inherent aversion to physical activity. And even then I mostly doggy paddled.

Not that I wasn't figure conscious. In fact, at one point in my life I'd had visions of being a sleek, svelte runway model, strutting the catwalks of Milan and Paris in the most haute of couture creations. However, when my last adolescent growth spurt topped me out at 5'1 ½", those dreams faded faster than a pair of acid-washed jeans. Instead, I'd turned my passion for fashion to design. Specifically, designing shoes. After a rocky start in the business, I was finally starting to come into my own. Okay, so I wasn't Michael Kors. But, I did have my very own line being stocked in chic boutiques throughout Beverly and the West Side. And, there was even a rumor that a certain unnamed mega-actress might be considering wearing a Maddie Springer original to the Oscars this year. (Okay, it's Angelina Jolie. How cool is that, huh?!)

So, while I was about as fashion forward as a girl could hope to be, I generally left the whole kill-yourself-at-the-gym thing to

Dana. My philosophy: if the heels are high enough, everyone looks like they have runner's calves, right?

But with the Big Day looming in the not too distant future, Dana had worn me down. Especially when she'd accompanied me to the last dress fitting, where my heavenly white satin corset number had clung a little more "snugly" to my hips than I might have liked. (Read: squished into the dress until I looked like pale pork sausage.) While the willowy stick-figure fitter had assured me she could make a few "adjustments" to the dress, Dana's idea of making a few trips to the gym instead had sounded like a better plan. That, of course, was before I was sweating like a hog in heat and stepping endlessly to nowhere.

"That's it! Now turn to your right!"

I turned, almost colliding with a guy in short-shorts and a headband a la Richard Simmons. "Sorry," I mumbled between gasps.

"Now throw those hands up! Whoo! You're doing great!" Dana demonstrated, shooting both hands into the air and shaking them like she was at a holy revival meeting. "That's it. Feel that burn! Isn't it great?"

I could think of a few other adjectives to describe it. I raised my hands almost to head level, wincing in pain as muscles I didn't know I owned protested. I glanced up at the clock. Ten more minutes. If I survived that long, I was so rewarding myself with a mocha frappuccino when this was all over. With lots of whipped cream. I was pretty sure I was burning off a gazillion calories. I swiped an arm across my brow. Hell, with sweat alone, I'd probably lost three pounds.

"And, one more time. Let's really sprint now. Double time!" If she wasn't my best friend, I might have killed her. Dana flashed her perkiest smile, bobbing up and down like an energizer bunny on wheat grass-laced speed as she quickstepped up and down her orange stairs.

I tried to keep up, willing my feet to move as fast as they could. Up, down, left, right. I was almost in a rhythm when I slipped (probably on a drop of my own perspiration) and tipped to the right, knocking into Richard Simmons. Who was midstep and was thrown so off balance his arms flailed wildly in the air, swatting a woman in purple stretch pants in the face. Stretch Pants let out a yelp louder than a Lakers fan watching a free throw.

"That's it! Let it out. Wooo!" Dana encouraged.

I rolled my eyes, mumbling apologies to Richard Simmons as I scooted my stairs to the back of the room and ducked out the door. One midstep collision a day was enough for me.

* * *

After ten minutes in the sauna and a long, hot shower, I was beginning to feel human again. I was just stepping out of the shower, towel drying my hair in the ladies' locker room, when my cell chirped to life, displaying Ramirez's number. I flipped it open.

"Hey, you," I said.

"Hey. Listen, I've got a ton of stuff to do today."

I narrowed my eyes at the phone. "Stuff?"

"Yeah. I had to hit the shooting range this morning, and a buddy of mine called and asked if I'd help him paint his rec room."

"Paint a rec room?"

"Yeah." I heard traffic sounds in the background, cars honking and the tell-tale rumble of eighteen-wheelers.

"Where are you right now?" I asked, frowning into the phone.

"I'm on the 60. Running that guestbook for the reception out to my mom's."

I looked up at the utilitarian clock hanging on the tiled wall. 12:15. Uh-oh.

"You better not be trying to bail on me, mister."

There was a short pause. Then, "Wouldn't dream of it."

"Hmmm." I made a noncommittal sound in the back of my throat.

"But, I am running a few minutes late," he said. "Why don't we just meet at the studio?"

"You are going to show up, right?"

"Of course!"

Only the way his voice rose half an octave didn't reassure me any. "Jack…"

"I'll be there. I promise. I'm looking forward to it. I want to be involved in our wedding, and I can't wait to sample the cake."

"You're so full of shit."

"Yeah, I know. But I'm showing up anyway. See you at one."

And with that, he disconnected.

I stared down at the phone, still feeling my forehead do a Botox-worthy wrinkle between my brows.

As much as I got Ramirez's whole guy-aversion to white lace and buttercream, it left me with a distinctly unsettled feeling somewhere in the pit of my stomach. I know, I know, it's normal, right? I mean, he's a guy, and a cop guy at that. Weddings are about as girly as things come. But the fact that I had to nearly twist his arm into a pretzel to get him to even taste cake (Seriously, it's cake. How bad did he think it would be?) made a small part of me worry that maybe the aversion wasn't solely wedding related. That maybe it carried over into being married related. I mean, he *had* proposed kind of suddenly. It wasn't like we'd ever discussed marriage; we'd just sort of jumped into it. Headfirst. In the shallow end. And I wondered if maybe now that the rosy glow of Paris and stolen café au lait-flavored kisses had turned into the reality of mile-long guest lists, meeting wedding planners, and running a guestbook out to his mother's in midday traffic, maybe he was regretting that leap.

"Hey, got time for lunch?" Dana asked, jogging into the locker room, still fresh faced as ever.

I'm woman enough to admit it. I hated her just a tiny bit.

"I do now." I shoved my phone back into my purse, trying to shove doubts about Ramirez and wedding bells to the back of my mind.

"Great. I've got a reading at one for that new DreamWorks cartoon, but I'm free till then. And there's this new vegan café down the street I've been dying to try. They've got a whole menu full of negative-calorie foods."

I threw on a black sweater tank and pair of dark denim jeans, visions of my mocha frappuccino fading like a mirage. "Negative-calorie foods?"

"Ohmigod, they're so cool. Like, they contain less calories than your body uses to digest them. You can eat them all day and actually be losing weight."

Hey, that didn't sound so bad. "Are cheese doodles by any chance negative calorie?"

Dana scrunched her ski-jump nose at me. "Get real. Anyway, what do you say? You game for vegan today? My treat?"

I thought about begging off, but, thanks to Ramirez's "running behind," it wasn't like I had anything better to do. And besides, who was I to turn down free food?

* * *

After making my way through a bowl full of lawn (Sure, Dana had *said* it was exotic sautéed greens, but it smelled like the grass in Griffith Park to me.), a cold purée of squash soup (Cold. Squash. Two words that should never be thrown together in the same recipe.), and a platter of seared kelp (I'm sorry, anything that washes up onto the beach is not considered food in my world.), I pulled up in front of L'Amore, tired, sore, and still hungry. I parked at the curb, feeding the meter a handful of quarters and scanned the street for Ramirez's black SUV. Not surprisingly, it was absent.

I narrowed my eyes, looking down at the readout on my cell. 1:03. He was late. I did a silent curse, swearing that if he didn't show, I was going to disconnect the cable through all of March Madness.

I contemplated going in alone, but facing Gigi minus backup was like going into a military zone with only a pop-gun for protection. I was liable to be assaulted with centerpieces, wedding singers, and four-foot ice sculptures of nuzzling swans before Ramirez even showed up.

If he showed up.

I tried to shake that disconcerting thought, instead leaning against my Jeep and letting the wisps of winter sun warm my face as I counted off the seconds, tapping one suede boot-clad foot anxiously against the pavement.

He'd show. I had faith. I mean, he had promised. I'd never known him to break a promise to me.

Well, except if his captain called.

Or if he was on an important case.

Or if some new homicide cropped up that needed his attention.

Okay, fine. He broke promises all the time. They were like fine china in a bullring to him. Sure, I knew he meant well, but following through was a lot harder in his world. Not that I totally blamed him. Before I came along, homicide was his life. He'd been lucky to remember to eat, let alone make time for a girlfriend. He was trying. I knew that. Deep down, I was sure Ramirez loved me and wanted to be with me.

It was the surface stuff that was still a little murky.

I looked down at my cell readout again. 1:11. He was officially very late.

As much as I tried to tell myself he'd show, panic starting flirting with my gut as the seconds ticked by. I let out a long sigh at the thought of braving iced rosettes, raspberry cream filling and matching bride and groom cake toppers alone. A sigh that ended in a loud hiccup.

And another.

I took a deep, calming breath…ending in a hiccup. Crap. I did another deep breath and held it, slowly counting to twenty before letting it out. Nothing. I did a sigh of relief.

Ending in a hiccup.

"Shit."

All right, fine. I tilted my head back, closed my eyes, held my nose, and sucked in my diaphragm as hard as I could. I stood like that until I felt my cheeks turning red and my ears start to pop. Then held it ten seconds longer.

"What are you doing?"

I opened my eyes and let out a long whoosh of air to find Ramirez standing in front of me, a look of amusement quirking one eyebrow north.

I bent over at the middle, sucking in long breaths. "Hiccups."

"Ah." Though his mouth twitched in a grin.

"What? How do you get rid of them?"

"Water."

"I'll remember that."

I straightened up, getting my breathing back to normal, and fixed my hair in the reflection from my passenger side window.

"You okay?" he asked.

"Dandy. You're late."

"Traffic."

"Uh-huh."

Ramirez spun me to face him, the grin taking over his whole face this time. "You didn't think I'd show, did you?"

"Of course I did!" I protested. Only it came out more like, "Of c-ourse I d-id," punctuated with two loud, yelping hiccups.

The grin broke, letting a chuckle flow out as Ramirez shook his head at me. "Come on," he said, steering me by the elbow toward L'Amore. "Let's get you that glass of water."

I would have protested, but the hiccups were too strong.

Instead, I followed Ramirez through the glass front doors of Gigi's studio, hearing the little bell chime above the door as we walked in.

"Hell-(hiccup)-o?" I called. The place was dark, the only light coming in from the two back windows as the sun struggled to maintain its precarious hold on the weather. All the overhead lights were switched off.

"Gigi?" I tried again, scanning the interior of the studio for any sign of her.

"Maybe she's late?" Ramirez suggested.

"Ha! Obviously you haven't met Gigi yet. Precision is her middle name."

Ramirez shrugged. Then nodded toward the conference room. "Maybe she's in there already?"

I followed his lead, crossing to the room.

But only got as far as the doorway.

That's where I froze, my boots suddenly encased in cement, refusing to move. I opened my mouth, but the only sound that came out was a sort of strangled cry in the back of my throat. I felt Ramirez's arm go around my waist. A good thing. Because, at the moment, my legs were doing their Jell-O imitation, threatening to crumple into a heap on the floor as I took in the scene before me.

Sitting at the sleek black conference table in the middle of the studio, surrounded by thick tulle, embossed invitations, and centerpieces made of delicate baby's breath, was Gigi. Facedown in the buttercream frosting of a carefully sculpted wedding cake.

A knife sticking out of her back.

CHAPTER THREE

It's a terrible thing for a girl to have to admit, but the fact was this wasn't the first time I'd ever found a dead body.

Not by a long shot.

In the months since Ramirez and I had first met, I'd been, as he put it, a bit of a magnet for trouble. (Okay, he'd used stronger language than that, but I put it down to stress.) In fact, that's how Ramirez and I had originally met, when he'd been investigating the disappearance of my last boyfriend, which had ended in a double homicide and my ex behind bars.

And that proposal in Paris? It had come right after I'd landed myself in a wee bit of trouble with a homicidal European fashionista. And that was right after I'd been involved with a Hollywood strangler. Which was right after getting mixed up with a group of Prada smuggling drag queens and the Vegas mob. (You can see where Ramirez's stress comes from.)

So, I guess you could say death was something I'd become more acquainted with in the last few years than I'd ever thought possible. And, after bearing witness to victims of drowning, falling off buildings, strangulation, gunshot wounds, and, most recently, stabbing by stiletto heel, you'd think I was immune to the sight of another dead body.

You'd think.

Despite Ramirez's arm around my waist, I felt myself going limp as he pulled me back outside. He gently lowered me to the sidewalk as he grabbed for his cell, shouting codes at the dispatcher and calling for backup.

I dragged in deep breaths, scented with car exhaust and pepperoni from the pizza joint across the street. I willed my lawn lunch not to make a repeat appearance as tears of hysteria backed up behind my eyes. Instead, I tucked my knees up close to my chest, hugging them to me for warmth, despite the sunshine beating down on my bare shoulders.

"You okay?" Ramirez asked, flipping his cell shut.

I nodded.

"You sure?"

I nodded again, bobbing my blonde hair up and down. Which would have been a whole lot more convincing if a pair of tears hadn't picked that moment to slide down my cheeks, probably taking a generous helping of mascara with them.

"Come 'ere." Ramirez crouched down next to me, running the pad of his thumb along my wet face. "You look a little pale."

"Uh-huh."

"You're shaking."

"Uh-huh."

"You gonna throw up?"

"Uh-huh."

Ramirez shook his head, hauling me to my feet. "Come on. Let's walk for a minute; you'll be all right."

He slipped an arm around me, propelling me forward as I continued the deep breathing thing. A few steps to the right, and then we turned around and stepped back to the left. The whole time Ramirez keeping a close eye on the door to L'Amore. After a few paces, feeling started to seep back into my limbs, and my stomach stopped rolling like a Six Flags coaster. I took in a deep, shuddering breath.

"Better?" he asked, loosening his hold on me to brush an errant strand of hair from my forehead. "You gonna be okay?"

I put on my best brave face. "Eventually."

Apparently it wasn't that brave, as he pulled me in tight again. Not that I minded. The solid warmth of his chest was settling my stomach better than any antacid could.

"Was she…" I trailed off, not wanting to put the obvious into words but needing to know all the same.

I felt Ramirez nod. "No question. DOA."

I pulled back, looking up at him. He was in full-on cop mode. His eyes scanning the street for possible evidence, his body tense with nervous energy, itching to get at the crime scene, his face set into those grim, unreadable lines that betrayed nothing of his thoughts.

"Jack, our wedding planner is dead."

He looked down at me, attempting (poorly) a smile. "Well, at least I got out of cake tasting."

I kicked him in the shin. "Not funny."

I knew he was just trying to make me feel better, but at the moment nothing about this was going to feel good. A woman I'd just spoken to yesterday was dead, her entire life over in one brief moment, leaving a lifeless heap where her sharp-as-a-tack personality had just been.

I shivered again, wrapping my arms around my sides as I heard the distant wail of sirens approaching.

As soon as the boys in blue got there, Ramirez handed me off to a uniformed officer whose nametag read "Hobbs" and told him to take me home. I started to protest, but as much as I wanted to know what happened to land Gigi facedown in my bridal cake, I really didn't have the energy to stick around and watch them wheel the human Hefty bag that was her final legacy out the front door. Besides, the press vultures were already starting to circle, and the last thing I wanted was my mascara streaked face on the 5 o'clock news. Thanks to one tabloid reporter in particular, I had a distinct love-hate (mostly hate) relationship with the press. Instead, I let Hobbs follow my little red Jeep home, making sure I got all the way up the stairs to my studio before his cruiser took off down the street.

Once inside, I immediately flipped on the TV. So far the death of Beverly Hills' most prominent wedding planner had yet to make the airwaves. But I knew it was only a matter of time. A story like this didn't chill for long. Obviously Gigi hadn't expired from natural causes. And last I checked, it was pretty hard to stab one's self in the back. That only left murder. Murder in a Beverly Hills wedding studio! The paparazzi would have a field day with this one.

And here I was, smack in the middle of it. Again.

I fought another round of nausea at that disconcerting thought as a knock sounded at my front door.

I flipped off the TV and crossed the room to open it. Only to be attacked in a rib-crusher hug that knocked the air out of me.

"Oh, baby," Mom said, squeezing me like a boa constrictor. "It's just too awful. I can't believe this is happening to you."

"Karma. Karma's a nasty bitch sometimes," said the large, muumuu-clad woman wedging her way into my apartment behind Mom. Mrs. Rosenblatt.

Mrs. Rosenblatt was a three hundred-pound, five-time Jewish divorcee, who read tarot cards and talked to the dead. Eccentric didn't even begin to cover Mrs. Rosenblatt. 90% of the time, she could be found wearing either Birkenstocks or Crocs, and the only thing louder than her Lucille Ball hair color was her muumuus. Today's was no exception. Hot pink with neon blue polka dots all over.

Next to her, Mom's outfit almost seemed subdued.

"Mom, can't breathe," I choked out, my face squished up against her boobs.

Mom eased up and stood back. "Baby, I'm so sorry. I don't know how this could happen but—"

I held up a hand. "Wait. Before you say anything else, let me just assure you that this was totally not my fault. I was just minding my own business, going to taste cake, and then Ramirez was late, and then I was worried he wouldn't show, but he did, but I already had the hiccups by then, and when we tried to go inside to get a glass of water, there she was with a knife in her back."

Mom blinked. Then her face drained of all color, going a shade of pale even Casper couldn't attain. "Knife?" She swayed on her feet, leaning on the back of my futon for support. "What do you mean, 'knife'?"

Oh hell. "Uh…exactly why were you so sorry a minute ago?"

Mrs. Rosenblatt put a steadying hand at Mom's elbow. "We were sorry that the restaurant we booked for the rehearsal dinner cancelled. Said the health inspector came in and found a roach in the kitchen; shut the whole place down. So, we gotta have it someplace else."

"Oh." If I ever learned to shut my big mouth, it would be a miracle.

"What knife?" Mom persisted, grabbing my arm in a death clutch.

I bit my lip. Well, if the cat was out of the bag, I couldn't very well stuff it back in clawing and screaming. Reluctantly, I filled

Mom and Mrs. R in on the events of the afternoon. Even though I tried to gloss over the more gory details, Mom's eyes were still dilated to an unhealthy size by the time I was finished, and Mrs. Rosenblatt's mouth was hanging open, showing off her lipstick stained teeth.

"Oy, your karma really sucks, *bubbee*. You musta been Hitler in a former life or something."

"Great. Thanks."

"Oh, my stars, I can't imagine how awful it would be to find her like that," Mom said, a hand going to her heart.

I cringed as the all-too-fresh memory of Gigi's limp body knotted up in my stomach. "It wasn't the best day ever. But Ramirez was with me," I added.

Which seemed to calm her a little.

"Oh, my poor, poor baby. Why do these things always happen to *my* baby? I tried to raise you right. You had a good home, went to a good school. Granted, I might have been a little lenient with bedtime and maybe let you have one too many sweets now and then, but I did my best. So why, oh why, is it my daughter who always finds the dead bodies?"

Okay, a very little.

"Look, Mom, I'm okay." Mostly. "Ramirez is handling the case, everything's fine."

"You're sure you're okay?" she asked again.

"Yes." And, actually, the more I said it, the more I started to almost believe it myself.

"In that case, we'll handle the rehearsal dinner," Mrs. Rosenblatt piped up. "Now that I think about it, I seem to remember my second husband, Carl, had a cousin who works in a place just down the street from the Beverly Garden. Italian joint. Has a live accordion player and everything. Classy."

While accordion didn't exactly scream "classy" to me, I let it go. In light of a dead wedding planner, the details of ambient music at my rehearsal dinner took a backseat.

"Call me if you need anything," Mom said as she and Mrs. R made for the door. "I mean it. *Anything*."

"Thanks." I gave her another hug, glad to see a little color returning to her cheeks.

As soon as the door closed behind them, I dug into my purse and pulled out my cell, speed dialing number one.

Three rings later, Dana's breathless voice answered.

"Hello?"

"Hey, it's me. And have I had a hell of an afternoon."

"Oh, man, tell me about it," she shouted. "I just finished that cartoon reading, and my throat is so raw! You would not believe the high, squealy voice they wanted me to do. I mean, please, do flamingos even talk that way?"

"Listen," I said, "I need pedi therapy. Want to meet me at Fernando's in twenty?"

"God, yes."

* * *

Fifteen minutes later I pulled my car down Beverly and parked on the street, a block south of Fernando's Salon.

Mom met Faux Dad a couple years ago when, after twenty some years of being a single mother, she'd decided to reenter the dating scene with a whole new look. She'd gone to Fernando's where Faux Dad had used his cut and color talents to not only give her a stylish makeover, but to win her heart as well. Mere months later, they'd exchanged vows in a beautiful ceremony with yours truly as the maid of honor. Which shocked the hell out of me, let me tell you, since at that point I'd been 99% sure Faux Dad was gay. But, as dads go, he's been stellar. Mom glows like a teenager, her roots have never looked better, and I get all the free pedis I want. What more could a girl ask for?

As I pushed through the glass front doors of Fernando's, I saw that this season's theme was Rock 'n' Roll retro. Think Happy Days and the Fonze.

In addition to Faux Dad's talents with a blow dryer, he was also a bit of an amateur interior decorator. (See what I mean? For a straight guy, he totally had the queer eye.) He'd painted the walls in alternating vibrant pinks and blues, with a smattering of old vinyl records tacked up along the ceiling. The reception desk was a chrome and

Formica piece that looked straight out of a '50s diner, and the stylist stations were each adorned with cardboard cut outs of Marilyn Monroe and James Dean. From somewhere doo-wop was being pumped into unseen speakers, and the front chairs had been upholstered to look like they were wearing giant poodle skirts. I suddenly had the urge to order a double malted, Daddy-o.

"Mads!"

Faux Dad's receptionist, Marco, came gliding in from the back. Marco was slim, Hispanic, and wore enough eyeliner to single handedly keep Maybelline in business.

In keeping with the theme, he was wearing skintight blue jeans, ending a good two inches above his white socks, a white T-shirt and a black leather jacket, a la *West Side Story*. His jet black hair was slicked back from his forehead, and on his feet were—I kid you not—roller skates. He skidded to a stop just inches from me, leaning on the reception desk for balance.

"Dahling, it's been ages since you've been in. Color touch up?" he asked, eyeing my roots.

Self-consciously, I fluffed my hair. "No. Actually, I wanted to see if you could get Dana and me in for pedis."

Marco frowned. "You know it messes up my whole schedule when you drop in like this, Maddie." He consulted his big black book.

"Pretty please, Marco. I need comfort today."

"Oh?" He lifted one drawn-in eyebrow. "Do tell, honey."

Marco was the current frontrunner for biggest gossip in all of L.A. County. I knew if I told him, within minutes it would be on every blog, Yahoo! loop, and MySpace bulletin in cyberspace. But, since the press would be running with it soon enough anyway, I figured I'd give him the pleasure of breaking this particular story.

"It's Gigi Van Doren."

"She's your wedding planner, right?"

"Was."

"Was?" There went the other eyebrow. "What happened?"

"Someone killed her."

Marco took in a shocked breath, his hands flying to his mouth. "No!"

"Yes. This morning. Ramirez and I walked in to taste the cake and found her there."

"Heart attack?" he asked.

I shook my head. "Not unless it was brought on by a knife in her back."

"Oh, my God, the poor thing!" Though Marco's eyes were shining like he'd just won the gossip lottery.

"Ramirez is with her now. So…a pedi-worthy emergency?"

"Good, God, yes! I'll fit you both right in. Come on, come soak and tell Auntie Marco all the gory details."

Ten minutes later my toes were encased in a lavender-scented foot bath, and Marco was on gossip overload, his eyes glazing over like he was high. He was just beginning to look truly feverish when Dana walked into the salon and plopped down in the pedi chair next to me.

"God, what an afternoon. I swear I'm going to be hoarse for the next week."

I turned to look at her. And blinked. Twice.

She was clad in a pink leotard covered in feathers that started at her throat and ended just above her derriere. Hot pink stockings and pink boots covered her legs, while her arms were encased in long, loose sleeves that seemed to be molting pink feathers all over the black and white checkered floor.

"Hey, Big Bird," Marco said.

Dana looked down at her outfit. "Very funny. I had a reading."

"A *voice over* reading," I reminded her,

"Right. I'm playing a flamingo."

"For a *cartoon*. You do realize that they usually *draw* cartoons right?"

Dana waved me off. "Ricky says the best way to know a character is to live like that character. We're taking this new method acting class together. It's at the Uta Hagen studio."

Ricky was Dana's boyfriend of the past year and star of the prime-time soap *Magnolia Lane*. Ricky had recently won a People's Choice Award for his portrayal of the hunky gardener on the show, after which Dana had vowed to follow any and all advice he had for her own acting career (such as it were). I hesitated to point out that Ricky's popularity probably had more to do with the fact that he took his shirt off in every episode than it did his amazing acting skills. But I had to admit, Uta Hagen was the premier acting coach to have. Though…

"Wait, I thought Uta Hagen passed away?"

"Oh, she did. It's being taught by one of her student's cousin's coaches. Bernie Sholpenstein. But it's so her method."

"Ah." I'm proud to say, I totally didn't roll my eyes here. See what a good friend I am?

"Anyway, what's the pedi emergency?" she asked, slipping off her boots and letting her toes settle into a bath of hot bubbly water.

Marco and I quickly filled her in. (Okay, mostly Marco. He was already embellishing the scene with blood spatter, ominous music in the background, and a feeling of foreboding creeping up my spine as I walked into the studio. Needless to say, I didn't even try to hide the eye roll this time.) When we were finished, Dana's eyes were as big as two round ostrich eggs.

"How traumatic! Maddie, are you okay?" she asked.

I nodded. And here in the bubbly, warm, lavender-scented comfort of Fernando's, it was almost true. Seriously, there was something magical about pedis. I swear if more people took time out for their toes, we'd have altogether less war and crime in the world.

"So, who do you think killed her?" she asked.

I shrugged. "I dunno."

"I bet it was one of her clients," Marco said. "You know she did the Spears wedding last spring."

"Britney?"

"No, Hank. Britney's cousin. But it was all over the *Us Weekly* special. Very tasteful."

"No," Dana said, shaking her head (prompting pink feathers to molt into her pedi tub). "No, why would her clients want her dead? I mean, without her, there's no wedding, right?"

Marco gasped, his hands flying to his face again. "Maddie, does this mean the wedding's off?"

I'd been so freaked out by encountering the dead body I hadn't even thought of that.

Was I a bad person that for a brief moment I was relieved I wouldn't have to order four hundred linen place cards after all?

"No, no way," Dana protested. "No, the wedding will go on. It's too late to cancel."

"But it's too late to book another A-list planner. Honey, those gals book moooooonths in advance," Marco said, drawing out the word and punctuating it with a sharp snap of his wrist.

"You know what? It's fine," I said. "We don't need a planner. I mean, we really wanted something small and intimate anyway. We'll just scale it down a little—"

"Oh!" Dana said, cutting me off as she popped up from her chair. "I know. We'll plan it ourselves!"

"Uh…we?"

"Marco and I."

I looked from Marco's roller skates to Dana's flamingo feathers. "Um, I don't know…"

"That is the most fabulous idea ever conceived!" Marco shouted, slipping forward in his excitement and grabbing the arm of my pedi chair to keep from skating away. "Surely most of the heavy work has already been done. The wedding venue, the minister, the caterer, all booked right?"

Reluctantly I nodded. "Yeeees. But..."

"So all we have to do is decorate, organize, and deal with the last-minute stuff."

"I totally know how to do this," Dana chimed in. "I've played a bride three times on the Lifetime channel. Oh, and I even auditioned for that J Lo movie about the wedding planner. I *totally* know weddings."

"Me too!" Marco squealed. "Oh, I saw this special on the Home and Garden Network about these tulle rose bouquets as gifts for your guests. They were daaaaaahling! We must do those!"

"Um, guys, I'm not sure..."

"Perfect! Oh, and I know one of Ricky's friends that has this band that's totally off the hook. Usually they do bar mitzvahs, but I'm sure they can do weddings, too."

I felt dread curling up from my pruney toes all the way to the tips of my fingers. "Guys, really, I don't think I need all this. I mean, the wedding's pretty planned already. We're good. Really."

"Oh, yeah?" Dana challenged. "When are the flowers arriving?"

"Uh…"

"And the limo?"

"What do I need a limo for?"

"The photography arrangements, the tux rentals," she said ticking items off on her fingers, "the makeup artist. Do you even know who's doing your makeup for the event?"

"Um…me?"

Marco and Dana gave me twin stares. Both said I was totally outnumbered. Again.

I threw my hands up. "Okay, fine. You two can plan my wedding."

"Eeek!" Dana said, engulfing me in a hug that sent feathers up my nose. "I'm so excited, this is going to be the best wedding ever. First thing is to sit down with you and Ramirez and pick a color scheme."

I snorted. "Fat chance of that."

Dana turned her head around. "What does that mean?"

I shook my head. The sad truth was that if I'd thought it was hard to get Ramirez involved before, it was going to be downright impossible now that a homicide was thrown into the mix. When it came to a case, he was like a pit bull with a big meaty bone—focused to a fault. As I voiced my concerns to my friends, I pictured his cop face earlier that day and had a horrible vision of me standing at the altar, staring down an empty aisle. Forget cake tasting, it would be a miracle if he remembered to show to the wedding at all.

"Surely he's not that bad," Dana said. "He'll show."

"Right. Remember my birthday? How I waited outside the opera for a full hour for him."

Marco clucked his tongue. "And they were such good seats."

"Double homicide in the West Hills wins out over *La Traviata* every time," I sighed.

"But this is his wedding," Dana protested.

I know she was trying to make me feel better. But I had a sinking feeling that tuxedos, slow dancing, and being barraged by four hundred well wishes while surrounded by delicate flowered centerpieces rated even lower on Ramirez's wish list than a night of listening to the fat lady sing. As he'd so aptly put it, he wasn't really a wedding-y guy.

"Well, we'll just have to make sure the case is closed by then," Marco said.

"He's right," Dana said, nodding. "If the death was solved, Ramirez would be free to focus on the wedding"

I bit my lip. "I guess."

"Good, then it's settled," Marco said, his eyes taking on a dangerous twinkle. "Oh, I just love it when we play Charlie's Angels!"

"Me too!" Dana squealed, molting more feathers as she clapped her wings together.

"Wait!" I held up both hands. If there was one thing in this world I had learned to fear it was when my friends used the term 'Charlie's Angels.' Ninety percent of the time it resulted in bodily injury.

Usually to me.

"Listen, as much as I appreciate the help, guys, there's nothing we can do that Ramirez and his crime scene buddies can't."

Dana put her hands on her hips. "Really? Tell me, exactly what did Ramirez say when you told him you were going cake tasting today?"

I felt my cheeks go hot. "He turned on a basketball game."

"Of course he did, because all men hate weddings."

Marco opened his mouth to protest.

"Present company excluded, of course."

He shut it, giving her a nod.

"My point is," she continued, "Ramirez doesn't know the first thing about weddings or wedding planning. He wouldn't even know where to begin looking for Gigi's killer. Maddie, we totally have the advantage over him."

I looked from Marco's beaming face to Dana's smug smile.

Oh boy.

For a brief moment, I almost felt sorry for Gigi's killer. The poor man had no idea what he'd gotten himself into.

CHAPTER FOUR

———

Once our toes were passion pink and ruby rendezvous, respectively, Dana and I settled down on the poodle skirt sofas in the front of the salon while Marco skated back and forth in front of us with a pad of lined yellow paper, outlining our strategy.

"So, where do we start?" Dana asked.

"With centerpieces! We must have floral centerpieces at each reception table. Roses? Carnations?" Marco asked, pen poised.

"Actually, I meant where do we start looking for Gigi's killer?" Dana pointed out.

Marco stuck his lower lip out in a pout. "Oh."

"Roses," I said.

Marco perked up immediately, making a note on his pad.

"What about the husband?" Dana asked.

"Ramirez?" Marco cocked his head to the side. "You think he'd rather have carnations?"

Dana rolled her eyes. "No, *Gigi's* husband. The husband is *always* the first suspect on *Law & Order*."

"You do know that's a fictional show, right?" I pointed out.

"She might be right, though," Marco added. "I'd look at the husband first. Marriage drives people crazy. I mean, you spend that much time with someone, odds are you're gonna want to kill them at some point."

Dana shot a wary glance at me, then stuck a foot out and kicked Marco in the shin as he skated past.

"Ow!" He looked at me. "Oh." Marco's face went red. "Oh, right, well, I totally didn't mean *your* marriage, Maddie."

"Uh-huh. Sure. Thanks."

"Back to Gigi," Dana said, clearing her throat loudly. "Do we know if she was married?"

I shrugged. I had to admit, I didn't know much about Gigi except that she didn't understand the word 'understated.'

"Leave it to me, dahlings," Marco said, skating around his desk to the slim, black computer behind it. He pulled up a Google screen and typed in the name "Gigi Van Doren."

As Marco scrolled through pages of hits, we learned that Gigi was on the alumni committee at UCLA, had signed an online petition to save the polar bears, and had an aunt named Eloise who'd recently died of lung cancer in Poughkeepsie. Finally we hit jackpot as Marco pulled up the online presence of the *L.A. Informer*.

An article about Gigi Van Doren separating from her husband of two years hit the front page last July, the reporter cruelly pointing out the irony of Beverly Hills' hottest wedding planner not being able to keep a marriage together herself.

"So much for the husband theory," Marco said.

"Well, an ex-husband is even better than a husband. Alimony is a great reason to want someone dead," Dana pointed out.

"Does it list his name?" I asked.

Marco scrolled down. "Seth Summerville. Says he's a real estate developer." He opened a new window, bringing up a yellow pages site, then typed the name into the search engine. A page of Summervilles popped up, ranging from dry cleaners to attorneys. Marco scrolled until he hit on "Summerville Development" in downtown L.A. He clicked the link, printing the address out on a giant printer hidden under a Styrofoam jukebox.

"Perfect, let's go pay the ex Mr. Gigi Van Doren a visit," Dana said, clapping her hands. And molting a few more feathers.

"Uh, maybe you'd like to change first there, Daisy Duck?"

Dana looked down. "Oh. Right. K, we'll stop by my place first, yeah?"

"Definitely."

"Call me the moment you know something!" Marco called out after us as we pushed through the front doors.

* * *

Half an hour later, Dana had ditched the poultry look and was dressed in a leather mini and ankle boots, once again looking human. I took the 101 south from her Studio City duplex into downtown, then wound down Figueroa until I hit the address on Marco's printout. It was a big chrome and glass building looming over the street, shimmering in the afternoon light, as if to say it was way more important than the other office buildings vying for space in the few short power blocks of downtown.

I circled the structure and parked my little red Jeep in the garage at the end of the block. After clubbing my steering wheel, Dana and I made our way down the street, passing two Starbucks (one on each side of the street, because heaven forbid you'd have to cross) and one Jamba Juice before hitting the Summerville building.

Yeah, he owned the whole building.

"Wow, I hope she had a good prenup," Dana said, as we pushed though the glass front doors into a spacious air-conditioned lobby. "This guy's loaded."

"No kidding." Though from Gigi's designer shoes and nip-tucked appearance, I figured she hadn't made out too poorly.

"How about you, Mads?" Dana asked, consulting the directory by the elevator. "You and Ramirez signed a prenup yet?"

"A what?" I asked, giving her a get-real look.

"A prenup. Have you signed one yet?"

"Me? Um. No. God, no. I mean, why would Ramirez have me sign a prenup?" While Ramirez did own a cozy little two-bedroom in West L.A., it was far from an entire building with his name on it. And his cop salary was at least a few zeroes short of Richie Rich.

"Not *him. You,*" Dana emphasized. "Maddie, you've got to protect yourself."

I choked back a laugh as we stepped into the marble tiled elevator.

"Me? Seriously? Have you seen my studio?"

"Mads, your designs, girl."

"What about them?"

"Well, what are they worth?"

I bit my lip. I guess my career had been looking up a bit lately. But I was still a far cry from a wealthy mogul. "Dana, I really don't think I need to worry about that yet."

"Oh, please, Maddie, *everyone* gets a prenup these days. You've got to protect yourself girl."

"From Ramirez?"

Dana turned to face me, a frown settling between her strawberry blonde brows. "Maddie, California is a community property state. Did you know that half of any design you create while married to Ramirez will belong to him?"

I paused. "Seriously?" I hadn't actually thought about it before.

"Seriously. This screenwriter friend of mine, his wife was always bitching at him to go out and get a real job. Eventually she left him. He sold the script two months later and, guess what? She got half his royalties. Turns out since the script was written while they lived together, it was technically a marital asset. Talk about irony, huh?"

"Ouch."

Dana nodded vigorously, her bangs bobbing up and down as the elevator doors slid open at the seventh floor. "When you're married, Ramirez will own half of *everything* you have. Split down the middle.

Even half of your tampons will belong to him."

I opened my mouth to protest just how ridiculous that was.

But only a hiccup came out.

"Think about it, Maddie," Dana said as she pushed through the glass doors with the word "Summerville" stenciled in curvy script. "Everyone who's anyone gets a prenup these days."

I clamped my lips together. No doubt that I loved Ramirez. But I hadn't actually given thought to the idea of sharing *everything* with him. Sure, he had his own shelf in my medicine cabinet, but it had taken me months to get used to even that.

I tried to shove those disconcerting thoughts to the back of my mind and calm my jumping diaphragm as I followed Dana across the posh reception area of Summerville's front office.

My heels clacked on the hardwood floor leading up to a massive wood desk so tall I feared my petite frame might not be visible behind it. The gargantu-desk was manned by a small, slim man in a pink dress shirt and bright green plaid sweater vest. A pair of wire rimmed glasses perched on the end of his nose as he talked into a headset glued to one ear.

"Yes, Mr. Summerville will be at the planning commission on the third, but the groundbreaking in Tokyo will have to wait until he comes back from his trip to New York.

"Yes, thank you for calling Summerville, please hold.

"I'll transfer you to HR immediately.

"May I help you?"

His speech was so rapid fire it took me a minute to realize he was talking to me. But his pointed "What?" look, one eyebrow cocked up, head tilted to the side finally clued me in.

"Oh, uh, yes. I was wondering if we could speak with Seth Summerville?"

"Do you have an appointment?"

"Um, not exactly—" I started.

But Mr. Sweater Vest cut me off. "What is this in regards to?"

"Uh…"

Luckily Dana was faster on the draw. "Mr. Summerville wanted to talk with me about modeling for him in their next brochure. You know, for the project in Tokyo?"

Sweater Vest narrowed his eyes. "Hmm. Well, Mr. Summerville is indisposed at the moment. But if you'd like to make an appointment, I'm sure he'd be happy to see you."

"Okay, I guess." Not the immediate gratification I'd been looking for, but not a 'no' either.

Sweater Vest opened a window on his computer and consulted the screen, all the while chatting away to his headset.

"Summerville, please hold.

"Yes, I'll transfer you to Mr. Peterman in accounts receivable.

"No, no the plans for the Fairfax building were messengered over Thursday.

"I have one opening on the twelfth."

Sweater Vest looked at me expectantly.

"Oh, you're talking to me?"

He cocked an eyebrow, tilted his head. Yep, he was talking to me.

"Right, sure. The twelfth will be fine."

"Of April."

I blinked. "April?" It was only February!

"Mr. Summerville is a very busy man."

I felt my heart bottom out my toes. So much for our prime suspect. But unless I was approaching him with a badge and a warrant, it looked like we were SOL.

"Are you sure he doesn't have just a few minutes for us?" Dana asked.

Sweater Vest gave us a stern look that said he was positive. "Shall I pencil you in?'

I shrugged. "Yeah. Sure," I said and gave him our names.

"Fine. See you on the twelfth.

"Yes, the offices are open until five today.

"Mr. Summerville will have to call you back after his conference call this afternoon.

"You'll have to consult local zoning regulations.

"Are you still here?"

I jumped a little at his pointed gaze, realizing he meant us. "Right. Just leaving."

Thusly dismissed, Dana and I marched back to the elevators.

"Well, that was a bust," she said once we got back outside.

I looked up at the building. Then down the street at the twin Starbucks.

Hmm…

"You in the mood for a latte?" I asked Dana.

She shrugged. "Sure."

I pulled out my cell, dialing Marco.

"Yes, dahling?" he answered on the first ring.

"Hey, Farrah. The angels need you. Meet us at Summerville?"

Marco did a happy squeak. "I was just getting off. I'll be right there."

I flipped my phone shut and grabbed Dana by the arm, dragging her down the street to Starbucks number one.

The barista behind the counter wore about fifteen different piercings, half of which were in her lower lip, silver rings jingling with each breath. I tried not to stare (much) as I ordered two grande lattes—one nonfat soy (for Dana), one extra whip (for moi) and three empty paper cups in a cardboard carrying case (for entry to Summerville).

Forty minutes later Dana and I were appropriately caffeinated and waiting again in the lobby of the Summerville building, when Marco showed up. While he was still in his greaser chic garb, I was relieved to see he'd traded in his roller skates for a pair of sensible loafers. Well, as sensible as Marco got. They were iridescent silver with red velvet hearts on the top.

I handed him the three empty cups and quickly filled him in on my plan to get past Sweater Vest as we rode the elevator back up to the seventh floor.

Marco strode through the glass doors, Dana and I hanging back. We waited through a five-Mississippi count, then followed, crouching low as we pushed through the doors, then crab walked across the hardwood floor, ducking below the desk.

"Are you sure Jennifer Moss doesn't work here?" I heard Marco saying. "I swear she said to bring the lattes to the conference room on the seventh floor. You know how much trouble I'm gonna be in if she isn't here?"

Sweater Vest let out a loud sigh. "I'm sorry, but she doesn't work here."

"Maybe she's new?"

Another sigh. This one even louder. "I'll check again, but I can almost guarantee you've got the wrong building."

The sound of fingers clacking on the keyboard sounded above, and Marco glanced down to give me a wink.

While Sweater Vest had his full attention engaged with the names on his computer screen, Dana and I continued our crabwalk around the right side of the desk, slipping down a hallway and to the left before straightening up to our full height.

Wow. It worked. Whatta ya know?

I glanced around the hallway, getting my bearings. It was punctuated by offices on either side, each filled with men and women in tailored suits talking into Bluetooth sets. I gingerly peeked my head around each doorframe, checking out the nameplates on the doors until we hit a large one in the corner with the words "Seth Summerville" stenciled in flowing script.

I stuck my head in. Seth Summerville had his back to me, his full attention on the floor to ceiling glass windows overlooking bumper-to-bumper traffic on the 110 freeway as he shouted into his headset.

"No, go low. We want to cut off their assets at the ankles, Bob. We can't have this coming back to bite us in the ass with the fourth-quarter returns."

Dana squared her shoulders beside me and, before I could stop her, knocked loudly on the doorframe.

Seth Summerville spun around, and I got a good look at him. Salt-and-pepper hair, a long face, pointed nose, sharp eyes to match his sharp features. I put him in his mid-fifties, that age when men start becoming "distinguished" and women start going away for weeks at a time to have stuff "done." He wore a white button-down over navy slacks, a matching blazer carelessly thrown over the back of an enormous leather desk chair. He had a broad, solid build and an aura about him that said he was used to getting his way, positively reeking of power in a manner that was more than a little intimidating. I suddenly felt about twelve in my jeans and tank. Like I was playing at being a grownup, but this guy was the real deal.

Luckily, Dana didn't intimidate that easily.

"Mr. Summerville?" she asked.

His brows hunched together. "Call you back in five, Bob," he told his Bluetooth.

Then directed his attention toward us. "Can I help you?"

"Hi, my name's Dana Dashel and this is my colleague, Maddie Springer."

Colleague? I raised one eyebrow at her as Seth waited for the punchline.

"We're looking into the death of your ex-wife, Gigi Van Doren. We're working with the police," she added with a solemn nod.

Oh, brother.

And Seth didn't seem to buy it either, taking in my high-heeled boots and Dana's micro mini with a pair of narrowed eyes.

"Any statement you need from me can be obtained through my lawyer."

"Fine, then we'll just come back with a warrant," Dana countered.

"Uh," I stepped forward, elbowing Dana in the ribs.

"Ow."

"Ix-nay on the arrant-way," I whispered out the side of my mouth. "Actually, Mr. Summerville, we're not actually police officers."

"You don't say." Wow, the man had deadpan down to a science.

"No. I'm...well, I was a client of Gigi's."

"And good friend," Dana piped up, stretching the truth just a tad again.

I was about to give her another elbow, but the friend bit seemed to soften Seth's features.

"I was very sorry to hear of her passing," he said. Though whether that was part of his press release or an actual sentiment I'd be hard pressed to say.

"We know you divorced last year. Had you seen Gigi lately?" I asked.

"No. No, I hadn't. Not since we bumped into each other at a charity function a couple months ago. Uh, sit, will you?" he asked, gesturing to a pair of leather club chairs as he sank into the executive version behind his desk.

Dana and I complied, her bare thighs making a little farting sound as she shifted on the leather.

"Had you had much contact with her?" I asked

"No. Our divorce wasn't what you'd call a friendly one."

This piqued my interested. "Oh?"

Seth frowned, looking out the massive window again as if searching back into a memory he'd just as soon forget. "No. It was…tumultuous to say the least."

"You fought?"

"Constantly."

"About?"

He drew in a deep breath. "Her health."

Not the answer I had been expecting. I bit the inside of my cheek. "If you don't mind me asking, what was wrong with Gigi?"

"Absolutely nothing. That was the problem. When I first met Gigi five years ago, things were wonderful. Life was like one long honeymoon. But a few months after we married, she started obsessing about her appearance. Her wrinkles, her hair, her pores, her skin. Every inch of her body was under constant scrutiny. Finally, I suggested she see a doctor if she was so worried. Huge mistake on my part."

"Why is that?"

"She saw one all right. A plastic surgeon. At first, it was just a simple chemical peel. Then it turned into an eye lift, a brow lift, implants in her cheeks. She had so many procedures I can't even remember them all. And after each one I had to watch her go though the agony of a painful recovery, just to hear her pick apart another body part the next month. Finally, I couldn't take it anymore."

No wonder I'd had such a hard time determining her age. It sounded like Gigi had gone to the plastic surgeon like most people go the supermarket.

"Exactly how old was Gigi?"

Seth shook his head. "Beats me."

"Wait, you didn't know how old your wife was?"

"Like I told you, she was obsessed with being younger. She said there were some secrets women never tell. Frankly, it didn't matter to me, so I dropped it."

"Well, she must have had a good surgeon," Dana piped up. "I never would have known she had all those procedures."

"Oh, she did," Seth said. "The best money could buy. The revenue from her little wedding business," he said, flicking his wrist as if her million-dollar-a-year enterprise was nothing more than a blip on his radar, "every cent went into her looks. The woman was obsessed with staying young."

"What about your money?"

"Ha!" He let out a sharp laugh. "No way. I had her sign an iron-clad prenup."

I tried to ignore the I-told-you-so look Dana shot me.

"Gigi didn't see a dime from me once the divorce papers were signed."

So much for motive. The way he spoke of her, it was more like she was a minor annoyance, like a pesky mosquito that had buzzed through his life more than a passionate entanglement. Our husband theory was sinking faster than the *Titanic*.

"Do you know if she was seeing anyone new?" I asked, totally fishing now.

He steepled his fingers under his chin. "She was with someone at the charity gala last fall." He did a laugh slash snort thing. "Young guy, probably half her age. But I guess that's why her plastic surgeon now drives a Bentley, right?"

"Any idea who he was?"

He shrugged. "She said he was a musician or something. I didn't really pay attention. Attention was what she wanted, so that was the last thing I was willing to give her."

Spoken like a true bitter ex.

"Well, thanks very much for your time. And, again, sorry for your loss."

A flicker of emotion passed across his features, and he mumbled a, "Thank you," as Dana and I slipped out of his office.

Once down the hallway, we power walked past Sweater Vest with our heads down. Luckily, since it sounded like he was simultaneously on four different calls, he didn't even notice.

Marco was bouncing on his toes in the lobby waiting for us. We quickly filled him in on what Summerville had told us as we walked back to the parking garage.

"I still think he's a possibility," Marco said when we'd finished.

"I don't know." Dana shook her head. "From what I heard on *CSI*, stabbing indicates a crime of passion. Summerville didn't seem all that passionate."

"You do know that the shows on TV are fiction, right?"

Dana waved me off. "It's all art imitating life."

I shook my head. But I did have to agree that Summerville seemed about as over Gigi as a man could get. Which didn't leave much in the way of motive.

"What about the new guy? The musician?" Marco asked.

"Maybe her assistant would know who he is?" I said, remembering the way Gigi's right-hand gal had been the designated keeper of the schedule.

"Any idea how to contact her?" Dana asked.

I shook my head. "Other than at the studio, no." And considering that place was probably still crawling with <u>real</u> police officers, that was not an option.

"Google to the rescue," Marco piped up, pulling something from his pocket.

"You carry Google around in your pocket?" I asked.

"iPhone. Hello, honey, who doesn't have internet in their pocket these days?"

I was ashamed to admit the only thing lurking in my pockets was likely lint and a stale sick of gum.

"What's her last name?" Marco asked, already punching things into his touch screen.

I scrunched my nose up as I thought back to when Gigi had first introduced us. "Quick. Allie Quick."

I watched Marco's lips move as he typed it into his phone, silently spelling the name out. A few clicks later, he hit pay dirt. "I've got a MySpace page for an Allie Quick in Glendale. This her?"

Marco passed the phone forward, and I squinted down at the photo on the screen. Sure enough, it was the same blue-eyed blonde who graced Gigi's front office.

"That's her! Can we call her?"

Marco snorted as he took his phone back. "Yeah, like she'd put her number on her page. We'll friend her, then message her. What's your username?"

"Username?"

"Yeah, your MySpace name?"

"Um…I don't have one?" I said. Though it sounded more like a question.

Marco rolled his eyes at me.

"Geeze, Maddie. I bet you still dial 411 instead of doing Yahoo Local, too," Dana said.

I declined to answer. Mostly because I had no idea what Yahoo Local was. "I don't do networking sites for twelve-year-olds, so sue me."

"Well, you do now," Marco informed me, stabbing at his phone with his index finger. "I just signed you up. You are now Maddie626 and your password is Manolo."

"Swell," I mumbled under my breath. I was now officially a member of the cyber age.

"K, I messaged her—" He paused. Then enunciated very slowly as if he were talking to a two year old. "Which means sending her an email…"

I gave him the finger.

"…telling her that you need to speak with her as soon as possible."

"Great. So, now what?"

"Actually," Dana said, stealing a glance at her watch, "I've got to get home. Ricky and I have class tonight, and I promised I'd go over our scene together first."

She was right. It was getting late and, on the off chance Ramirez actually came over tonight, I wanted to be at my studio to pump him for information.

"Okay, let's wait till we hear back from Allie and go from there tomorrow," I said

Marco agreed, hopping into his little Day-Glo yellow Miata with a promise to call me for updates tomorrow from the salon. I jumped on the 101 and dropped Dana back off in Studio City before pointing my Jeep toward the ocean. Of course, it being rush hour (meaning gridlock the entire way down the 405) it took me over an hour before I pulled my Jeep up to my own apartment.

Where I almost hit my neighbor's trashcan with a lurching halt.

While I'd been expecting Ramirez's SUV to fill the other half of the drive, the beat up blue Dodge Neon parked there instead had me swerving in surprise.

As did the man lounging against the dented back fender. White button-down shirt, wrinkled khaki Dockers, shaggy rumpled blond hair, and a kill-all cocky grin that became ever so slightly bigger as I gaped at him.

Felix.

CHAPTER FIVE

———

My fingers clenched the steering wheel so tight my knuckles went white. I took two deep breaths and steeled myself for what might happen when I got out of the car.

Felix was the *L.A. Informer*'s star reporter, and we had what you might call a complicated history.

My first contact with him had been after my ex-boyfriend went to the slammer, and I'd caught a killer by popping her breast implant with a nail file. Admittedly, it was the kind of sensational story the *Informer* lived for. But that still didn't excuse the fact that Felix had run the article with a photo of my head pasted on Pamela Anderson's body and the headline, DOUBLE D'S BEWARE!

He'd endeared himself to me even less when I'd had the pleasure of meeting him in person, this time while investigating the disappearance of my biological father, Larry. Felix and I had formed a reluctant alliance to outwit the mob, which had ended with us getting kidnapped and Dana blowing a hole through some thug's chest. Again, not one of my finest hours.

Recently, however, Felix had been conspicuously absent from my life. Probably due to the fact that a completely accidental kiss in Paris had prompted me to realize that Felix's feelings might go a bit beyond friendly. Rumor had it he was even in love with me.

I hadn't seen Felix since we were backstage at the Jean Luc LeCroix show at fashion week. Right before someone had tried to kill me. (See what I mean? No exaggeration, I am a total trouble magnet.) Felix had been staring deep into my eyes, ready to confess his true feelings for me. It was a moment that was a little too honest, a little too intimate, and a little too fresh in my mind. One which *should* have made me feel icky, squeamish, and like washing my tonsils out with soap. Oddly enough, it didn't. In fact, if he hadn't been interrupted by a homicidal manic, I'm not sure how I would have responded to his confession.

As it was, my feelings toward Felix were…well…complicated.

And what all that translated into now that I was engaged to Ramirez, I had no idea. Though the word "awkward" immediately came to mind.

A knock sounded on my car window, and I jumped in my seat, giving off a little terrier-esque yelp.

"Hey." Felix's crooked smile and dimpled cheeks filled my vision.

Willing my heart rate to return to normal, I cracked the window.

"Yeah?"

"You gonna come out?"

"I was thinking about it."

His blue eyes crinkled at the corners, and I was pretty sure they were laughing at me. "Come to any conclusions yet?"

I took a deep breath and shook off the part of me that wanted to put the car in reverse, pretend I'd never seen him, and drive straight to the nearest comforting Ben & Jerry's ice cream parlor. I was being ridiculous. We were two grown adults. Well,

I was grown. Sometime I wondered at Felix's maturity level. He did work for a tabloid after all.

I opened the door, sliding out of the car and planting my feet on the sun-warmed pavement with as much dignity as I could after being caught cowering in my driver's seat.

"Felix," I said by way of greeting.

"Maddie. Nice to see you again," he responded in his impeccably articulated Hugh Grant accent. Then he gave me a slow up and down, taking in every inch of me from my swanky suede boots to my barely B's hinting at the neckline of my sweater tank.

I felt my cheeks flush, rethinking that whole getting out of the car thing.

"You look good, Maddie."

"You—" I started, but for some reason my voice stuck in my throat. I cleared it loudly, trying again. "You, uh, you look good, too."

Liar. He looked great.

Despite his lived-in look, even I had to admit Felix had a certain charm about him. He was such a study in dichotomy you couldn't help but be intrigued by him just a little. You'd never know from his appearance that he was an actual British Lord with his own castle and a distant relation to the Queen of England. Felix was what I called a cheap rich guy. He was sitting on a boatload of old family money from his father, yet inherited the penny-pinching gene from his Scottish mother. And by penny-pinching, I don't mean buying the small yacht. I mean the driving-a-ten-year-old-beat-up-car, wearing-the-same-pair-of-wrinkled-pants-for-a-week, drinking-watery-gas-station-coffee-instead-of-Starbucks cheap. No joke, I'd actually seen him tip a valet in nickels once.

"So," Felix said, "I hear we've had some excitement, yes?"

I guiltily looked down at my diamond-clad left ring finger. "Yeah, about that…" I trailed off, clearing my throat again.

"Yes? Care to fill me in?"

"Look, Felix, I was going to tell you. But it just all happened so fast. We were in Paris, and there was the Eiffel Tower, and it was all so romantic, and then there was the ring, and, well, I just kind of said yes without thinking. I mean, I wanted to say yes; I'm glad I said yes, but I didn't really think about saying yes before I said yes; I just said it. And then, well, afterward, I didn't really know what to say to you and, like I said, it all happened just so fast. It wasn't like I'd planned it or thought about it or anything like that. It just kind of happened. Fast."

I paused for a breath to find Felix chuckling softly, shaking his head at me.

"What?"

He continued laughing, letting the question hang in the air just long enough for my cheeks to heat again before replying.

"Actually, I meant Gigi's murder."

Oh. Great.

What was it about men that made me instantly stick my size-seven pumps in my mouth?

"Right."

"But congratulations on the upcoming nuptials. Sorry I won't be able to attend. Got big plans that day."

"Oh, hell, don't tell me my mother invited you, too?"

"No. She didn't."

"Well, then who… Oh." I blamed it on the effect of those two dimples still staring back at me from his grinning cheeks that I didn't detect his sarcasm straight off. Felix was apparently the only person in L.A. County *not* on my guest list. Damn if I didn't blush even harder. "Sorry. I was going to invite you, but, well, I wasn't sure…I mean after…well, you know…"

Felix cut me off, his grin widening considerably at my discomfort. "You know you're adorable when your face goes all red like that. Kind of like a choking victim."

The words every girl longs to hear.

I shook off my guilt and embarrassment, reminding myself that Felix was the kind of guy who made up stories about Bigfoot's secret love child with the crocodile woman. He was a big boy. He could handle a little rejection.

"Exactly what are you doing here, Felix?"

"I told you. Wanted to hear your big news."

"Wanted to hear as in you're a concerned friend, or a nosey reporter?"

Felix cocked his head to the side. "Oh, you know me better than that, Maddie, love."

"Right. Just as I thought. Reporter."

"Cute and smart. Ramirez really is a lucky guy."

For a fraction of a second I could have sworn I saw real emotion flicker across his face. Something like regret mingled with envy mingled with just enough of a hint of unexplored lust to make me blush again.

But just as quickly as it came, it was gone, the teasing glint in his eyes returning so quickly it made me wonder if I hadn't imagined the whole thing.

"So, how about it, Maddie? Want to unburden your day on the *Informer*'s most sympathetic ear?"

"Hmm. Tempting."

I brushed past him, heading up the flight of wooden stairs to my second story studio.

"Was that a note of sarcasm I detected in your voice?" he asked, following a step behind me.

"Oh, look who's the clever one now."

I fit my key in the lock, and before I could stop him, Felix slipped into the apartment behind me.

"Just tell me one thing: is it true she was facedown in buttercream icing?"

I bit my lip, images of the scene that morning flooding my brain. I nodded.

Felix threw his head back and laughed. "Too delicious, the irony. What ultimate revenge for the lovelorn."

I opened my mouth to protest, but something in Felix's words sent the little hamster running on my mental wheel. Could this have been a case of revenge against the wedding planner? A jilted bride or groom? A ceremony gone terribly wrong? I made a mental note to look into that. Had aborted wedding plans resulted in someone with a grudge against Gigi?

"What color?"

"Excuse me?" I asked, Felix's voice jolting me back to the present.

"What color icing?" His eyes were shining with the kind of glee usually reserved for a six-year-old with a shiny new Christmas bike.

"This is not some joke, Felix. A woman is dead."

"It most certainly is not a joke. Do you know how many copies the *Informer* will sell once this story breaks?"

"Okay, we're done here. Out." I pointed, straight-armed at the door. "I'm feeling sleazier just being in the same room with you."

"Flatterer. I see why Ramirez scooped you up."

"Oh, please. You were seconds from trying to scoop me yourself."

The moment it was out of my mouth I regretted it, clamping one hand over my lips as if to stave off any further verbal diarrhea.

But before I had the chance to apologize, Felix threw his head back and laughed out loud again. "Wow, we do think rather highly of ourselves, don't we, Maddie? Every man's madly in love with you, eh?"

I bit my lip. "No! That's not what I meant. I mean…well, at the LeCroix show…it seemed like you were about to…I mean I thought you were going to say…"

Felix's blue eyes twinkled at me, mischief dancing through them like a cat with a fresh ball of string. "You thought I was going to say what, Maddie? That I was madly in love with you? That I'd been secretly pining for you all this time? That I couldn't possibly live another day without you?"

His mocking tone turned that blush into a full-bodied thing. "No," I mumbled. "Of course not. Don't be silly."

And listening to him talk now, it seemed just that. Silly. Maybe I'd imagined the whole thing in Paris. Maybe the romance of the city had done funny things to my perception. Maybe the way Felix looked at me was just what he said it was—lust over a juicy story.

Talk about feeling ridiculous. I said a silent prayer that the floor would open up and swallow me whole.

"Don't worry, Maddie," Felix went on as I marinated in mortification. "I'm well aware that you prefer the tall, dark, and caveman type."

Hey! "Ramirez is not a caveman!"

Felix quirked an eyebrow my way as if challenging that statement.

"All right, so he can be a little macho at times. But at least he doesn't make a living exploiting innocent people. He's one of the good guys."

"And I suppose that makes me a bad guy?" Felix took a step forward.

Instinctively, I took one back, my tush coming up against the cool tile of my kitchen counter.

"In this case, yes."

He moved forward again, his smile taking on a decidedly wicked glint. "Goody. I always wanted to play the villain."

Oh, boy.

I licked my suddenly dry lips. "I-I think you should go now," I squeaked, my voice coming out a full octave higher for some odd reason.

"Do you *want* me to go?" he asked, emphasizing the one word I really didn't want to explore.

I opened my mouth to respond…

Only it wasn't my voice I heard.

"Yes, she does."

I whipped my gaze to the front door and found Ramirez's broad shoulders filling the frame. His hand hovered just over the gun I knew he kept strapped under his jacket, his brows hunkering down in a way that made his dark eyes fairly growl with menace.

I did a dry gulp. Then put on my best innocent face and did a little one finger wave. "Hi, honey."

But Ramirez ignored me, his gaze locked on Felix like a homing device. On a bomb. About to go off.

I can't say I completely blamed him. As complicated as my history with Felix was, throw Ramirez into the mix and…well, let's just say that the last time Ramirez and Felix were in the same room, Felix's lips were on mine, and Ramirez was dumping me. A memory that, as evidenced by the vein starting to bulge in Ramirez's neck, hadn't faded from his mind.

"Felix," he hissed through clenched teeth.

"Jack, lovely to see you again," Felix said breezily, as if the two were old friends meeting for a pint at the pub. He was doing an excellent impression of a man unfazed by a pissed-off cop, though how much was acting, I wasn't sure.

He grabbed my left hand, holding up the two-carat rock resting there. "I hear congratulations are in order."

Ramirez's nostrils flared, his eyes shooting from Felix's face to his hand holding mine, then narrowing. I had the distinct feeling if I squinted hard enough I could actually see the testosterone crackling in the air.

I shook off Felix's grip, lest he tempt Ramirez into actually using that gun.

"Felix just dropped by to discuss Gigi's death," I said, trying to defuse the situation.

Ramirez tore his gaze from Felix's smirk (with obvious difficulty) to me.

"Of course, I told him I had nothing to add and that he'd have to go sniff out a link to the Loch Ness monster on his own."

I gave Felix a pointed look. Now would be an excellent time to make an exit, pal.

But he seemed pleased as punch to remain in the line of fire, shoving his hands in his pockets and rocking back on his heels.

"Oh, Maddie," Felix said, "don't you worry your *pretty* little head…"

Ramirez growled deep in his throat. Actually growled.

I rolled my eyes.

"…one bit about it. I've always got a Nessie angle up my sleeve."

"I'll bet," I mumbled. "Well, as fun as this has been, time to go, Tabloid Boy."

I grabbed Felix's sleeve and physically propelled him the three feet to the front door. All the while Ramirez staring him down as if he were a bug he'd like to put a boot to. They sidestepped past each other, and I held my breath, knowing just how easy it would be for Ramirez's fist to accidentally shoot out and catch Felix in the jaw.

Felix must have realized too, as, despite the cool grin still cracking his cheeks, he scuttled out double time.

"I'll see you soon, Maddie," he called over his shoulder.

Prompting another growl from Caveman.

I shut the door, internally sighing with relief that we'd avoided bloodshed.

"Care to tell me what that was all about?" Ramirez ground out.

I spun around to find his arms crossed over his chest, narrowed eyes now zeroing in on me.

"Oh no, pal. Don't play mad with me. How about you tell me what this," I said, gesturing between him and the closed door, "was all about?"

"What?"

"The silent pissing contest. 'Grunt, grunt, hands off my woman.'"

He softened his stance, uncrossing his arms. "I didn't grunt."

I raised a challenging eyebrow.

"Much."

Despite playing the hard-ass, I couldn't help a smile tugging at the corner of my mouth.

"Thanks for not hitting him."

"You're welcome. But no promises about next time."

"Fair enough." The way Felix had taunted Ramirez, next time I might hit him myself.

Ramirez sank down onto my futon and flipped on the TV, the tension leaking out of his shoulders and instantly being replaced by a look of fatigue.

"How did it go at L'Amore after I left?" I asked, settling down beside him.

"Fine."

"Fine? Like, fine how? Anything interesting at the crime scene? Any witnesses crop up?" I asked, trying my best at casual curiosity.

Unfortunately, Ramirez knew me better than that.

"No way."

"What?"

"There's nothing I'm willing to share with a nosey blonde who hangs out with tabloid reporters."

"Hey!" I stuck out my lower lip in a mock pout. "We don't 'hang out.' I was ambushed."

He grinned, tilting my chin up to face him. "You're a lot of trouble, you know that, Springer?"

I nodded.

"Good thing you're so cute."

I couldn't help my insides from doing a squealy girly thing. The hot guy thought I was cute.

"So…how about cluing the cute girl in on your case?"

Ramirez shook his head, but the grin remained in place. "All right, I give in."

My turn to grin.

"Cause of death was one stab wound to the back with a cake knife, wiped clean of prints. No defensive wounds, which indicates the killer was someone she knew and trusted. Time of death was approximately 10:32 am."

"Wow, that's a specific approximation."

"Her watch stopped."

I raised an eyebrow.

He shrugged. "Got clogged with buttercream."

"What about DNA?"

"Have to wait for lab techs to finish processing."

"Okay. What else?"

"That's it."

"That's it?"

"Yep."

I sank back in my seat, suddenly thinking Dana and Marco were right. If that was all he had so far, Ramirez really did need our help.

Having divulged all he knew, Ramirez focused on the TV. Me—I had no interest in guys in squeaky shoes putting a ball in a net. Instead I wandered over to my drawing table, picking up a sketch for a pair of ruby red slingbacks I'd been working on. On the floor next to my drawing table sat a brown package that I'd swear hadn't been there this morning.

"Where'd that come from?" I asked, nodding with my head.

"UPS brought it after you went to the gym. Looks like a wedding present."

I dropped my sketch with a squeal. "We have unopened gifts in the house? Why didn't you tell me?"

I didn't wait for an answer, instead grabbing a pair of scissors from my drawing table and attacking the box. It was addressed to "the Future Mrs. Jack Ramirez" (which elicited another high-pitched squeal on my part) from Uncle Cal, my Mom's oldest brother. In a flurry of packing peanuts and bubble wrap, I dug into the sucker, pulling out our very first wedding gift, the first thing that belonged to us as a couple. I felt anticipation building in my stomach, as I emerged with a crystal…um…

"What the hell is that?" Ramirez asked, staring at our first wedding gift.

It was clear, angular, and…kinda shaped like a duck. With a spout coming out of its beak. And a handle made of crystal tail feathers.

"Gravy boat?"

"It looks like a duck."

"A duck-shaped gravy boat?"

Ramirez grinned. "Does this mean you're gonna learn how to cook when we get married?"

I resisted the urge to throw the gravy boat at him (I threw a packing peanut instead.), shoving our anticlimactic first gift back into the box.

"Tell you what," I said. "I'll learn to cook when you learn to scrub toilets."

"Takeout it is."

"So," I said, joining him on the sofa. "Dana and Marco agreed to help plan the wedding now that Gigi's…well, you know…" I trailed off, not able to actually make myself say the words.

Ramirez narrowed his eyes. "Marco? He's the guy with the eyeliner?"

I nodded.

Ramirez shook his head. "God help us."

"They promised they'd keep it tasteful. Small."

He shot me a 'yeah right' look.

I would have argued with him, but honestly I had my own doubts.

"So…um, we still need to let the caterer know about the cake. I know we didn't actually get to taste it, but, well, they still need to know what to make."

Ramirez's eyes took on that dark, hooded cop-face look. That unreadable gaze that left me forever guessing the emotion hiding behind them.

"They left a message on my voicemail saying a sample would be ready at the bakery day after tomorrow. So, how about it?"

"Look, Maddie, I can't think about a wedding right now. Can't you just…handle it?"

That squealy feeling faded instantly.

Our wedding was now something to be "handled."

Okay, I know he probably didn't mean it that way, but right then I didn't quite trust my voice. Instead, I just nodded, avoiding his gaze.

"Thanks." He wrapped one arm around me, grabbing the TV remote with the other and flipping on some basketball game in progress.

I closed my eyes and leaned against his chest, focusing on his steady heartbeat against my cheek and not the tiny bubble of anxiety those unreadable eyes had instigated in the pit of my stomach.

Probably Ramirez was just tired. Probably he was preoccupied. Probably it was that he just didn't have the energy to think about white organza-strewn aisles and not that he was having second thoughts about actually walking down them.

Probably.

But one thing was for certain—if I wanted my groom back, I was going to have to find Gigi's killer.

And fast.

CHAPTER SIX

———

Organ music filled the air, echoing off walls peppered with bright red roses and delicate white baby's breath. Silky ribbons knotted into intricate bows made a clear pathway down the aisle. I followed them, slowly walking forward, my feet moving as if through molasses. I could feel everyone's eyes on me, watching me, waiting breathlessly.

My hands began to sweat as I neared the end of the aisle. A line of bridesmaids in black stood to one side, their dresses somehow morbid against the white background, the blood red roses in their bouquets suddenly appearing sinister. To the other side, a line of groomsmen, again in unrelieved black. One stood out from the rest, his back to me, apart from the other tuxedo-clad-men. The groom.

I swallowed a nervous lump in my throat, my heart beating way too fast. Somehow the organ music had morphed from the wedding march to something out of a B-horror movie. Shadows seemed to gather along the walls, shifting the flowers and ribbons into grotesquely distorted shapes. I wanted to run, to leave, to get away as fast as I could. But I couldn't make my feet respond. No matter how I tried to flee, they continued their steady forward motion toward the man waiting for me at the end of the aisle.

I watched in fascinated horror as he came closer and closer, until I was standing right behind him.

I held my breath as he turned around.

Only it wasn't a him.

It was Gigi, the front of her suit covered in sickly yellow buttercream, her lifeless eyes staring out at me as her lips mouthed the words, "Don't forget to order place cards."

*   *   *

I shot bolt upright in bed, sweat trickling down my spine, breath coming out like a marathon runner's. I whipped my head around the room. No organ, no blood-red roses, no gory corpse groom.

I let out a deep breath, sinking back onto my pillow.

Instinctively I rolled over toward Ramirez…only to find his side of the bed conspicuously empty.

I opened my eyes, swallowing down a lump of disappointment. But what did I really expect? With an open homicide, he'd probably been strapping his gun on well before the sun had come up.

I got up and padded into the kitchen to my Mr. Coffee, filled to the brim, giving off the heavenly aroma of freshly brewed French Roast. A yellow Post-it was stuck on the side.

Had to run.

XO

R

Okay, so I didn't get to wake up in his arms. But he had made me coffee. Gotta love the man for that.

I downed a cup, then showered and dried my hair before stepping into a pair of cropped jeans, an Ed Hardy T-shirt with pink skulls and rose vines creeping over the shoulders, and a pair of cute, pink wedge heels I was determined to wear despite the fact that spring was still a good month and a half off.

Pouring myself a second cup of Ramirez's caffeinated offering, I flipped open my laptop and booted it up.

As I may have mentioned, I'm not what you'd call technology savvy. I'm an artist—give me a pad of paper and a set of drawing pencils, and I'll create you the most to-die-for designs you ever saw. But sit me in front of a computer, and my IQ drops about twenty points. What makes a computer tick is a total mystery to me. Part of me still has this irrational fear I'll push the wrong button and smoke will start coming out of my monitor.

With no small difficulty, I've stumbled my way through learning the basics. I can check my email and order shoes from Zappos.com. And, I'm proud to say that, after a particularly frustrating afternoon with my laptop, I'd figured out how to make the songs on iTunes miraculously appear on my iPod. But download, upload—it was all gobbledygook to me.

Needless to say, MySpace was way out of my league.

I took a fortifying breath before typing the web address into my browser. It only took me two tries to realize that MySpace was all one word (Whatever you do, don't put an underscore in there. Shudder. That was way more than I wanted to see of anyone before my second cup of coffee in the morning.), but finally a blue welcome screen came up. I typed in my email address and the password Marco had given me.

My personal page came up next, along with the information that I had two friends. Some guy named Tom and Allie Quick. I clicked on the little link below my name that read "inbox" and saw Allie's smiling face at the top of the queue.

Look at me, navigating the internet like a pro!

Feeling pretty darn proud of myself, I opened the message.

It was short and to the point, saying how horrified she was about what happened to Gigi and that she'd be happy to meet with me this morning. She suggested her apartment at 10:00 and gave me an address in Glendale.

I glanced up at the clock above my drawing table. 9:30. I downed my coffee and I prayed traffic on the 5 was light.

* * *

10:12 I pulled up in front of a two-story tan, stucco building hunkered against the side of a hill on Verdugo. It was one of those nondescript seventies buildings that conformed to the utilitarian shoebox school of architecture. Three units on the bottom, three on top, one set of rusted metal stairs climbing up the right side. On the left was a covered car park, where a pair of sedans squatted beneath the overhang.

I parked at the curb and clubbed my Jeep, taking a cement walkway to the building through overgrown agapanthus and a lawn that was 90% crabgrass. The mingling scents of curry and onions wafted from beneath the first door, the distant wail of an unhappy toddler bellowing from the second before I reached unit F on the end. I gave a sharp rap, hoping Allie was still home.

Two beats later Gigi's former assistant opened the door. Her blue eyes were red and rimmed with dark circles that spoke of a sleepless night. She held a tissue in one hand. A pair of white cargo pants hung limply on her slim frame beneath a black Daughtry concert T-shirt that hugged her generous D cups in a way that made me wish I'd thrown on a Wonderbra this morning.

"Oh, Maddie, doesn't this just suck?" she said, her voice threatening to crack.

I nodded sympathetically. "Thanks for seeing me. Do you mind if I come in?"

She nodded, sniffling loudly before stepping back to allow me entry.

The inside of the apartment was as square and uninteresting as the outside, a small kitchen done in olive green tile and peeling linoleum to the right, a living room to the left and a single bedroom visible beyond that. While the gray shag carpeting and at-one-time-white vertical blinds were an eyesore, she'd tried to make the most of it with the furnishings. A colorful sheet covered the sofa on the far wall, red and yellow throw pillows adding a cheery feeling. A TV sat in one corner on a stand painted in white and yellow, a matching coffee table sitting in the center of the room, a vase full of bright pink daisies gracing its top. Someone was obviously making the most of a meager salary.

Next to the flower vase sat a slim, silver phone with about a hundred more buttons than mine and a textbook, open to a page filled with equations that made my eyes cross just glancing at them. Algebra had never been my thing. Math was numbers as far as I was concerned. As soon as they started throwing letters in there, they'd lost me.

"Taking a class?" I asked.

Allie sank down onto the sofa, pulling one leg up underneath her as she nodded. "At UCLA. Algebra two."

I suppressed a shudder as I took a seat beside her. "You're ambitious."

"It's required. If I want to graduate this June, I have to suck it up and take math."

"I didn't know you were still in school." Though it made sense. She looked about twelve today, minus her makeup and tailored work clothes.

Allie nodded. "Working with Gigi was just a part-time gig. I'm actually majoring in journalism. I only worked at L'Amore on days I didn't have class. Which is why I wasn't there yesterday when..." She trailed off, her eyes filling with big fat tears.

"I'm so sorry," I said, laying a sympathetic hand on her arm. "Had you worked for Gigi long?"

Allie shook her head, blonde hair swaying against her cheeks. "Not really. I just started last quarter."

"Do you have any idea who could have done this? Anyone have a grudge against Gigi?"

"No! No one." Allie pressed the tissue to her lips. "I can't think of a single person who'd want to harm Gigi. She was wonderful. The woman was an amazing artist."

While I personally didn't exactly see party planning as art, I bit my tongue, instead making more sympathetic noises.

"What about businesswise? Any debts she hasn't paid, financial trouble?"

"Just the opposite. Business was booming lately. After she did that football player's wedding to the pop star last month, she was featured everywhere. *Entertainment Tonight*, E!, even TMZ mentioned her by name. She couldn't keep people away."

"What about past clients?" I asked, not yet ready to give up my fishing expedition. "Any weddings gone awry? Anyone who might have blamed Gigi?"

Allie shook her head. "No. The police asked me all this yesterday, too."

"The police were already here?" Duh. Of course they would have been. Ramirez was a trained homicide investigator. I felt a tiny prickling in the back of my head that I was wasting my time. If Allie knew anything worth pursuing, chances were Ramirez was already pursuing it.

"Yeah. They were really pushy, wanting to know if Gigi and I got along, where I was that morning, if anyone could verify it. It was almost like they were accusing me of something."

"How awful," I said, appropriately horrified.

"They were. Except for the tall one. He was actually sorta nice. Kind of a hottie, too. Hispanic, tattoo on his bicep, nice butt."

I narrowed my eyes. Hey, that was my hottie!

"Anyway," she continued, "they wanted to know all about who Gigi did business with, who might have been angry at her. But, honestly, I can't imagine anyone being angry at her, you know? She was just the most wonderfully sweet woman ever."

While I was sorry to see Gigi gone, 'sweet' wasn't exactly a word I would have used to describe Gigi. Efficient, yes. But sweet? I wondered if maybe we weren't dealing with a minor case of hero worship here.

"Allie, Gigi's ex-husband mentioned that she was seeing someone new. Do you happen to know who he is?"

Allie bit her lip, cocking her head to one side. "Gosh, I dunno. Gigi wasn't real open about her private life."

"He may have been in a band of some sort?" I prompted, mentally crossing my fingers.

Allie looked up at the ceiling, searching her memory. "Um, let's see…well, I don't know if it's the person you're looking for, but this one guy did come by the office a few weeks ago. Said he could get me tickets to his concert if I wanted."

I felt myself sit up straighter. "What concert?"

"The Symmetric Zebras."

I had to admit, I'd never heard of them. But, then again, the last time I'd aspired to be a groupie was when I was fifteen and drooling over my Skid Row posters.

"Any idea how I can get hold of these Zebras?"

Allie shrugged. "Sorry, I'm not really a fan."

I was about to press more, when Allie's phone rang, vibrating across the coffee table.

She picked it up, flipping open the top. "Sorry. Text," she explained, reading the little screen. Then she did some fancy maneuver, flipping the screen sideways and turning the screen into a mini-keyboard. She quickly typed back some message using her thumbs with a speed that I'd swear rivaled the best receptionists in the known universe.

"Wow, cool phone." Even though it would take me a year to figure out how to use it.

"Oh, thanks. Gigi gave it to me for Christmas. Same one she had. She said the bulk of her business was about organizing and timing. Double booking is like death to a wedding planner." She paused, cringing at her own word choice. "Uh, anyway, she said I needed a way to keep track of everything on the go."

"You don't happen to have Gigi's schedule on there as well, do you?" I asked, leaning forward to get a better look.

"Uh-huh. Hang on a sec." She slipped a stylus from the side and stabbed at the little screen. "Gigi wanted to make sure I avoided any conflicts, so I always kept a copy of her schedule."

"Any idea what she had planned the morning she died?" I know, it was unlikely the killer had made an appointment to murder her. But it was possible someone she'd been meeting with had stabbed her in the heat of the moment. At the very least it might be worth questioning the people who'd last seen her.

"Let's see," Allie said, pursing her blonde brows together, "no clients that morning. But she had an appointment the afternoon before with Mitsy Kleinburg." Off my blank face, she added, "You know, the daughter of that guy who directed Johnny Depp's last movie? She's marrying some stockbroker in June, and the chick is a total nightmare. Changes her mind like every five seconds, then blames us when things get delayed."

"Really?" I asked, making a mental note. So not *everyone* had been on hunky-dory terms with Gigi. I wondered just how nightmarish Mitsy could get. Enough to actually kill over a fouled-up table setting?

Yes, I was reaching. But it was a start at least.

"I don't suppose you have Ms. Kleinburg's number, do you?"

Allie bit her lip, then looked up at me through her enviably long lashes. "I'm really not supposed to give it out," she said. "A lot of Gigi's clients are high-profile personalities. I had to sign a confidentially agreement and everything when I came to work for her."

"Right." So much for Bridezilla.

"Sorry," Allie said, looking like she actually meant it.

"Anything else? She didn't have anything scheduled for that morning?"

Allie stabbed a little more with her stylus. "Just Paul."

"Another boyfriend?"

She laughed. "Hardly. Paul Fauston does all our wedding cakes. He was probably delivering the sample that morning that…" She trailed off, her eyes going watery again as she left the rest unsaid.

I patted her arm awkwardly.

While I'd yet to actually meet Mr. Fauston, I recognized his name right away. Gigi had said he was the best in the business, creating virtual sculptures out of sugar and egg whites. I may have been iffy about place cards, but the cake was one place I was not skimping. We'd taken Gigi's advice and ordered from him straight off. From what I remembered he had a bakery just a few blocks from Gigi's studio.

"Listen, I don't mean to be rude, but I've got a test later," Allie said, gesturing toward her algebra book, "and I didn't get a whole lot of sleep last night."

"Of course. Thanks for seeing me," I said, rising from the sofa and crossing the tiny room to the doorway.

"If you think of anything else, here's my number," I said, slipping Allie my card.

She took it with a sniff, then shut the door behind me.

Once back in my Jeep, I opened my purse, pulling out a notepad and pen. While Mystery Rocker Boyfriend was still my number-one suspect, I wrote down Paul Fauston's name. I know. The baker visiting the wedding planner before a cake tasting was hardly in the arena of suspicion. But he'd likely been the last person to see her alive. And it *was* his cake knife that she'd been killed with. Which definitely bore looking into. Luckily, I had an appointment with him tomorrow to taste that cake sample, an excellent excuse to grill him.

I felt a little pang in my gut that I'd be doing it alone this time instead of with Ramirez, but I shoved it down, telling myself I was a big girl. I could taste wedding cake alone. So what if Ramirez wasn't interested in the minute details of our wedding? As long as he showed up, it would be fine.

I just prayed he'd show up.

Under Fauston's name I wrote, *Mitsy Kleinburg* with a notation, *bitchy bride.*

If Mitsy had really been as bad as Allie said, maybe she and Gigi had had a falling out? Maybe Gigi had ordered the wrong hors d'oeuvres? Booked the wrong chapel? Maybe in a fit of bridal induced rage, Mitsy had offed Gigi? As I well knew, getting married was more than enough to stress a person out. Maybe Mitsy had just snapped?

Allie may not be at liberty to divulge Mitsy's number, but, thanks to my addiction to celebrity gossip magazines, I did know where to find Mitsy's famous father. Al Kleinburg was wrapping up production on a period piece already being hailed as next season's Oscar frontrunner. It was the angsty saga of one family's fall from grace during the depression and, according to *Access Hollywood's* Nancy O'Dell, was currently being shot on the Sunset Studio's lot.

With new purpose, I flipped a U-ey on Verdugo and hopped onto the 134 heading west. I was just merging at the 101 interchange when my cell chirped to life from the depths of my purse. Driving with one hand, I used the other to navigate around a tube of lipstick, a sheaf of credit cards, and some old mints until I finally laid hands on my phone, flipping it open just as it was about to go to voicemail.

"Hello?"

"Maddie?" Mom shouted on the other end.

I cringed, pulling the phone away from my ear. "Hi, Mom."

"What?"

"I said 'hi.'"

"Speak up, baby, I can hardly hear you," she shouted.

I rolled my eyes.

"I said 'hi!'" I yelled.

"Oh. Hi, baby. Listen, where are you?

"I'm on the 101. Why?"

"Oh, thank God. I was worried with all that had happened you'd forgotten."

Oh. Shit. "Forgotten?"

"The fitting. You didn't forget, did you?"

Mental forehead smack. The dress fitting.

Four months ago Mom and I had spent three full weekends scouring every boutique in town for the perfect wedding dress. I'd tried off the shoulder, one shoulder, spaghetti strap, empire waisted, pleat waisted, long sleeved, puff sleeved, lace, beaded, satin, silk, and everything in between. For once in my life, I had to admit, I'd been shopped out.

Finally, we'd found this new boutique started by none other than Austin Scarlett, one of Heidi Klum's *Project Runway* cast-offs. The most gorgeous couture gowns you ever saw. On the very back rack, the last dress I tried on…I found my perfection. Never mind Ramirez, I was pretty sure that this dress was my soul mate. A slim, corset waist, cut low in the back with a full skirt and delicate beading around the hem in a lovely white satin that made my skin feel like it was indulging in a silky bubble bath every time I put it on. Only better. 'Cause I got to wear a tiara with it.

Today was the final fitting to check every nip, tuck, pin, and seam. As much as the last twenty-four hours had taken out of me, I felt my mood lifting just a little at the thought of putting it on.

"Right. The dress. Of course. Uh, what time is the fitting again?" I asked, glancing down at my dash clock.

"It's in half an hour. You didn't forget, did you?"

"Me? Forget? Never," I said, taking the next exit. "I'm on my way."

CHAPTER SEVEN

———

Austin Scarlett's bridal salon was located in an unassuming white-stuccoed building off Beverly, sandwiched between a trendy French bistro with an outdoor patio and the Lucky Happy Time nail salon. The front window featured headless mannequins in gorgeous, flowing gowns of bright white satin holding large, foam geometric shapes in primary colors that looked like they should be in a preschool block bin. The contrast was striking, bold, and oh-so-very high fashion.

I pushed through the glass front doors and inhaled deeply the scent of fresh couture as my eyes scanned the small interior for my merry band of wedding misfits.

I spied Mom right away, her neon green stretch pants standing out like a sore off-the-rack thumb among the soft, beaded gowns.

While I loved my mother dearly, I thanked
the gods on a daily basis that I hadn't
inherited her fashion sense. Though I had to
admit, lately she'd been trying. After
experiencing Paris Fashion Week last year,
Mom had finally seen the fun in fashion.
She'd absorbed every outfit she'd seen go
down the runway. Then had promptly come
home and started downloading fashion
shows from YouTube.

Unfortunately, she'd taken the outfits just
a little too literally. Anyone who's ever seen
a runway show will know what I mean when
I say the outfits are for *show*, not necessarily
ready for the racks at Nordstrom. They're a
jumping off place for the wearables that hit
stores that season. Not even models could
get away with wearing show outfits around
town for an afternoon of brunch and gossip
with the gals without catching snickers and
stares.

And I could see Mom already eliciting a
few from the other shop patrons.

She'd paired the neon stretch pants
(because, as she'd told me, "Bold color is in
this year, Maddie!") with a long, billowy
white shirt that was just a tad on the see-

through side ("This spring is all about sheers!") and a leopard print bra that was way too visible beneath (Apparently she hadn't downloaded any lingerie shows yet.). A pair of iridescent silver boots covered her feet and long, dangling neon green earrings hung from her ear lobes. She'd capped the effort off with matching green eye shadow that went all the way from the line of her chunky mascara to her penciled-in eyebrows.

I did an internal shudder, thankful she hadn't been kicked out of the boutique by now.

"Mads!" she cried, rushing across the shop and enveloping me in a hug. "Oh, I'm so glad you made it. Almost on time, even."

I generously let the comment slide.

"BillyJo just left," she continued. "Her dress fits fine, and Marco's helping Molly and Dana get dressed now."

BillyJo, Molly, Dana, and Marco were the girls I'd convinced to be my bridesmaids. (Yes, I lumped Marco in with the girls. Trust me, he was thrilled.) BillyJo was Ramirez's sister and, while I got the distinct impression she wasn't all that fond of me, she'd seemed pleased to be included in the wedding party. Especially since all five hundred of Ramirez's brothers and male cousins were groomsmen.

Molly, or The Breeder, as I liked to call her, was my cousin. She'd popped out five rugrats in just under six years. I was pretty sure I didn't have one recent photo of Molly where she didn't either look like she was smuggling watermelons under her shirt or have a kid glued to one hip. Or both. After the last munchkin, had been born, Molly told her husband he had two choices—either he could make an appointment with their doctor to get a vasectomy or he'd have to sleep with one eye open and hide all the kitchen knives. 'Cause one way or another, the guy was getting snipped. Wise man that he was, he made an appointment the next day.

"Come on, everyone's in the back," Mom said, leading me to a private section of the shop that opened up to three fitting room doors. I could see tiny feet beneath two of them. Beneath the third, pink loafers. On a plush sofa to the side sat Connor "The

Terror", my faveorite of Molly's brood, sucking on a Tootsie pop.

"Hey, Connor," I said giving him a little wave.

He stuck his artificially grape colored tongue out at me. Connor wasn't what you'd call a master conversationalist.

"Mads, is that you, dahling?" Marco called.

"Yep. Almost on time, even," I said, sending my mom a playful look.

"We'll be out in a second. Wait until you see what Dana and I did to the bridesmaid outfits!"

Did? Uh-oh.

"Um, they were kind of done already, weren't they?" I called back, taking a seat on the sofa as far away from Connor's sticky fingers as possible.

I'd gone with simple yet flattering gowns for all three ladies. They were long, flowing white, with touches of red along the hem and sleeves. Dana had wanted to do spaghetti straps, but Molly had vetoed that, saying that after breastfeeding for five years straight her boobs hung somewhere around her belly button. Without her ultra industrial strength support bra she looked like a mutant. After we'd measured the width of said mega bra's straps (two inches of the strongest spandex modern man could make) it was pretty clear spaghetti straps were out of the question. We'd gone with flirty little cap sleeves with a red trim instead, then dressed Marco in a white suit with a white shirt and red tie.

All in all, simple, elegant, tasteful.

Which is why a knot of dread was forming in my stomach now.

"What do you mean 'what you did' to the bridesmaid outfits?" I asked again.

"Weeeeell," Marco said, drawing out the word, "we realized your wedding didn't have a theme."

"Theme?"

"Yes, a theme," Mom piped up. Apparently she'd been in on this.

"Oh, Mads!" Dana popped her head out of door number two. "You have to have a theme to your wedding."

"She's right," Molly's voice chimed in from behind door number one. "I read it in *Good Housekeeping*. Themed weddings are in. Boring traditional weddings are out."

"Boring?" I asked, the dread growing.

"Boring," Dana repeated.

"You don't want a boring wedding, Maddie," Mom said, shaking her head.

"And since you're taking your honeymoon in Tahiti…" Marco said.

"…island paradise…" Dana added.

"…so romantic…" Marco, said, popping his head out of door number three.

"…we decided on a Romance in Paradise theme!"

"It's perfect, dahling."

"Tropical chic."

"Do we love, or do we love?"

I blinked at the two of them doing their disembodied heads version of Abbot and Costello.

"Tropical chic?" Suddenly visions of plastic grass skirts and coconut bras danced before my eyes. "Uh, I don't know…"

"Oh, it's going to be fab! We've already ordered the flower leis," Marco informed me.

"And hula dancers."

"And two giant tiki heads."

"Tiki heads?" I asked. Only it sounded more like, "Ti-iki h-eads," as loud hiccups interrupted my speech.

"Uh-huh," Dana nodded. "So, going with the new theme…"

"…we made a few changes to the bridesmaid outfits…" Marco said, fairly bursting as he danced on the tip toes of his loafers.

"You're going to love them," Dana clapped her hands together behind the door. "Ready, Molly?"

"One more zipper," Molly huffed behind her door. "Okay, got it."

As one, the three of them stepped out of their fitting rooms.

"Ta-da!" Marco said, striking a Madonna Vogue-worthy pose.

My eyes ping-ponged from one of my "simple, elegant, tasteful" dresses to another.

Someone had glued tiny sea shells all along the red trim at the hem and sleeves. Fake red hibiscus flowers had been sewn all up and down the skirts and the necklines were now trimmed with braided hemp rope.

And Marco's tuxedo was dyed red. Head to toe red. With a hula girl appliquéd on the tie.

"Well, what do you think, Maddie?" Dana asked, rocking onto her toes.

Luckily, I didn't have to answer as a loud hiccup erupted from my mouth instead.

Connor giggled, grape-colored drool sliding down his chin.

"We made the changes ourselves. Total retro island girl, don't you think?" Dana did a twirl. Prompting the tiny clam shells at the hem to clink together like a wind chime. "So romantic." She sighed. "Just what I'd want at my wedding."

"I think a hibiscus is caught on my bra," Molly said, twisting in the mirror and tugging at an industrial strap.

"Well? Say something," Marco said. His eyebrows drew together and his Vogue started to fade.

I opened my mouth to speak.

But only a sort of strangled sound in the back of my throat came out.

Mom clapped her hands together with glee. "She's speechless. Oh, we knew you'd like them. See, you're not the only one with an eye for fashion." She winked at me.

I hiccupped again.

"Mads, have you got the hiccups again? Dana asked, pointing out the obvious.

"Here, try holding your breath," Marco said, pinching my nostrils together.

"Ow."

"No, no, she has to tip her head back," Molly instructed, elbowing her way toward me. She grabbed a generous handful of my hair and yanked backward.

I tried to protest, but only another hiccup came out.

"Someone get her a glass of water," Mom instructed.

"Here, I've got a sports drink," Dana said, reaching into her bag and pulling out a bottle of orange stuff with lots of lightning bolts on the label.

Mom shoved it under my nose while Molly held my head back.

"Hold your breath and drink as quickly as you can," Mom said, pouring the bottle down my throat.

It tasted like liquid vitamins and I coughed, sputtering orange junk down my chin.

Connor wailed with glee, clapping his hands until his lollipop stuck to the sofa.

"I'm fine. Really," I said, breaking free from the oh-so-helpful trio. "I'm f (hiccup) ine."

"Geeze, you really have them bad." Dana cocked her head to one side, studying me.

"No kidding." I pulled a tissue from my purse, wiping sticky stuff from my chin.

"Hello?" a voice called from beyond the door. "Everyone decently clothed?"

I looked at Marco's tie. That was debatable.

But before I could answer, Austin Scarlett came striding flamboyantly into the room, a black garment bag over one arm. "There's our blushing bride!" he cried, descending upon me with a pair of air kisses.

Take every fashion industry cliché you can think of, roll it into one divalicious package, and you'd have Austin Scarlett. From his blonde bouffant, to his faint uppercrust accent, to his flared waistcoat and heeled boots, he was fashion with a capital F-A-B.

Mr. Fashion's eyes flickered to the horror that was my bridal court, but, like a true professional, he didn't even roll his eyes, instead looking away before any snarky comments could slip out.

"Sweetie, you look divine today," he said, draping his bag on the seat beside me. "We're ready to try your dress, yes?"

I nodded, praying he hadn't let the Theme Squad get their hands on it.

And, as he unzipped with the flourish of a true artist unveiling his latest masterpiece, I let out a sigh of relief that God was on my side today.

It was flawless.

I felt my breath catch. Yeah, I know that's what all brides say. But I seriously couldn't breathe for a full two seconds. It was that beautiful. I reached one hand out and reverently stroked its silky smooth surface, all my childhood fantasies of Cinderella princess dresses suddenly realized in front of me.

In a magical whirlwind moment I will treasure for the rest of my life, my own clothes came off and the dress slipped over my head. I stared at my reflection in the three-way mirror and couldn't help grinning like an idiot. All those sessions at the gym with Dana had paid off. The bodice fit perfectly, and I didn't even have to suck in. (Much.) The skirt draped like a dream, the train flowed stunningly, the tiny accents of crystal beads shimmered in the light like diamonds.

"Oh, Maddie, it's lovely," Mom said, tears backing up behind her eyes.

Okay, so maybe I was getting married in a cheap version of the Disneyland Enchanted Tiki Room. Maybe my bridesmaids would look like they'd been attacked by a Tahitian craft fair. Maybe letting Dana and Marco plan the wedding wasn't on the list of Maddie's finest moments.

But one thing was for sure.

The bride would look fabulous.

* * *

By the time we completed all the last-minute tucking and pinning, I was starving.

Dana suggested this smoothie bar she knew down the street. While my stomach was crying for a Big Mac and a large fries, the memory of how snugly the corset waist had fit prompted me to follow her lead and order a strawberry banana shake instead. Honestly it wasn't all that bad. Could have used a generous helping of whipped cream on top, but not bad.

"So," Dana said, leaning back in her white plastic chair outside the smoothie bar, "get anything out of Ramirez last night?"

"Not much." Other than a gut full of worry. But I quickly filled her in on my interview that morning with Allie.

"I wondered if you've heard of the band. The Symmetric Zebras?"

"Sure." Dana sucked the last of her shake so that her straw made loud slurping sounds against the bottom of her plastic cup. "I went to a show of theirs a couple months ago at the House of Blues. Pretty cool, a little on the heavy side, but not bad melodies."

"Know how I could get a hold of them? One of them may be our mystery boyfriend."

Dana puckered up her brow. "I got the tickets from an ex-roommate who roadies for them."

I perked up. For once Dana's endless stream of roommates paid off.

Dana lived in a tiny place in Studio City I'd come to think of as the Actor's Duplex, because it was home to a bevy of actors. Or, more precisely, actor-slash-waiters, actor-slash-valets, actor-slash-security guards…you get the picture. And since actors aren't exactly known for their steady income, the place usually smelled of cheap Top Ramen, and there was a constant turnover of roommates. Over the last couple of years Dana had lived with No Neck Guy, Stick Figure Girl, and, my personal faveorite, Overweight Guy Who Lives on Subway Sandwiches. Lemme tell you, that guy ate so many of those suckers that he started sweating out pastrami.

"Which one was this?" I asked. "Bandanna Guy?"

Dana shook her strawberry blonde head. "Nope. That was the biker. This one was Smokes Dope All Day Guy."

"Ah." I didn't remember much about him except the thick pungent cloud that wafted down the hall every time his bedroom door opened.

"Anyway, I'll give him a call and see if he can put me in touch with the band. Cool?"

"Very."

In the meantime, I shared with her my plan to visit Mitsy's father and have a chat with bridezilla.

"Do you have a pass?" Dana asked, tossing her cup into one of the nearby recycling bins.

"Pass?"

"You know, to get on the studio lot."

Oh. I hadn't thought of that. "No."

Dana grinned. "Good thing you have me, then."

I raised one eyebrow at her, begging explanation

"Ricky shoots *Magnolia Lane* there, remember? He's got me permanently on the guest list."

"Dana, I love you."

She grinned, showing off a tiny strawberry seed stuck between her front teeth. "What's not to love?"

Ten minutes later we were in her tan Saturn, cruising down Sunset Boulevard until we hit the impressive iron gates that enclosed the Sunset Studios. We made a right and pulled into the drive at the main gate where the five hundred-year-old guy with a clipboard checked Dana's ID against his list, then pushed a button allowing us entry onto the lot.

The best way I could describe Sunset Studios was like a giant playhouse. You were never quite sure if things were real or just made to show well on camera. Beyond the front gate, the lot opened up into a huge roundabout with a park in the center with tall oak trees (real) and large decorative rocks (fake). Off the roundabout were different roads that served as the main studio arteries leading to the stately executive offices (real), the filming studios (mostly real), and the famous Sunset Studios backlot (totally fake), a virtual city of hollowed out buildings made to look like New York,

Boston, San Francisco, and, of course, a generic middle-American suburb.

Dana pulled off to the left where a large parking lot for actors, crew, and guests sat, then grabbed a golf cart (the preferred mode of lot transportation) and headed toward the rows of squat warehouses with the names of hit shows painted on the outside. *Magnolia Lane* shot in 6G, nestled between that new crime drama and the latest celebrity game show. A group of guys in headsets smoking cigarettes stood in front next to a guy in a chicken suit (I hoped he was with the game show and not the crime drama), while Wardrobe and Makeup filtered in and out of the side entrance.

Dana parked next to a craft services truck and motioned me to follow her inside.

The last time I'd been on the *Magnolia Lane* set, I was being chased by the Sunset Studios Strangler and running for dear life. Not exactly a memory lane I was dying to stroll down. But, as we walked onto the set, I noticed not much had changed since then. A few of the actors had been changed out for new ones, most notably the show's star Mia Carletto who'd been replaced by a newcomer with the hots for Ricky's character. But, for the most part the sets (fake) and crew (real—well, as real as people got in L.A.) and general air of crazed creativity in the air was still the same.

"Ricky!" Dana called, hailing a shirtless guy by the camera.

He turned, giving her a lopsided smile that would make any woman with a pulse melt. As much as I was a one-Ramirez kind of woman, I had to admit, Ricky was hot. Sizzling. He had to be, because his ratings banked on it. He played the hunky gardener, trimming the hedges of *Magnolia's Lane*'s most desperate housewives as he preened and smiled his way into the hearts of middle America every Tuesday evening. With his heartthrob looks and boyish charm, he was hard to resist.

And shirtless, well…let's just say some of us didn't resist.

Dana flung herself at him, wrapping her arms around his neck as he picked her up in a full bodied hug.

I tried not to be envious, shoving down the memory of my very empty bed that morning.

"Hey, babe, what's up?" Ricky said, setting Dana back down on the ground.

"Oh, I just missed you." Dana twirled her hair around one finger. I wasn't sure if it was cute or pathetic the way she instantly turned into a sixth-grader with a crush around Ricky.

"We've got a few more shots to get today," he said. "But I'll meet you at your place later?"

"Perfect!" Dana bit her lip and giggled.

Ah, young love.

"But, in the meantime," she said, "I was wondering if you know which studio Al Kleinburg is shooting in today?"

Ricky puckered his forehead. "Hey, Jay," he yelled to a grip in a backwards ball cap. "You know where Kleinburg is today?"

"New York."

"Thanks." Ricky nodded at the guy, then turned his attention back to us. "He's on the backlot. Why? You girls want his autograph?"

"Something like that," I mumbled.

"Cool, well I'll catch up with you later then," he said, planting a kiss on Dana. That quickly turned from a peck into something you'd see on pay per view.

I turned away, blushing.

Once Dana had untangled her tongue from Ricky's, we hopped back in the golf cart and sped through the maze of warehouses until it opened up onto the studio backlot. We parked behind a foam replica of a taxi cab in the New York section. (Conveniently located between Boston and *Leave it to Beaver* suburbia.)

A large crane (real) was set up at one end of the street (fake) while a group of extras dressed in 1920s outfits mingled below, sipping bottled water and talking on their cell phones. Countless grips and production assistants ran back and forth, checking the lighting, the sound, and every other detail of the shot, their tool belts stuffed with duct tape and walkie-talkies jangling against their hips.

Off to the side stood a bank of black monitors and fancy computer equipment. Behind it three guys in suits squinted at the playback. Beside them stood the director, Al Kleinburg.

I'd seen plenty of pictures and *Access Hollywood* footage of him attending premieres, but in person he was a lot smaller than I'd expected. I guess due to his high profile I was looking for a larger-than-life figure. In reality he was 5'5" if an inch, balding on top, growing paunchy in the middle, with a pair of wire-rimmed glasses perched on his oversized nose, giving him a slightly Mr. Magoo look.

"Mr. Kleinburg?" I asked, gingerly stepping over a length of cable as we approached the monitors.

"Yes?" he asked, without tearing his gaze away from the scene on the screen. A man was being chased down the faux New York street by what looked like Al Capone's gang.

"I'm Maddie Springer."

"Who?"

"Uh…the fashion designer," I said.

Kleinburg turned to me, a perplexed look crossing his features. "Is there something wrong with wardrobe?"

"No, no. I, uh, I actually worked with Gigi Van Doren," I said. Which was almost true.

"Oh. Right." Kleinburg adjusted his glasses, inspecting me more closely. I suddenly felt like I was auditioning for his time. "Yes. Tragic about that. What can I do for you Ms. Springer?"

"Actually I wanted to speak with you about your daughter, Mitsy. She was a client of Gigi's?"

Kleinburg nodded, his bald spot gleaming in the sun. "Yes. Poor thing's just completely distraught over it. You are going to find her another planner, right?" he asked.

"Me? Oh, well, we…"

"Of course," Dana said, jumping in.

I resisted the urge to elbow her in the ribs.

"That's actually what we wanted to talk to her about," I said. "I understand she didn't get on well with Gigi?"

"Well, I wouldn't go that far. Mitsy is a very strong-willed girl. Always has been. She knows exactly what she wants. Gigi sometimes had trouble delivering it, that's all."

"Had they argued over anything in particular lately?" I asked.

Kleinburg narrowed his myopic eyes at me. "Why do you ask?"

"Um…well…"

"We just want to make sure we pair her with the right planner this time around," Dana said, jumping in again.

I nodded. Even though I was a little worried about promising a new planner to Mr. Hollywood's finicky daughter. As Marco so aptly pointed out, these women booked months in advance.

"I see. Thorough of you," Kleinburg said, nodding. "Honestly, though, I don't really know. I can't keep track of all that wedding stuff. I just sign the checks. And let me tell you, there were plenty to sign. This wedding is costing me a fortune. You know I've spent more on flowers than I did on Mitsy's entire college education? It was quite a racket Gigi was running there."

I raised one eyebrow. "A racket?"

Kleinburg shook his head. "Every week Mitsy came back from that place with one more thing we just 'had to have' at her reception. A flutist, an ice sculpture, engraved stemware. I swear Gigi took one look at my daughter and saw dollar signs."

I had to admit, I'd seen that look in her eyes, too. Fleetingly, I wondered how much Kleinburg might have resented it.

"Mitsy had an appointment with Gigi the day before she died. Do you know what they discussed?"

Kleinburg shrugged. "You know, maybe you should speak to my daughter about this." His eyes started to wander back toward the monitors where the gangster had just caught up with our hero.

"Any idea where we could find Mitsy this afternoon?" I asked.

"Same place she is every afternoon. Shopping."

I raised an eyebrow. Maybe Mitsy wasn't so bad after all.

"She and her mother have been filling out that damned registry for months," he went on. "You want to find her, check Bloomingdale's. Century City Mall. Now if you'll excuse me…" He gestured toward the dailies.

"Of course. Thanks for your help," I called as he turned away.

"He's a lot shorter than I thought he'd be," Dana said as we walked back to our cart.

"Seriously." I navigated around the foam taxi and slipped into the passenger side of the golf cart. "Though I'm liking the idea of Mitsy as the crazed homicidal bride more and more."

"So," Dana said, doing a three point turn back toward the front gate. "I guess we're going to the mall?"

I grinned. "It's a tough job, but someone's got to do it."

CHAPTER EIGHT

———

The Century City Mall was as close to my Mecca as you could get. Row upon row of funky one-of-a-kind stores mixed with the standard mall fare like Abercrombie and Banana Republic, all in an outdoor setting that capitalized on our California surplus of sunshine.

Dana and I parked in the structure and walked through the corridors sheltered by a canopy of white, wooden latticework toward the center flagship of the mall, Blooomingdale's. I tried to put blinders on as we passed through accessories and handbags to the housewares section.

"I always wanted to register at Bloomie's," Dana said, her voice wistful as she eyed a pair of his and hers brandy snifters.

"Well, all you have to do is get some Hollywood mogul to adopt you, and you're set."

She did a sigh, running her fingertips along a silver cake server.

"Come on, let's find Mitsy." Only, as the words left my mouth, I realized there was one fatal flaw in our plan. "Um, any idea what she looks like?"

Dana shook her head.

Shit.

I scanned the rows of crystal decanters, silverware patterns, and china plates for an expensively dressed girl who looked like she 'knew exactly what she wanted.' Unfortunately, that covered just about everyone. (We were, after all, in Bloomingdales.)

Then, near the back, I spotted a sign that read *Bridal Registry*.

Bingo.

I grabbed Dana by the arm and steered her toward the sign. A short, older woman with wiry salt-and-pepper curls sat at a desk beneath it. She wore a pair of thick glasses on a beaded chain around her neck, and a nametag that read *Beatrice* was pinned to the lapel of her maroon suit.

"May I help you?" she asked.

"Yes, I'm purchasing a wedding gift for a friend," I lied. "I'd like to see her registry."

"Of course," Beatrice said, turning to the computer station behind her and tapping her computer to life. "The name, please?"

"Mitsy Kleinburg."

A frown settled between Beatrice's brows. "Oh, I'm terribly sorry, but her registry isn't complete yet."

"Oh, really?" I asked in mock surprised. "Darn."

"Actually," she continued, "Mitsy's out on the floor with her mother right now."

"What a coincidence! Do you think you could point her out to me so I can congratulate her in person?"

Beatrice cocked her head at me. "You don't know what she looks like?"

"Oh, we're with the groom's family," I quickly covered.

"Right. Of course." She turned to her keyboard again, tapping away until a screen with Mitsy's name popped up. Beatrice lifted her glasses to her nose and squinted up at it.

"The last item she logged was from the fine china department." She stood up and gestured the opposite way we'd come in. "It's through barware there and to the right. Mitsy's the lovely young brunette. Long hair, and I believe she's wearing pink today. She's with her mother, in Chanel. You can't miss them."

"Thanks," I said, as we followed her lead through rows of tinted martini glasses and fine champagne flutes.

Just to the right were the displays of china plates, teacups with dainty saucers, and delicate little sugar bowls. All in various floral patterns—lilies, roses, green snaking vines. It was a veritable Eden of dinnerware.

And smack in the middle were the Kleinburgs.

As Beatrice had promised, they were hard to miss. Not that a Chanel suit and a brunette stood out in Bloomingdales. But the volume of their conversation did.

"Marion Lester has the Rose of India pattern. I will not have the same pattern as Marion Lester."

"Well, this one is hideous. What will people say when you serve them on something so pedestrian?"

"Royal Rose is a modern pattern. I'm not serving dinner on some old lady ware. And certainly not the same one Marion Lester has!"

"Well, what about Ivy and Rose?"

"Snoozeville."

"Ivy and Rose is a perfectly respectable china pattern."

"For the near dead!"

"Um, Mitsy?" I asked, coming up behind the pair.

Mitsy spun on me. "What?" she barked.

While her tone was abrasive enough to make me jump, there was no denying Mitsy was a lovely girl. Smooth skin touched with just the right amount of time in a tanning booth, lips any collagen devotee would die for, and long, sleek, brown hair that fell well past her shoulders in a perfectly layered cut that was both trendy and classic all at once.

Maybe money couldn't buy happiness, but, in this case, it could sure buy good looks.

"Hi, I'm Maddie." I stuck a hand out toward her.

She gave it a bland so-what stare.

"I'm a fashion designer. I, uh…worked with Gigi," I said, sticking with the same story I'd spun her father.

Again with the so-what stare. Gee, a big talker, huh?

Luckily, her mom had the society manners thing down pat. "We were both just so shocked to hear about Gigi," she said, putting a hand to her heart as if the very thought may make it beat right out of her chest. "What a horrible incident."

Somehow the word 'incident' made the whole thing sound like a missed luncheon or quarrel with the dry cleaner over a stubborn stain. It sanitized all emotion out of the equation. Which, I decided as I watched Mrs. Kleinburg, I'd bet is just what she meant for it to do.

"Yes, horrible," I echoed. "You were a client of hers?" I asked, turning to Mitsy again.

"I was. But I fired her," she responded, sticking her chin up in the air.

"Oh?"

"Yes, she was impossible. I mean, she said she would give me my dream wedding. Those were her exact words. 'Dream wedding.' Then whenever I asked for something, she couldn't deliver."

"Really?" I asked. "Anything specific she didn't deliver on?"

"God, everything!" Mitsy rolled her brown eyes toward the ceiling. "First she said we couldn't change the flowers this close to the wedding, even though I pointed out that they would now clash with the new color we picked out for the bridesmaid dresses. Then she said the Italian pastry chef I wanted to do my cake wouldn't fly in from Milan to bake it. Then there was the whole orchestra disaster."

"Orchestra?"

"Yeah, I wanted a nine-piece orchestra. Gigi said the reception hall we'd booked could only accommodate five. So, I told her to find a new place. Well, of course she went up in arms saying it was too late to book the size venue we needed. But the last straw was when I was supposed to meet with her at the church to discuss the ceremony arrangements and she totally blew me off. Canceled at the last minute."

"When was this?"

"Saturday."

"The day before she died?" Dana piped up.

"Yes. Why do you ask?" Mrs. Kleinburg stepped in, eyeing Dana and I. Apparently she wasn't as open as Mitsy with her dirty laundry.

"Well…we just want to make sure that this sort of thing doesn't happen again with your new planner." I cringed. I was not the world's best liar, and I had a bad feeling the more fibs I told, the sooner they'd come back to bite me in the butt. But in for a penny, in for a pound.

Mitsy nodded vigorously. "Thank you! I've gained two and a half pounds from the stress! I need someone who is way less pain in the ass."

"Mitsy. Language," her mother said, visibly flinching.

"Had she ever missed an appointment with you before?" I asked. With the way Gigi had emphasized the importance of an organized schedule to her assistant, I had a hard time picturing her forgetting a client meeting.

Mitsy shook her head. "Never. She told me something had come up at the last minute."

"Hmm." I wondered if that something had anything to do with her death the following morning. "She didn't happen to say what had come up, did she?"

"No. She sent me a text, so she didn't elaborate. Just, 'unavoidable' and 'terribly sorry.'" Mitsy snorted as if she didn't believe it. "Old hag probably needed an emergency Botox or something."

"Mitsy," her mother chided again.

"Anyway, I was so done with her after that," she said

I made a mental note to ask Allie about it later. Maybe it was wrinkle related, but then again, maybe not. Unexplained absences the day before the victim's death were the things those *Law & Order* guys salivated over.

"Hey, which pattern do you like?" Mitsy asked, gesturing to a row of plates. "Royal Rose, Rose of India or Ivy and Rose?"

I looked down. All three plates had a yellow background spotted with red roses. I squinted hard, trying to see some difference among them. "Umm…Royal Rose?"

Mitsy gave her mother a smug I-told-you-so look. "See?"

Mrs. Kleinburg looked hardly convinced. "Well, it was lovely to meet you," she said, clearly not meaning it at all.

"Thanks. And same to you," I said, giving a nod Mitsy's direction.

She shot me a wan smile, then turned back to her china.

As Dana and I made our way out of the breakables section I watched Mitsy from behind. While she was clearly a nightmare client, I had a hard time putting her in the role of murderer. She seemed more the type to hire out that sort of unpleasantness. Besides, if she had really fired Gigi on Saturday like she said, I didn't see the motive in it.

Then again, I only had her word that Gigi had missed the appointment at all. I wondered if Allie could confirm it. While I'd asked her for Gigi's schedule, I hadn't thought at the time to ask if Gigi had actually kept to it.

"Which pattern did you pick?" Dana asked, pulling me out of my thoughts as we stepped outside.

I shrugged. "Honestly, all those roses looked the same to me."

"No, silly, not just now. I mean which china pattern did you and Ramirez pick out?"

"Oh. We didn't."

Dana stopped in her tracks as we passed The Gap, grabbing my arm in a vise grip. "Seriously? You didn't pick a china pattern?"

"Um. No?"

"Well what are guests supposed to give you?"

"Um…regular plates?"

She shook her head, giving me a look like I'd just suggested Dixie cups.

"Look, we're not really the china type of people," I explained. "I mean, it's not like we're giving Kleinburg style dinner parties. Most days it's takeout pizza."

"Maddie it's not for *you*."

"O-kaaaaay. Then it's for…?"

Dana shook her head at me, silently giving off the 'you're hopeless' vibe. "You're supposed to pick out a china pattern when you get married so that everyone can buy you that stuff for your wedding, then you can put it in a curio, where your children will admire it their whole lives, and you can leave it to them when you die so they'll always have that reminder of your wedding day."

I stared. "Um. Right. That makes total sense now."

Dana sighed. "Oh, well." She linked her arm through mine and propelled me toward the parking garage. "At least there's always your anniversary. You know, it's never too early to start registering for that."

Lord help me.

* * *

By the time I got back to my studio the sun was just starting to set over the water, creating one of those picture postcard perfect California moments as vibrant oranges and pinks melted into the deep aqua horizon. I wistfully sighed at the thought I'd soon be coming home to a nice little suburban pad instead of my ocean-side escape. Not that I was knocking living with Ramirez. The stay three-nights-at-my-house-then-I'll-stay-three-nights-at-yours thing we'd been doing the last few months since returning from Paris was a pain in the butt. More than once I'd had the perfect outfit picked out only to realize I'd left that pair of shoes in his closet.

But there was some tiny part of me that, despite how happy I was merging from a Me to an Us, was going to miss Me's view.

I parked my Jeep in the drive and trudged up the flight of stairs, happy to see a light on under the door. Amazingly, Ramirez had beaten me home. I slipped my key into the lock, turning the handle to find my guy standing at the kitchen counter hunkered over a bowl of Frosted Flakes.

He raised his head, licking milk from his lower lip. "Hey."

"Hey. You're home early," I said, planting a kiss at the corner of his mouth. Mmm. Kellogg's flavored. Yum.

"Just came by to change my clothes."

"Oh. Right." I tried to hide my disappointment.

"You're disappointed."

Hey, I didn't say I tried *hard*.

"No, it's fine," I lied. "I understand."

"Hmm," he said. But let it go. "Another box came." He gestured to the coffee table. A brown, rectangular package almost as long as the table itself.

Despite feeling just a little frustrated that Ramirez's plans for the evening didn't include spooning with me while we watched *American Idol*, an unopened gift always lifted my spirits.

I checked the return address. My grandmother.

In a large Irish Catholic family there is no greater sin than being single. At every family gathering since I started menstruating, my grandmother regaled me with stories of how she'd had nine children before the age of thirty. As I marched through my twenties unmarried, the stories turned from tales of my ancestors to warnings that my ovaries were drying up like little barren prunes.

Which is why Grandmother had actually fallen to her knees, grabbed her rosary, and said a prayer of thanks when I'd shown her my engagement ring. Her last single grandchild was finally tying the knot. And to a good Catholic boy no less. (Okay, a Catholic boy at any rate. The jury was still out on the "good" part.)

I grabbed my scissors and dug into the package, ripping away tape and fishing around in the layers of packing peanuts until I came away with a soft bundle wrapped in pink tissue paper.

"What's that?" Ramirez asked around a bite of flakes.

"I don't know." I untied the pink ribbon, and out fell a white lacy dress. Size zero. And no, not as in supermodel zero. I mean zero. As in zero-to-three-months baby sized. Underneath it sat a tiny white bonnet with lacy frills down the side and a pair of matching booties.

I looked up at Ramirez, horror bubbling in my throat. "I-I think it's a Christening outfit."

He coughed, choking on his cereal. "A what?"

"A Christening outfit. For a baby."

"Why would she give us that?" He froze. "Wait, you're not pregnant, are you?"

"No!"

He let out a long sigh. "Jesus, don't scare me like that."

"My grandmother's just a little…overanxious." I turned the frilly outfit over in my hands. "You think maybe we should have registered for china?"

Ramirez gave me a blank look.

"Never mind." I shoved the box into the corner next to my crystal duck gravy boat. Did my family know how to do gifts or what?

"So, when are you coming home?" I asked, purposely changing the subject.

"I probably won't be back until late. We've got some leads to follow tonight."

I raised one eyebrow. "Oh?"

Ramirez gave me a warning look. Then stuffed an oversize mound of flakes in his mouth, crunching down with purpose.

"Oh, come on. I'm good at this stuff. I could help," I said, rushing on while his mouth was too full to argue. "In fact, I'll bet I know something you don't know about Gigi."

He paused midchew. Then narrowed his eyes at me and swallowed loudly.

"Please don't tell me Lucy and Ethel have been on the case again?"

"We prefer Cagney and Lacy. But, yes, as a matter of fact we have."

Ramirez shook his head and muttered something in Spanish under his breath.

"What was that?"

"You don't want to know," he responded.

He was right, I probably didn't.

"Do you want to hear what we learned or not?"

He turned around, abandoning his cereal, and crossed his arms over his chest, leaning back against the counter with an assessing stare. "Okay. Shoot, Cagney."

"Ha ha. Very funny." But I filled him in on everything I'd learned so far from Allie, Mitsy, and Summerville.

His bad-cop poker face remained firmly in place until I got to the part about Dana and me ambushing Summerville in his office.

"Wait," he said, holding up one hand. "Are you telling me that you told Seth Summerville you were working with the police?"

"Um, well, technically Dana told him that. But I'm pretty sure he didn't believe it."

He shook his head and started muttering in Spanish again.

"Quit doing that. At least swear at me in a language I can understand."

"Maddie, these are high-profile people with high-profile lawyers and short fuses. You can't just go impersonating an officer like that. You know how much trouble you could get into? If he pushed it, you could get arrested for something like this."

I bit my lip. I hadn't actually thought about that.

"Not to mention," he continued, picking up steam now, "piss a lot of people off. You know what happens when you go prying into people's personal lives?"

"Um, I figure out their motives and eventually find the killer?"

He shook his head. "You end up getting shot at, stabbed, kidnapped, drugged…" He ticked off on his fingers. "Do I need to go on?"

No, he didn't. Because I couldn't argue that all of those things had, indeed, happened to me. "But you have to admit, it's always led to the killer before. Without me, who knows if you'd have solved those cases," I countered instead.

He did a laugh-slash-snort thing. "I think I would have managed."

"So, what, you're saying I've never been any help to your cases before?"

"Maddie, you are not a police officer. You are a fashion designer. You draw little shoe pictures all day."

My turn to narrow my eyes. "You make it sound as if I use crayon. I'll have you know designing shoes is very hard work. It takes a lot of skill and years of training. Not to mention the business savvy it takes to get your own line going. Not just anyone can do it."

Ramirez rolled his eyes.

"I saw that!"

"Fine. I'm sure drawing shoes—"

"*Designing* shoes," I corrected him. Loudly, I might add.

Another eye roll. "Fine, *designing* shoes, is very hard, very important work."

"Now you're just being sarcastic."

He threw his hands up in the air. "What do you want me to say?"

"I want you to say that what I do is every bit as challenging as what you do."

He cocked his head to the side, a smirk playing at his lips.

He wasn't going to say it.

I could feel adrenalin pumping through my veins, every feminist bone in my body rankling. Okay you wanna play hard ball, pal? Fine. Let's play.

"Okay, you think anyone can do my job? Let's see *you* do it?"

"Excuse me?"

"You heard me. I bet you that I'm better at police work than you are at designing shoes."

"Oh, you do, do you?"

I crossed my arms over my chest. "Yep."

He shook his head as the smirk turned into a full bodied grin. "Okay, what do you have in mind, Springer?"

"You let me investigate Gigi's death—"

He opened his mouth to protest.

"—without impersonating any officers."

Reluctantly, he shut it with a click.

"At the same time, you have to design a pair of high heels. If the heels are fab, you've proven your point. But if I catch

Gigi's killer, I win and you have to admit that what I do takes skills, and you actually have respect for my intellect."

Something flickered behind his eyes. "You know I respect you, Maddie."

"I 'draw little shoe pictures'? Yeah, right. I'm feeling the admiration in big steaming piles."

He bit the inside of his cheek and cocked his head to one side, unable to come up with a decent rebuttal to that one.

Finally he said, "And exactly what do I get if I win?"

Damn. I hadn't thought that far.

"What do you want?"

His faced morphed from doubtful to devilish in seconds flat, a wicked smile dancing in his eyes.

"Oh no. No way am I making a bet for sexual faveors," I said, quickly shutting those unspoken thoughts down.

"Okay, then," he said, the mischievous look undaunted. "How about this: I win, and you promise never, and I mean never, to stick your cute little nose into one of my cases again."

"But—" I protested.

But he ran right over me. "No more following witnesses, no more questioning suspects, no more Lucy, Ethel, Cagney, or Lacey."

I bit my lip. Those were high stakes. But this little game of chicken had escalated beyond Gigi and worrying about the wedding. It had become apparent that if I ever wanted him to take me seriously, there was only one answer to his question. I clenched my jaw and thrust my chin toward the ceiling, trying to stretch an extra inch out of my 5' 1 1/2" height.

"Fine."

"Fine?"

"*Fine*."

Surprise flickered across his features. As if he hadn't expected me to woman-up to the challenge. I felt a little lift of pride already. Ha! Take that pal. You're playing with the big girls, now.

"Good," he said. "Then you don't mind if we up the stakes a little."

Oh swell. "As in?"

"As in I not only design a pair of shoes, but you have to wear them to the wedding."

I felt my face drain of color. "My wedding shoes?"

He nodded, that self-satisfied smirk returning. "Yep."

"But I already picked out a pair." They were a simple white satin with a cross cut woven pattern along the top. Elegant and stylish all in one three-inch package.

Ramirez shrugged. "Okay, then all bets are off. And you stay the hell away from the Van Doren case."

He turned back to his abandoned bowl of cereal.

"Wait!" Dammit. I scrunched my eyes shut, sucked up every last ounce of pride I had, and said a silent good-bye to my perfect wedding outfit. "Fine. You can design my wedding shoes."

I opened my eyes and crossed the room, sticking my hand out at him. "Do we have a deal or what, Ramirez?"

For half a second I thought he might back out. Common sense and the thought of having his cases Maddie-free on into eternity warring behind his dark eyes.

Finally he shoved his palm into mine. "Deal."

I shook on it, silently gulping down a little voice telling me I was going to live to regret this.

CHAPTER NINE

———

The next morning I awoke to the sound of jackhammers digging away up the street. I rolled over to see that I was once again alone.

Feeling just the teeniest bit abandoned I got up and trudged to the coffee maker. Another yellow Post-it was stuck to the side.

Took sketch book to work. Will call your manufacturer this morning. Happy hunting.
XOXO
R

I stuck my tongue out at it. But since he had made coffee again, I couldn't hate him too much. Instead, I showered, dressed in a cute pair of capris, peep-toe sandals and a white cashmere sweater, and, with renewed energy, picked up where I'd left off with my suspect list yesterday.

Paul Fauston, the baker.

I took Santa Monica east, past the 405 and into Beverly Hills. I was just veering into the left lane to avoid a pickup with Playgirl bunnies on the mud flaps when I spotted a flash of blue in the rearview mirror.

I narrowed my eyes.

He wouldn't.

I accelerated, pulling two car lengths ahead and moving back over into the right lane. Two beats later a blue Dodge Neon followed my lead, tucking itself behind a silver SUV filled with kids who kept sticking their hands out the window.

That bastard. He was.

Thinking really bad thoughts, I wove in and out of traffic past Wilshire, trying to lose him. But since I was a blonde in a conspicuous red Jeep, and he was a guy who was used to dealing on the shady side of life, by the time I pulled off at Beverly he was right on my bumper, not even attempting to be sneaky now.

I pulled my car up to the curb in front of Fauston's Bakery and got out, slamming the door behind me.

Felix unfolded himself from his little Neon and shot me a smile that I supposed was meant to be charming.

"Good morning, Maddie."

"You're following me."

He rocked back on his heels, his eyes twinkling. "My, my, we are a clever detective, aren't we?"

If looks could kill, he'd be in the morgue.

"What do you want, Felix?"

"I told you. A story. If you won't give me one, I'll just trot around after you until I catch one myself."

I pursed my lips together. "What makes you think I'll lead you to a story?"

Felix threw his head back and laughed. "You're joking, right? Wherever Maddie goes, trouble follows. It's only a matter of time, love."

I bit back a nasty retort on the tip of my tongue. Mostly because he was right.

"Sorry to disappoint you," I said gesturing to the bakery, "but I'm simply tasting a wedding cake today."

Felix glanced from the building to me, his eyes narrowing.

"Really?"

"Really."

"Great, I'm starved."

And before I could stop him, he'd pushed through the front doors to Fauston's.

That's it. I seriously needed to get new friends.

I contemplated turning around, getting back into my car, and driving off. But the thought of Felix questioning Fauston without me shut that idea down. Instead, I followed a beat behind him, listening to a bell chime over the door as we entered the store.

A long bakery counter took up most of the room, running in an L shape along the walls. Inside sat a variety of chocolates, cookies, and tarts that had my mouth instantly watering. Layer cakes, tortes, brownies, and cupcakes taunted my diet from behind their gleaming glass case. The air was filled with the sweet scents of sugar and creamy icing, and I closed my eyes and just inhaled for a moment, getting a kind of sugar rush contact high. My stomach growled out loud in response.

"May I help you?"

I opened my eyes to find a young brunette emerging from the back room, wiping her hands on the starched white apron tied around her waist. I put her in her mid-twenties, just a hair younger than I was (okay, fine, a very thick hair), with dark, serious eyes beneath brows that would make Brooke Shields jealous. She wasn't a whole lot taller than I was, but I'd venture to guess she was at least twenty pounds lighter—a virtual stick figure. I instantly wondered how someone could possibly be so thin surrounded by such heavenly foods all day. Me, I'd be downing half the inventory for lunch.

"Hi, I'm Maddie Springer," I said, offering a hand to the girl.

She shook it in a grip that was deceptively firm for such a slim thing, as her eyes flickered with a spark of recognition. "Oh, right. You're the Valentine's wedding this Saturday?"

I nodded, the nearness of the event hitting me full force. Could it really be this Saturday?

I did a loud hiccup that echoed off the glass cases.

Stifling a laugh, Felix stepped forward. "Felix Dunn," he said, offering his hand to the woman.

"Hi. I'm Anne. Paul's niece. So, you're the groom?" she asked.

I opened my mouth to respond, but only another hiccup came out. Damn these things!

"That's me," Felix answered. He threw one arm around my shoulder, pulling me close to him.

I did another hiccup. Then plugged my nose, holding my breath and counting to five Mississippi as I shot him another death look.

"The little lady and I," Felix went on, giving me a wink, "were so disappointed we never got to taste the other sample you made for us."

"Oh, riiight," Anne said, nodding. "Wow, so sad about Gigi, wasn't it? Almost surreal."

"Almost."

"Um, yeah, let me go tell my uncle you're here."

"That would be much appreciated, love," Felix answered, giving me another squeeze.

Anne returned to the back room, and I let out the breath I was holding with an unladylike heave as air rushed back into my lungs.

I turned on Felix, shoving his arm from my shoulder. "My groom?"

"Well, I couldn't very well tell her I'm the tabloid reporter who's been following you around all morning, could I?"

"I swear to God, I'm going to—" But I didn't get a chance to finish that threat as Anne emerged again, this time with a tall, older man in tow.

Paul Fauston looked to be in his mid-to-late forties, though his height and broad shoulders gave him that timeless Carey Grant sort of appeal. His forearms were dusted with just the finest sprinkling of light hairs, well muscled from years of manipulating dough. He wore a crisp apron as well, only his was layered over a pair of white trousers and a white button-down shirt, giving him a monochrome look that even carried to the pale white/blonde color of his hair. A pair of watery blue eyes stared back from a face that was angular to a fault, a long slim nose, sharp cheekbones and a jaw that time had yet to work its gravitational pull on.

"I'm Paul Fauston," he said, offering his hand. I shook, noting the firmness in his grip. I saw where his niece got it from. "Pleasure to meet you, both. Though I wish it were under different circumstances."

I nodded, mumbling a subdued, "Same here."

Instead of returning to the back room, Anne moved to the bakery case, rearranging a display of fudge squares while pretending (badly) not to eavesdrop on the conversation.

"Such a tragedy about Gigi," Fauston went on. "I really can't get over it."

"Incredible, isn't it?" Felix responded. "Maddie finding her in your cake like that?"

I jabbed him with an elbow. I could already see him mentally concocting a juicy headline: FATAL FEASTS FROM FAUSTON'S BAKERY.

But Fauston just nodded, a solemn look on his sharp features. "We often worked with Gigi. I delivered that particular sample earlier that morning."

"Oh?" I asked.

"Yes. And I have the new sample ready if you'd like to follow me," he said, gesturing toward the backroom.

I followed his apron-clad form around the counter and into the kitchen, trying to ignore the feel of "my groom's" hand at the small of my back as he steered me through the pair of swinging doors.

Fauston's kitchen was a vision in white. White tiled floors, white marble countertops, and a fine dusting of white flour and powdered sugar covering it all. The only relief in the polar look was the array of gleaming stainless appliances and cakes and pastries in various states of dress. The scent of baked goods was even stronger back here, and my stomach growled again as I spied a chocolate torte in the corner just waiting for the final fudge icing.

Fauston led us to a counter where a miniature, one-layer version of my wedding cake sat. A simple, delicate white frosting, surrounded by tiny pink rosettes. In the center were the porcelain little man and wife toppers Gigi had helped me pick out. I noticed Fauston frown as his eyes flickered from the dark haired miniature groom to the blond man whose hand was currently straying precariously closer to my tush.

"It looks lovely," I said, wiggling from Felix's grasp.

"Well, it's just a mockup," Fauston said, cutting the tiny cake in two and handing a slice to each of us.

I took a bite. And sighed out loud. Raspberry filling, light fluffy angel food cake, creamy frosting with just the slightest hint of vanilla. Heaven.

"Mm, delicious," Felix said, licking a dab of frosting off his lower lip. "Snookums, this is the perfect cake."

I swallowed a snort. Snookums?

"Thank you," Fauston replied, clasping his long fingers in front of his apron. "I'm glad you like it. Gigi told me you wanted something simple and traditional."

I nodded, feeling a little ball well in my throat at the fact Gigi had really listened to me after all. "Did you know Gigi well?" I asked, taking another bite of cake to help swallow down the emotion.

Fauston's pale eyebrow drew together as if he were searching for just the right wording. "We've known each other for a number of years."

"Intimately?" Felix asked.

I kicked him in the shin.

"Ow!"

"I'm not sure I know what you're implying," Fauston said. But by the way his ears went bright red, I was pretty sure he did.

"He just meant we're sorry you lost such a close friend," I said as Felix bent down to rub his leg.

"Er, right. Sorry," Felix offered. "British to American translations aren't always clear." He shot Fauston a smile that was all charm.

"Oh." Fauston clasped and unclasped his hands. "Well, yes, we were good friends."

"What time did you say you delivered the cake that morning?" I asked.

"Ten. Why?"

I perked up. If Gigi had died at 10:32, Fauston was likely the last person to have seen her alive.

"I guess that makes you the last person to see her alive," Felix remarked, echoing my thoughts.

Paul went a shade paler. Then, slowly and deliberately said, "No, the last person to see her would have been the monster who did this to her."

He had a good point. But it didn't escape my notice just how strongly he was making it. Methinks he doth protest too much?

"Where did you go after Gigi's?" I asked.

He narrowed his eyes at me. "I'm not sure I feel comfortable answering that question."

Felix stepped in, throwing an arm around me again. "Sorry, the little lady has a tendency to be a bit nosey. I keep telling her, curiosity killed the cat, darling."

I gritted my teeth together. "I think it's time we were going, *darling*."

"Well, if this is all right, I'll have the cake delivered Saturday, then?" Fauston asked, gesturing to our plates.

I was surprised to see mine was empty, though my stomach was growling considerably less. I glanced at Felix's. He'd barely tasted it. I resisted the urge to finish it off for him.

"Yes, please. It's perfect," I answered.

"Good. Well, if you'll excuse me then, I have an order waiting..." Fauston trailed off, gesturing back toward the front of the store.

Taking the cue, Felix and I pushed through the swinging doors back into the store.

Nearly colliding with Anne.

She quickly stepped away and began rolling out a mound of cookie dough on the counter as if she hadn't just been caught eavesdropping red-handed. "How'd you like the cake?" she asked, averting her eyes.

"Delicious." Felix showed off his pearly whites, waving a good-bye to Anne as he steered me out the door.

Once we were out of earshot, I turned on him.

"'The little lady'?"

He grinned. "I thought we made a cute couple in there."

"We made a disastrous couple, Felix."

Something flickered behind his charming smile.

"I meant *in there*," I quickly added, remembering just how close to a real couple we might have been under different circumstance. "Just now. You know, with Fauston."

"I'm aware of the place we just came from, Maddie."

"Right." I ducked my head, awkwardness suddenly hanging like a thick fog in the air between us. "Yeah, of course you are."

"So, what do we think of Fauston?" he asked, deliberately changing the subject.

I was happy to comply. "I think he's a bit shifty."

"Agreed." Felix nodded his head. "But I'm not sure he's our killer. I still like that Mitsy character better. Really we have only her word that she fired Gigi at all."

"That's what I was thinking. But I'm not sure she—" I paused mid-sentence. "Wait. What do you mean 'that Mitsy character'? Were you following me yesterday, too?"

A big toothy grin was my only answer.

"I hate you."

"Sticks and stones, love."

"That's it, I'm leaving."

"Off to where?" he asked, leaning on my passenger side door.

"None of your business."

"Now, don't be that way." And before I could stop him, he had the Jeep door open and his bony butt sliding onto my passenger seat.

I gave him a look that could freeze a penguin. "Out."

"Come on, love, you know I'll just follow you anyway."

"Then follow me, but get out."

"This way saves me gas."

"No!"

"Now, what will Anne think if she sees you throwing your fiancée out, huh, love?"

I ground my teeth together in a way that would make my dentist shudder as I threw a glance at the bakery. Sure enough, Anne was at the window watching our every move while pretending to roll out cookie dough. I hated it when Felix was right.

"Stop calling me love," I hissed.

"You prefer snookums?"

"I—" I started, but the sound of my phone trilling from the depths of my purse halted that thought. Still shooting mental daggers at Felix I flipped it open.

"Yeah?"

"Hey, it's me," came Dana's voice. "Listen, I talked to my old roommate."

"Smokes Dope All Day Guy?"

"Yep. He says the Symmetric Zebras are the warm-up act tonight at the Inca Theater. Seven o'clock. He's got passes waiting for us at will call."

"Dana, you rock."

"Yeah, I know. Hey, listen, Marco and I need your opinion on something."

"Shoot."

"Um, well, you see there's this one thing that we can't agree on."

"Okay…"

I heard Marco pipe up in the background. "You know I'm right. It's just too tacky."

Oh, great. If *Marco* thought it was tacky, we were in real trouble.

"What is it that you disagree about?" I asked.

"Well, I think you should come look for yourself."

"You're worrying me."

"No, it's no biggie," she said. Only the forced lightness in her voice didn't make me feel any better.

"It's a very big, biggie," Marco yelled in the background.

"Dana…"

"Listen, just meet us here in an hour," she said, rattling off an address. I grabbed a pen from the glove box and quickly wrote it down on my hand. "We'll show you everything then," she promised, "and you can make a decision. 'K?"

"Okay, but Dana—" It was no use. She'd already hung up.

"Trouble with the dream wedding?" Felix asked, crossing his hands behind his head and leaning back against the headrest.

"Everything's peachy."

"You're a terrible liar."

"So I've been told," I mumbled.

"So, where are we off to then?"

I punched him in the arm.

"Ow. You've been working out, haven't you?"

Was it awful that a little part of me was pleased someone noticed my newfound gym body?

"All right, if you won't spill it," Felix went on, "I'll tell you what I'd like to know. I for one would like to know who Gigi was meeting the day before she died who was so important she cancelled on Mitsy Kleinburg."

I bit my lip. I had to admit I'd been wondering that, too. "We could go ask Allie."

"Allie?"

"Gigi's assistant. She kept a copy of Gigi's schedule on her phone organizer thingie, but I didn't actually ask which appointments she kept."

The corners of Felix's mouth tilted up. "'Phone organizer thingie'?"

"Shut up."

"Is that a technical term?"

"Shut. Up."

"See, what I'd like to know is how you can tell a thingie from a doohickey. Or a thingamabob for that matter."

"You are really annoying, you know that?"

He shot me his most charming grin, showing off two perfect little dimples.

I gave him the finger. "As I was saying, Gigi was in the habit of scheduling everything. If something came up, maybe Allie would have a guess who or what that something was."

"It's certainly worth a try. Let's have a chat with her, shall we?"

As much as I'd rather have "chatted" with Allie alone, it was clear Felix was in this for the long haul. I shrugged, resigned to my tag-along.

"Fine. But you're pitching in for the gas."

CHAPTER TEN

———

I dialed Allie's cell as I pulled away from the curb. She answered on the third ring and informed me she was at school today but had a break between classes in half an hour. I hopped back on Santa Monica, heading west toward UCLA, snaking my way through Westwood until I hit the ginormous campus. After parking in a lot near the building she'd indicated and spending a full ten minutes trying to figure out the complicated parking voucher machine (I finally gave up, crossing my fingers the lot Nazis didn't catch me), Felix and I made our way across the campus to the student center, where Allie was waiting for us at an outdoor café, iPod buds in her ears, a Red Bull in one hand and a textbook in the other.

I waved as we approached.

She looked up, her eyes still rimmed in the same dark smudges as the last time I'd seen her. Apparently between Gigi and algebra, Allie still wasn't sleeping. She was dressed today in a pair of faded jeans, Ugg boots, and a V-neck sweater dipping low enough to illustrate just how much kinder the boob fairies had been to her than they had to me.

"Hey, Maddie," she said, pulling her headphones out and letting them dangle around her shoulders

"How are you doing?" I asked, putting on my most sympathetic voice.

"Oh, you know..." She trailed off, looking at a spot on the ground.

Felix cleared his throat. I turned to find his eyes riveted to Allie in a way that clearly spoke of V-neck approval.

"Allie, this is a...uh...a friend," I said, almost choking on the word. "Felix."

"Hi," Allie said, extending a hand his way.

He took it. Holding on just a little too long. "Charmed."

"He's a reporter," I told her.

Suddenly Allie's big brown eyes lit up, taking Felix in with renewed interest. "Cool."

"Allie's a journalism major," I explained.

Though, I probably could have said, "Allie's a two-headed dragon who can fart rainbows" and it wouldn't have made any difference. She was blonde, perky, and had big boobs. Felix was riveted.

"Well, any tricks of the trade you'd like to learn, I'm happy to impart my wisdom."

I'd bet my Manolos that wasn't all he'd like to impart.

"Who do you write for?" Allie asked, leaning so far forward I feared the girls would pop out any second.

"The *L.A. Informer*."

And just like that the interest tanked. "Oh. A tabloid." Allie sat back in her seat again, all but sneering out the word 'tabloid'.

My thoughts exactly.

"Listen, Allie," I said, pulling out a chair, "I was wondering if we could ask you something about Gigi's schedule?"

Allie nodded. "Sure. What's up?" She pulled her super phone out of a book bag with little hearts on it resting on the seat beside her.

"Gigi's appointment with Mitsy Kleinburg the day before she died. Mitsy says Gigi cancelled it at the last minute."

"Oh. Wow," Allie said, clearly taken aback. "Gigi was a stickler about schedules; that's not like her."

That's what I thought. "She said something came up unexpectedly. Do you have any idea what that may have been?"

Allie pursed her lips together, wrinkling her forehead in a way that would surely mean chemical peels later, but was completely adorable on a perky co-ed.

"No," she finally said. "Like I said, that was really out of character. But it must have been something important."

"Any idea who would rate such importance? Could it be another client?" Felix asked. "Hot celebrity perhaps, bumping Mitsy?" I could see him fishing for a story.

But Allie shook her head from side to side. "No way. Gigi didn't do faveoritism. She treated all her clients the same way. One reason why she was so popular. Everyone felt like a celebrity with her."

I had to admit, it was true. I'd always felt like Gigi was there to cater to my every wedding whim when I'd been with her. Not that I had a lot of whims. But I'd always felt she was as invested in my having a fabulous wedding as I was.

For a brief moment I felt a pang of regret that Gigi wouldn't be around to see all her hard work come to fruition.

Then again, considering the way things were shaping up with the Theme Team, maybe that was a good thing.

"Sorry, I really wish I could help," Allie said, "but there were some things Gigi kept to herself, you know?"

"Any idea how well Gigi and Paul Fauston got on?" Felix asked, changing gears.

"Oh, they've known each other for ages," Allie said. "I got the impression there might have even been something between them at one point. Oh, but that was long over with," she quickly added, noting the juicy-gossip light flicker on in Felix's eyes.

"How long is long?" I probed.

"Before her ex-husband. I know Paul always resented him."

"The ex?"

She nodded. "Gigi didn't talk about him around Paul much. But a few weeks ago she mentioned his name, and Paul got all tense and red in the face. He said he couldn't wait until she was 'clear of the bastard for good.'"

"Any idea what he meant by that?"

She shrugged.

A lot of help she was.

But…if Paul still carried a flame for Gigi, it was possible he wasn't all that thrilled about her seeing a new guy, either. I wondered just how tightly wound the stoic baker was. Enough to snap at the idea of losing Gigi again?

I was about to ask her just how well she knew Fauston, when her phone vibrated to life in her hands. She flipped the little screen around.

"Sorry, text from my study partner," she explained, whipping her mini keyboard out and sending back a reply.

A light bulb went off in my head as I watched Allie's fingers fly across the keyboard. Mitsy had said Gigi texted her to cancel their appointment. I wondered how many other messages might be stored on Gigi's phone…

"Did Gigi do much texting?" I asked as Allie sent off her message and set the phone down.

She nodded. "Totally. It was her fave mode of communication. She rarely spoke on the phone, said it took too long wading through chit chat to get to the important stuff."

That sounded like Gigi all right.

"So, it's possible that whoever caused her to cancel on Mitsy might have sent her a text that day?"

Allie nodded. "And if she did, the message would still be stored on her phone."

"Which is likely in the hands of the LAPD," Felix reminded us.

Right. I slumped back in my chair. So much for my light bulb moment.

Allie chewed her lower lip. "But wouldn't the phone company still have a record of that stuff?"

"What do you mean?" I asked.

"She's right." Felix nodded. "Any information that gets sent from your phone has to go through your wireless company. While they don't like you to think about it, any data you have, they have as well."

"Wait—" I said, holding up a hand. "You mean if I text something to my boyfriend, some employee at T-Mobile is reading it?"

"It's not exactly that simple, but, yes, there is a record of the data buried somewhere in their server."

I felt my cheeks go hot, remembering the racy messages Ramirez and I had exchanged that night he'd been on a stakeout near the Hollywood Bowl.

That's it, I was never texting again.

"Generally they erase the data after a few days to make room for more, but," Felix said, leaning forward with excitement now, "if Gigi did receive a text from Mr. Anonymous that day, there should still be a record of it at the phone company. All we need to do is get the record."

"But I doubt they'd give that sort of information up to us," Allie reasoned.

"Give, no. But that doesn't mean we can't take a peek on our own."

Uh-oh. I knew that twinkle in Felix's eye.

Felix hadn't become one of L.A.'s most hated tabloid reporters without learning a few key skills along the way. Most of which I couldn't discuss in front of Ramirez without giving him a dozen different reasons to arrest Felix. While I didn't condone some of his practices, I had to admit they had come in handy on one or two occasions. Most notably, his ability to hack into anything with a USB connection.

As Felix explained the intricacies of slipping into the phone company's back door, my eyes started to glaze over from the techno babble.

Allie, on the other hand, was leaning so far forward I could see her bra color. Hot pink.

"You can really do that?" she asked, her voice a little breathless.

"It may take a bit of time, but, yes, I'm pretty sure we can."

"Wow, I'm impressed."

"Ah, er, thanks."

I looked over. Good lord, was Felix actually blushing?

"I will need some information about her account first, though," he added.

"Anything," Allie breathed.

Felix shifted in his seat. Yep, that was totally a blush. I swear to God if I saw a snake in his pants, I was leaving—bet or no bet.

"A copy of her phone bill should have all the account information I need."

Allie nodded. "Done. She kept copies of all that stuff at the office as well as at home. I can easily grab one from L'Amore."

"Allie, you are a gem."

She grinned, showing off a row of white teeth.

She took a sip of her Red Bull, then glanced down at her watch. "Oh shit. I've got class in five," she said, gathering up her books. Then she paused, turning her big doe eyes on Felix. "I've got a study group tonight, but maybe we could get together for lunch or something tomorrow, and I could bring you a copy of the phone bill then?"

"That would be lovely," Felix said, grabbing a pen and writing his address down for her on a napkin.

Why did I have the feeling I was witnessing some sort of hook up here?

Allie shoved the napkin in her book bag and gave Felix one more cute co-ed smile before chucking her Red Bull can in the trash and getting up.

"Bye, Maddie," she said. Though I noticed her eyes hadn't left Felix since he said the word "hack." Apparently that was one skill they didn't teach serious journalism students at UCLA. "See you later, Felix," she said, practically skipping away from the student center.

Poor kid. She had no idea what she was getting herself into.

I jabbed Felix in the side as he watched her walk away.

"I think you're drooling."

He didn't answer, mesmerized by the sway of her round little hips in those skinny little jeans.

"You know she's like twenty, right?"

Felix tore his gaze (with difficulty) away from Allie's butt. "And?"

"And she's way too young for you."

He grinned. "Is that a note of jealousy I detect?"

"No!" I said. A little louder than I meant to, I realized, as a group of pigeons fluttered out of my way. "No," I said again in a normal person's voice. "I'm just pointing out how ridiculous it would be to get involved with someone that much younger than you are."

"Your advice is duly noted," he said. Though I caught him staring at Allie's butt again as she rounded the corner of the student center.

I rolled my eyes.

"Listen," I said, glancing at my watch, "I've gotta go meet Dana. Wedding stuff," I added.

"Ah." He cleared his throat, quickly looking away. "Well, I suppose I'll be off. I think I've done enough groom duties for one day."

"Cute. Listen, let me know when you get something from the phone company."

Felix cocked his head to one side. "Does this mean we're working together again?"

I bit my lip. As much as I wanted to say 'no,' *I* was the one who needed *him* this time. I cringed inside as I forced my lips to form the word, "Yes."

Two dimples appeared in his cheeks. "I knew you'd come around."

I tried to ignore the conflicted feelings in my gut as his mega-watt smile aimed at me. Instead, I turned away, making for the parking lot.

"Call me," I shot back once more.

He nodded. But I noticed he didn't follow. Instead, he shoved his hands in his pockets, sauntering off the way Allie had disappeared.

A tiny undistinguishable feeling gnawed at my gut. I told myself it was disgust at seeing him make a fool of himself for someone who thought 'Pong' was something to be played at keggers.

Because one thing was for certain.

No way was it jealousy.

* * *

I hopped onto the 405 south and fifteen minutes of mid-afternoon traffic later, I pulled up to the address Dana had given me.

And blinked.

It was a small suite in one of those brand new retail complexes where all the stores looked the same. A Pier One sat at one end, a Payless Shoes and a Trader Joe's at the other. In the middle was Happily Ever After Animals, a sign on the window advertising ring-pillow dog collars for your canine best man.

My first urge was to drive away. Fast. My hand hovered over the gear shift.

But, knowing Marco and Dana, if I didn't go in there and rein in whatever harebrained scheme they'd come up with to make my "special day" more memorable, I'd likely end up with a toucan at my Romance in Paradise themed wedding.

How did I get myself into these things?

I parked in an empty space near the door and, clubbing my steering wheel, took a deep, fortifying breath.

A bell chimed as I entered and got my first glimpse of the place.

Racks of shelves held tiny little tuxedos and white dresses for animals of varying shapes, sizes, and species. Matching little top hats and bridal veils with elastic straps and ear holes cut out sat beside them. Silk leashes, collars, and brightly colored bows lined the walls, along with bags of environmentally friendly bird seed in little wedding bell-shaped cups. From somewhere near the back I could hear a bird squawking and the faint scent of animal droppings mixed with cedar shavings filled the air.

All in all, nothing about the place jived with the wedding I'd envisioned.

"Mads, I'm so glad you're here," Marco called, emerging from the aisles. He grabbed me by the arm and propelled me toward the back of the store, where the pungent animal scents grew. "Honey, we have got a *huge* dilemma."

"Uh-huh. Why are we here?"

Marco ignored me, racing on. "We have been going back and forth for simply *ages* and can't seem to agree. I told Dana you wanted a fun, modern wedding, but she's stuck on some old traditional thing."

"Uh-huh. Fun how?"

"See, I knew you'd agree with me. Wait until you see what we have picked out. You are just going to die, dahling!"

That's what I was afraid of.

Marco propelled me to a line of metal cages, all filled with birds. Dana stood at the last one, making little kissy faces through the bars at the occupant.

"Aren't they adorable?" she asked as I approached.

I looked into the cage. Four white doves sat inside, perched on a wooden twig.

"Doves?" I asked.

Dana nodded vigorously, her blonde bangs bobbing up and down. "Uh-huh. We're going to release them at the ceremony right after you say, 'I do.'"

"Or…" Marco said, turning me around to face the opposite wall.

I noticed it was lined with glass terrariums like the one my nephew kept his pet lizard in. Only these were filled with butterflies. Hundreds of butterflies.

"Or, we release butterflies! They're so much more colorful. Can you imagine the scene? Hundreds of tiny butterflies spreading their wings toward the heavens as you and Ramirez are joined as one." Marco looked up toward the stained ceiling tiles as if he could see them now.

"Yeah," Dana said, spinning me back toward the birds. "But doves are symbolic. The say 'love.'"

Marco grabbed my arm and spun me back the other way. "Doves are so overdone.

Butterflies are fresh, new. Like your life with Ramirez will be. A new beginning."

Dana reached for my arm to spin me again, but I quickly stepped back out of range.

"Halt!" I held up both hands in front of me to ward them off. "I'm getting dizzy."

Marco crossed his arms over his chest, glaring at Dana out of the corner of his eye. Dana put her hand on her hips, mirroring his combative stance.

"Look the doves are very nice…"

Dana gave Marco a triumphant look.

"…and so are the butterflies…"

"Ha!" Marco called.

"…but, I'm not sure we really need either."

"What?!" Both of them gave me twin looks of horror.

"What do you mean we don't need anything?" Marco said, his voice rising into a falsetto. "This is your wedding. You want people to remember it. *You* want to remember it. How can it be memorable if we don't release anything?"

"Oh Maddie, you have to have something. Think how romantic it will be."

"I know," Marco said, "If you're not into animals how about fireworks?"

"Right, we could time them to go off right over the wedding gazebo."

"Wait!" I got a sudden vision of my gazebo going up in firework flames as guests ducked for cover, showers of sparks raining down on them. "Okay. We can have one of these guys."

"Okay, doves it is?" Dana asked, gesturing to her feathered friends.

"Honey, butterflies."

Dana shook her head. "Butterflies are so bad for the environment. You know, releasing too many of them into a non-native environment can change their migration patterns for generations to come. Pretty soon the whole place will be overrun with butterflies with not enough for them to eat, and they'll all die off. You don't want to kill off the butterflies with your wedding, do you Maddie?"

"Uh…no?"

"I'm telling you, doves are classic. Classy. You can't go wrong."

"Doves are mean," Marco said, scrunching up his nose. "I heard they peck people. You want doves nipping at your guests?"

"No. Definitely no," I replied.

"They are not mean! They're peaceful. So sweet. Here, see for yourself."

She opened the cage, making soft, cooing sounds until one of the little white birds hopped from the twig to Dana's index finger. Slowly, Dana pulled her hand out of the cage and offered the bird toward me. "Look how tame they are. You can even pet them."

I reached out one finger and gingerly stroked it down the bird's back. It just sat there. I stroked it again. Actually, it was kinda nice. Soft, pure white. It might not be such a bad idea to have a couple of these fellows at the wedding, after all. I moved my fingers over the smooth feathers on his head and found myself making little baby talk sounds at him.

"Who's a pretty birdie? Who's the beautiful bird? You are. Yes, you are."

Unfortunately, it seemed he didn't agree with me as he took that moment to start flapping his wings. Taking Dana by surprise, who yelped, causing the bird to freak out even more.

"He's gonna start pecking!" Marco said, ducking behind a bag of birdseed.

I jumped back.

But not quickly enough. Mr. Dove flew from Dana's hand, straight at me, his little clawed feet landing in my hair.

"Get it off, get it off!" I yelled, flapping my arms up and down in what I'm sure was an exact imitation of his wing flapping thing.

Dana tried to grab him, all the while chanting, "Ohmigod, ohmigod, ohmigod," as he hopped back and forth, tangling his little claws in my hair. I looked wildly around for a store clerk, but, of course, they would have all chosen *that* moment to go on their latte breaks.

Finally, Dana managed to wrap her hands around the bird's little body, pinning his wings down as she lifted him from my head, taking a few choice strands of hair with her.

Unfortunately, she was just a second too late.

I felt something warm and wet hit the shoulder of my sweater.

"Ewwwwww," Marco cried, pointing at me. "It pooed on you!"

I looked down. Sure enough, a brown streak ran from my shoulder all the way down the front of my white sweater.

Dana shoved the offender back into his cage with a, "Bad birdie!" then turned to face me.

"Maddie, I am so, so sorry," she said, biting her lip.

I gave her a death look.

"So, um, maybe we should go with butterflies?" she asked in a tiny voice.

"Ya think?"

CHAPTER ELEVEN

After the shit hit the cashmere I decided I'd had enough wedding business for one afternoon. In an attempt to make amends, Dana offered to pick me up later to go the Symmetric Zebras concert and even offered to buy me a souvenir T-shirt. She seemed so genuinely sorry I couldn't help forgiving her. (Even though I noticed she didn't offer to buy me a new sweater.)

Clad in one of Dana's sports bras (the only spare clothing any of us had in our trunks) I hopped on Wilshire and took surface streets home to Santa Monica. The sun was setting into the sea in the distance, and as I trudged up the stairs to my studio, a large, square package on the front step caught my eye. Another wedding offering courtesy of the postman? I stooped down for a closer look at the return address. My Aunt

Lorraine in Idaho. I picked it up. It kinda rattled.

I entertained the idea of ripping it open right then and there, but remembered the moment of horror with the christening dress and shoved it on the kitchen counter, hitting the shower instead.

After a fresh shampoo and blow dry, I checked my messages (just one from Mrs. Rosenblatt offering to do a pre-wedding aura cleanse for Ramirez and I), then dug into my closet for an appropriate rocker-chick outfit. After trying on and discarding a couple (ten) outfits, I finally settled on a black miniskirt, black knee-high boots and a red clingy shirt with tiny silver fibers running through it that sparkled when the light hit it just right. I capped it all off with a little red lipstick and a lot of mascara, and I was ready to rock someone's world.

I contemplated adding a pair of black chunky earrings that dangled down to my shoulders, but wondered if that might be a bit much. I was still holding them up in the bathroom mirror when a familiar shave-and-a-haircut knock hit my front door. I dropped the earrings and crossed the apartment to the door, throwing it open.

And realized nothing I could put on would be a bit much.

Dana wore a teeny tiny spandex dress in electric blue with cutouts at her belly and back. The top part of the dress was held to the bottom part with big silver rings that would have given her a really funky tan line in the sunshine. On her feet were a pair of matching electric blue heels that made her tower over me by almost a foot. Not including her teased hair.

I gave her a slow up and down.

"You bought the dress just to have something to wear the shoes with, didn't you?"

"Wouldn't you? They're rockin' shoes."

She had a point.

"Ready to go?"

"Wait!" I ducked into the bathroom and grabbed the chunky earrings from the counter. "K, now I'm ready."

* * *

The Inca Theater was located in Hollywood, just down the street from the famous Mann's Chinese Theater and walk of fame. Once an icon of Hollywood architecture, the Inca had housed chorus girls and later black and white films, until it started to crumble in the 70s as much of old Hollywood died off. After a decade of being boarded up as an eyesore, new owners with a penchant toward preservation had come in and restored the old theater to its original glory—or at least something passable enough to draw the tourists back in. These days the Inca played host to Latin awards shows, reality TV dance-offs, and the occasional minor rock bands.

The outside of the Inca looked like any other building in Hollywood. It was tall, white stuccoed and sandwiched between Happy Hollywood Souvenirs and a talent agency touting open auditions for kids' commercials. The interior was just like the name would indicate—Incan.

Dark, stone walls carved with ancient totem-looking faces glared down at us. The high ceilings were patterned with intricate mosaics of half naked men with bronzed skin and dour expressions building temples in the sun, and lights fashioned to look like torches blazed in sconces along the walls. Deep blue, red and purple mood lighting shone through the theater, giving the Incan faces a gruesome, ominous glow in the shadowy interior.

I tried not to let them creep me out as I followed Dana to a spot on the floor where the crowd was eagerly watching the red curtains, waiting for a glimpse of their rock gods.

They didn't have to wait long. Almost as soon as we settled into place (between a guy with a green Mohawk and a gal in Docs with teardrops tattooed on her cheeks) the first chord struck, vibrating off the walls like 6.2 on the Richter scale. I grabbed Dana's arm for support as she threw one hand up in some two finger rock salute and shouted out a loud, "Wahooo!"

I tried to keep up as the band appeared and the mob started to gyrate in time to the pulsing beat, bumping into me on all sides, generating a mass of body heat until I could feel warm sweat break out on the back of my neck. While I wasn't the world's most private person, the thought of all these strangers touching me was a little icky. I tried to groove with it, focusing on the guys on stage instead, wondering which one of the Zebras Gigi might have been seeing.

The drummer was a guy with shaggy brown hair, pounding away with a vigor that had sweat darkening his gray T-shirt—one that sported a picture of a multicolored zebra on it. The guitar player was a blond with freckles, his hair tinted with green streaks, and the guy on keyboards was wearing the tightest pair of leather pants I had ever seen in my life. (Though I had to admit, he filled them out nicely. Hmm…I wondered how Ramirez would look in leather…) I had no idea what the bass player looked like—he moved too fast, dancing all over the stage like some hyper Chihuahua with a guitar. And the lead singer was a skinny guy with pink hair wearing a kilt. Honestly, none of them looked like he fit with the image of the Prada-wearing, schedule-toting Gigi.

But, as they say, opposites do attract.

Just about the point where I was starting to hear bells ring in my ears, they jammed out the last song, hitting the high ending note so hard the place nearly shook, and I had the irrational fear that the Incan gods on the wall might come to life, angered by the noise. The band threw their guitar picks into the crowd, and the curtain closed, allowing the roadies time to switch out the set for the night's main attraction.

"Come on," Dana yelled in my ear, grabbing me by the arm. She steered me to the side, skirting the line of the stage toward a door on the left.

Unlike myself, Dana was a pro concert-goer, having threaded her way through many a crowd with her backstage pass. Before meeting Ricky, my best friend had been a bit of a...well...okay, there was no nice way to say it. A slut. I loved her dearly, but let's call a spade a spade. It wasn't that she set out to bed-hop her way through L.A. It was that she was a blonde, blue eyed, 5'7" aerobics instructor. She was hawt. Men fell at her feet. And, while she had a heart of gold, Dana was a weak woman when it came to a well-built man.

At least, she had been before Ricky. Apparently Ricky and monogamy worked for her, for which I was eternally grateful.

(My midnight "Maddie, I'm such a bad person because I just slept with Mr. Blank and Mr. Blank in one night" calls had significantly decreased.)

However thanks to her many hours in the arms of rock stars, Dana knew her way around the backstage at just about any venue in Los Angeles.

And the Inca was no exception.

She pushed her way through the mob to a spot on the far side where a small staircase led to a level just below the stage. A big guy with bulging forearms stood there, an earpiece in his ear, sunglasses covering his eyes even in the dim horror house lighting.

Dana held up the backstage pass around her neck and he silently stepped aside, opening the door for us. A line of groupies behind us shouted, "No fair!"

I couldn't help feeling just a little cool.

We followed a corridor to a big room full of tables of pizza and beer, reams of wires and amplifier cords and guys in black jeans, flannel shirts, and backwards baseball caps skittering every which way.

A particularly large one in a black hat with a green pot plant painted on the brim and sporting a belly that looked like he was due in June spotted us right way.

"Dude, Dana!"

He grabbed Dana like she was a ragdoll and spun her around.

"Hey, long time no see," Dana responded once he'd put her down. "You remember Maddie. Maddie, Mort, my old roomie.

"Hi," I said, raising a hand in greeting.

"'Sup, dude?" Mort said, nodding my direction by way of greeting.

I took it to be a rhetorical question as his bloodshot eyes immediately went back to Dana. Or, I should say, her cleavage.

"Dude, you look good. Watcha been up to?"

"You know. Same old."

"Well, whatever you been doing, keep doin' it." He cackled at his own joke, showing off a row of teeth that didn't see much time at the dentist.

"I was wondering if it would be possible to talk to the band?" I asked him.

I was half afraid I was shouting, as that ringing was still echoing in my ears. But if I was, he didn't seem to notice. Or maybe he was just permanently deaf from one too many nights on the road.

"Yeah. Totally. They're chillin' in the green room. You wanna meet 'em?"

I nodded.

"Cool. Follow me, dude," he said. He grabbed Dana's hand and steered us down another corridor.

I heard them before we saw them. Loud laughter and female screeching, punctuated by the occasional song verse, poured out into the hallway as we approached an open doorway on the right.

As we entered the green room (which, by the way, was actually a dingy gray) the first thing I saw was vodka bottles. Lots of them. Mostly empty. A faint sweet scent hung in the air, like Mrs. Rosenblatt's incense burner, and a thin haze of smoke drifted near the ceiling. I tried to take shallow breaths, remembering my one not-so-swell encounter with pot in high school when I'd spent two hours giggling like a maniac, then polished off every box of Duncan Hines cake mix in the house.

The band—along with a generous helping of girls in miniskirts and tube tops—

sprawled on a pair of sofas that looked like they'd been salvaged in a Dumpster dive. Dana paused, adjusting her bra upward and her top downward before we approached.

"Rockin' set tonight, Alex," Mort said to the one in the kilt.

"Thanks, man," he responded, doing some sort of complicated handshake thing with him.

"Dude, this is Dana. She used to live with me, man."

"Right on!" the singer replied. He turned his attention to Dana, holding out a hand. "Hey."

"Hey. You guys are great."

He grinned like he already knew it. "Thanks."

"This is Maddie," she said gesturing to me. "We heard about your band from Gigi. Gigi Van Doren," she said, stretching the truth just a little.

I watched the lead singer's face closely for a reaction, but only the same slightly stoned one stared back at me. "Cool."

"Did you know her?" Dana probed. "Gigi?"

He shook his head. "Nope." He turned to his band mates. "Hey, any of you guys know a Gigi?"

The guy in the leather pants stood up, almost toppling over the brunette hanging on his arm in the process. "What about her?" he asked.

"I'm a friend of hers. Or…was…" I said, correcting myself. "Maddie."

He nodded. "Hey. Spike."

"You knew Gigi, Spike?"

He nodded again. "Yeah."

"You were dating?" I asked, realizing I was going to have to be direct with this guy. Though whether it was grief or vodka creating the one-word answers, I wasn't sure.

"Yeah, we went out," he said.

And as I got a closer look at him, I could see why Gigi had been drawn to him. He had jet black hair that curled a little near his ears. Uncommonly vivid blue eyes and small piercings in each ear that gave him a bad boy look while still being approachable. In addition to the assets highlighted by his tight leather pants, thick muscles ripped along his forearms and chest, contained by a loose-fitting black tank showing off biceps that made me check the corners of my mouth for drool. Intricate dragon tattoos snaked down both of his arms. All in all, Rock God personified.

"I'm sorry for your loss," I said.

His eyes darkened, hitting the floor. "Yeah."

"How long had you been seeing each other?"

"A few months," he said. "But it was serious, you know? I mean, we like felt a total connection right away."

I shot a quick glance back at his displaced brunette.

"For real," he said, following my gaze. "Look, I may hang with the groupies a little now and then, but with Gigi and me it was the real deal."

"I can't help but ask—she was a bit older than you, wasn't she?" Dana said trying to put it as delicately as she could that they were a virtual odd couple.

Spike grinned. "Hey, I dig mature girls," he said. Then glanced my way.

I threw my shoulders back, thrusting my barely B's a little higher. Hey, I was *not* mature.

"Anyway, she was generous," he continued. "She didn't mind throwing a little money my way now and then, you know. It's tough when you're just starting out. We've got all kinds of studio expenses and stuff. She was a doll about pitching in now and then."

"Ah," I said. Sugar Momma. "When was the last time you saw her?" I asked.

He bit his lip, his eyes turning watery before hitting the floor again. "Last week. We went to dinner."

"Not since then?" I asked, stopping myself just short of asking if he'd been her mystery meeting on Saturday.

He shook his head, black curls bobbing around his ears. "We had a gig last week. At some fundraiser in…uh…hey?" he called over his shoulder to his band mates. "Where the hell were we last week?"

"Topeka, man," the guitar player answered around an armful of redhead.

"Yeah, right. Topeka. It was a benefit for the library there. Those Kansas dudes were real cool."

I felt my best lead quickly slipping away. Topeka was a far cry from Beverly Hills. "When did you get back?" I asked, grasping.

"Last night. Night before. I dunno. It's kinda like a blur, ya know?"

From the number of empty bottles littering the room, I could see why.

"How were things between you and Gigi?" I asked.

His head snapped up. "Why? What did she tell you?"

I bit my lip. "Uh…I'd rather hear your side of it first."

He sighed deeply, rubbing his hands up and down his thighs as if I was making his palms sweat.

"Look, I…I'll be honest, I'm not sure how things were between me and Gigi. I was totally into her, you know? Like, I'd fallen hard."

My troubles seeing the two of them as a serious couple must have shown on my face as he continued.

"I know what you're thinking. And, yeah, neither of us set out to fall in love. But we did. At least…I did."

The way his eyes shifted away, I got the feeling there was a whole lot more to the statement.

"She didn't return your feelings?"

He let out a deep sigh. "Look, we'd been going through a rough patch, and I wanted to let Gigi know how I felt. When we went to dinner last week…well…I proposed."

I raised one eyebrow. "As in marriage?"

He nodded.

"And what did Gigi say?" Dana asked.

"She said she needed some time."

"Ouch."

"Yeah. Tell me about it," he sent me a rueful grin.

"So, after she had some time? What did she say?"

He took a deep breath, pursing his lips together. "Nothing. She…I didn't talk to her again until she…"

Was murdered.

I put a hand on his arm, genuinely feeling awful for the guy. "I'm so sorry."

He nodded. "Thanks."

"You mentioned you and Gigi were going through a rough patch?" Dana asked.

He blew a long breath out toward the ceiling. "Yeah. We were. But, look, it totally wasn't my fault. I didn't know."

"What wasn't your fault?" I asked, trying to follow.

"Okay, a couple weeks ago I think I'm gonna surprise Gigi by taking her out to lunch. I go to that wedding place of hers, but the chick at the front desk informs me she's with a client. You know the one—blonde, totally big boobs. Hot?"

I nodded. That seemed to be the general male consensus about Allie.

"Anyway," he went on, "I figure, might as well pass the time. I start talking to her. Turns out she's a music fan, so I offer her a couple tickets to our next show. That's when Gigi comes out and sees me talking up her assistant."

"She was jealous?"

"Dude, not even the word for it. She was really pissed."

"What did she say?"

"Nothing then. But after, at lunch, she was totally all over me about it. I said I was sorry, that I'd never even look at the chick again, that I was just trying to be friendly. But she was like on the warpath, man."

"What happened afterward?"

"I bought her flowers every day for, like, a week." He smiled at the memory. "Finally, she calmed down. But, like I said, I wanted her to know that she was the only woman for me."

"Are you sure all you did was talk to Allie?" Dana asked, popping one hip out as she eyed the brunette behind him.

"Dude, I swear on my life. I was totally faithful to Gigi." He paused. "I think she knew it, too. But, well, seeing me with Allie, she just went off. If it had been anyone else, I'm sure she wouldn't have thought twice about it."

"Because Allie is so hot?" I asked, really getting tired of that broken record. Geeze, just 'cause a girl's got enlarged mammary glands.

He grinned. "Sure she's hot. But that wasn't what set Gigi off. What set her off was she thought I was hitting on her daughter."

CHAPTER TWELVE

———

I felt my jaw drop open as my rusty mental wheels started to turn. "Allie was her daughter?"

Spike nodded, his eyes solemn. "Sucks, right? If I knew, I totally would have steered clear of the chick. I mean, I was in love with Gigi, you know?"

I shook my head, wondering why Allie hadn't mentioned this. Granted, it did explain the hero worship she'd exhibited and the deep grief she'd seemed to be experiencing. But if Allie was her daughter, that added a whole new layer to the puzzle. Maybe Allie had had a falling out with her mother? Over money? With the kind of dough Gigi was raking in, I could see Allie being resentful about her starving student's apartment.

On the other hand, maybe they'd fought over Spike.

I took a long look at the musician. He was a co-ed's dream, no doubt about it. Maybe Allie had been jealous of her mother? Maybe Gigi had been angry at Allie, too. Maybe they'd fought, and in the heat of the moment, Allie had stabbed her mother.

Had the hot blonde been playing me all along?

"Do you know if Allie and her mother got along?" I asked.

Spike shook his head. "Sorry, no idea. That day was the first I'd heard she even had a daughter. Gigi said she didn't tell people because she didn't want them knowing she was really old enough to have a grown kid. She fooled me. I had no idea how old she was. Not that I cared. Gigi was beautiful. Nature took real good care of her, ya know?"

I knew. Though I had a feeling it was more Dr. 90210 taking care of Gigi than nature.

"Did Gigi blame Allie? For flirting with you?"

He sucked in a deep breath, his eyes going to a spot past me. "I wouldn't say she was flirting. Maybe just kinda friendly like. But, in her defense, she didn't know Gigi and I were going out. Gigi kept our relationship real on the down-low. After the tabloids raked her over the coals with her divorce last year, she didn't want anyone butting into her personal life."

I didn't blame her. I knew firsthand how it felt to be raked by Felix.

"Dude, your brunette's getting cold," the bass player called, hailing Spike over.

Spike looked over his shoulder at the groupie in fishnets and short-shorts. Only the look in his eyes was more sad than lustful.

"Look, I don't know what else I can tell you," he said. "I loved Gigi, plain and simple. Life won't be the same without her." With that, he sauntered back over to the sofa and grabbed a stray vodka bottle, downing a generous swig.

And by the way the brunette's cleavage failed to gain his attention as we ducked out of the room, I was inclined to believe him. Whatever might have gone on between him and Gigi, the poor guy was visibly heartbroken.

"So, what do we think of Band Boy?" I asked, once we were out of earshot.

Dana shrugged. "Cute. Sad."

I nodded. "But he *did* have motive."

"You think?" she asked, wrinkling up her nose.

"Well, if Gigi declined his proposal, chances are that would be the end of his music bankroll. I mean, we really only have his word she didn't say no."

She nodded. "True. But he was in Topeka."

"Maybe. They seemed a little hazy on when they actually got back."

"Good point," she conceded. "So, what now?"

"Now? I wanna go home, soak in a long bath, and wait for my ears to stop ringing." I turned to make for a bright green exit sign at the end of the hall.

But Dana stopped me with a hand on my arm.

"Um, actually…" She trailed off, biting her lip as she shot a look back toward the theater entrance. "It *is* kinda early to call it a night."

Uh-oh. I could mentally see Miss Former Groupie and Miss Monogamy warring behind her blue eyes.

"Dana, you have a hunky gardener waiting for you at home."

She shook her head. "No, I totally know. I would never…I mean, I was just thinking of hanging out a little. To see the rest of the show. The other bands tonight look pretty good."

"Dana…"

But she'd already made up her mind, pedaling backward toward the pounding bass emanating from the Inca's stage. "I'll call you tomorrow!" she promised, disappearing inside.

I shook my head, praying she didn't ruin her first perfectly good relationship with one wild night of groupie sex as I made my way through the corridors alone.

Once outside, the cool night air hit me in sharp contrast to the muggy theater, and I felt instant goose bumps rise. Hugging my arms around myself, I hailed the first cab I saw and gave him my address.

As he snaked down Hollywood Boulevard, I whipped out my cell, dialing

Allie's number. Unfortunately, it went straight to voicemail. Probably at her study group.

I hung up and dialed Felix instead.

He answered on the first ring.

"Felix Dunn."

"Hey, it's me."

"Me who?"

I narrowed my eyes at the phone. "You know who. I just found out something interesting about your girlfriend."

"I have a girlfriend?"

"Miss Hooters. Listen," I said, filling him in on what Spike had told us. When I was done, he let out a low whistle.

"That was a key bit she left out, wasn't it?"

I nodded at the phone.

"Makes me wonder what else she hasn't told us," he went on.

No kidding. I bobbed my head in agreement again.

"Still there, Maddie?"

"I'm nodding."

"I'll tell you, love, I have a hard time picturing her actually harming her mother."

"Just because she has big boobs doesn't mean she's not capable of murder."

"Oh, Maddie, jealousy doesn't become you."

"I am not jealous!" I shouted.

Causing my cabbie to jump in his seat. I mouthed the word "sorry" at him in the rearview mirror.

"Look, just…watch your back with her tomorrow, okay?"

"If I didn't know better, I'd say you were concerned about me."

"Good thing you know better."

"Good thing."

"Just call me when you have something from the phone company, okay?"

"Done. Anything else, ma'am?"

I rolled my eyes. But instead of shooting back a smart remark, I hung up.

As my yellow chariot pulled up to a stop at my place, I felt a little bubble of happiness when I saw that Ramirez's black SUV was already parked in the drive. I looked down at my watch. Only 8:30. Wow, before midnight with an open case? I fairly skipped up the steps.

"Hi, honey, I'm home," I called as I opened the door.

Ramirez stood at the kitchen counter, munching his way through a slice of leftover pizza. He paused midbite, giving my slinky outfit a slow up and down.

"Please tell me you're not wearing that."

"What, I thought you liked short skirts," I teased. I stood on tiptoes, kissing him on the cheek as I felt him up.

He did a primal growl thing in the back of his throat. "I like the short skirt. My mother may have a thing or two to say about it."

I frowned. "Your mother?"

"We're supposed to be at her place in half an hour."

Mental forehead smack.

"You totally forgot didn't you?" he asked, shoving the last of his pizza into his mouth.

"No!" Yes. "Give me two minutes to change," I called, already digging into my closet for a more Mom-worthy outfit.

I could feel Ramirez rolling his eyes behind me. "I promised her we'd be there for dessert."

"Two minutes," I repeated, laying hands on a navy baby-doll dress with a modest knee-length hem. I stepped out of my skirt and pulled my top over my head, throwing it somewhere in the vicinity of my hamper. (Though whether it actually made it in or not I couldn't promise.)

I stepped into the baby doll and a pair of navy wedge-heeled canvas shoes, pausing only long enough to grab a little white sweater. "Ready?"

Ramirez leaned in close, his breath warming my cheeks, and planted a soft kiss on my lips.

"I really did like the short skirt," he murmured.

Making me go warm in all the right places.

"Rain check," I promised, letting him lead me outside.

I hoped dessert was fast.

*   *   *

Ramirez's mother, or Mama, as she had insisted I call her the first time we'd met, lived in the sleepy little suburb of Hacienda

Heights. The homes were older, ranch-style jobs that had seen generations of kids swing in the mature trees, tear up the lawn with neighborhood soccer games, and whip up and down the sidewalks on their big wheels. Aluminum siding and over-the-garage-additions abounded, as did late-model sedans and minivans with those little stick-figure families on the back windows.

Mama's house sat back from the curb, a patchy lawn surrounded by well-tended roses separating it from the sidewalk. A hula hoop, a very complicated looking Transformer action figure, and a couple of dolls who'd had one too many home haircuts littered the front walk as we approached. On the front door were three big red Valentine's hearts pasted to paper doilies. Ramirez rang the bell, then pushed in without waiting for an answer.

Immediately the scents of warm cinnamon and hot chilies hit my nostrils as we headed inside. An older guy in a cowboy hat dozed in a La-Z-Boy under a homemade afghan in assaulting pinks and greens while the muted TV showed some old western. And every surface around him was covered in knick-knacks. Mama was a bit of a pack rat. Anything that her number of nieces, nephews, grandchildren, or neighborhood kids gave her she kept and proudly displayed in her living room. Hand prints in clay, macaroni sculptures, and countless pictures in handmade Popsicle-stick frames of little brown-eyed children throughout the various decades littered the room.

"Hello?" Ramirez called. "Anyone home?"

"*Mijo*, is that you?"

Mama's round face popped out from the kitchen, lighting up when she saw Ramirez. Wiping her hands on a big white(ish) apron, she wrapped him in a hug around the middle.

I am what you'd call petite. In my wedges, I towered over Mama. She was almost as wide as she was tall, a comfortable sort of lived-in shape that made for an awesome kid-sitting lap and attested to her skills as a wonder in the kitchen.

"I was afraid you weren't going to make it, it's getting late."

"Stand you up, Mama? Never," he teased.

I tried not to be jealous.

"Is that our boy?"

Three more heads popped out of the kitchen, all identical to Mama. The Aunts. Swoozie, Cookie, and Kiki. Behind them came BillyJo.

BillyJo and I had gotten off on the wrong foot. It may have had something to do with the fact that the first time I had met her I'd been dressed as a hooker. Long story (involving dead guys in Dumpsters and Dana's idea of undercover investigating) but suffice to say, it hadn't endeared me to her. Over the past couple of years, I'd done my best to work my way into her good graces, but she hadn't thawed much. When she'd heard I was engaged to her brother, she'd muttered something in Spanish (eerily similar to the things Ramirez mumbled under his breath) and put on the same scowl she was wearing as she stared me down now.

I tugged at the hem of my skirt, infinitely glad that I'd changed as I gave her a wave.

She narrowed her eyes in response.

"You're late."

Ramirez kissed his sister on the cheek. "Good to see you too, sis."

"Now that you're here, Jackie," Mama said, her eyes gleaming, "you must try on the *guayabera*!"

"The what?" I asked.

Mama waved the question off. "Never you mind. Jackie, go with your aunts. Maddie can help me in the kitchen while you change."

Before either of us could protest, the aunts swooped upon Ramirez as one, rushing him off to a back bedroom with BillyJo leading the way.

"Come on," Mama said, slipping her arm through mine. "You come with me. We'll chat in the kitchen."

I followed. Partly because I had no choice. Partly because my stomach was growling again at the scents emanating from said kitchen. Did I mention how great a cook Mama was? If Mexican hadn't already been my favorite type of food, after eating from Mama's table, there would be no contest. She quickly put me to work rolling out cornmeal dough as she pulled a tray of cookies shaped like little folded envelopes from the oven and dusted them with pink sugar crystals.

"My boy's been working hard lately, no?" Mama asked. "I heard about that dead woman on the news."

I nodded. "He has."

Mama pursed her lips. "You make sure he no work too hard, yeah?"

As if I could stop him. But, instead, I nodded.

Which seemed to suffice. "Good. He's a good boy, my little Jack." She put a hand on mine, her eyes shining with pride. "You'll take good care of him, no?"

I nodded again. Truly meaning it.

"He's always been the one I worried about," she said. "Always in the fights at school. Always the broken bones, always the principal's office. Some days I wondered if he'd make it to a grown man."

I smiled, trying to imagine Ramirez as a kid.

"But now, I don't worry so much that he has you."

I felt a lump in my throat. "Thanks." I paused. Then added, "Mama."

She smiled, patting my cheek with one floury hand. Then a small look of concern flitted through her eyes. "Ah, you do know what's expected of a good wife, right?" she asked.

I paused. "Expected?" I looked around the kitchen, sorely hoping she didn't suppose I'd become Suzie homemaker after the wedding. I could heat up a frozen dinner like nobody's business, but actual cooking was, as Ramirez had pointed out, not on my list of finely honed skills.

She nodded. "There are certain…duties…a man expects of his wife."

I bit my lip. "Mrs. Ramirez, I don't mean to seem rude, but Jack can take care of himself. We're a modern couple. We do things for each other, but I'm sure he doesn't expect me to perform any 'duties.'"

Mama stared at me. Then grinned.

"I meant the sex."

I blinked. My cheeks going hot. "Oh."

"On the wedding night. He's gonna want some sex."

"Oh."

"You do know how that works, right?"

"Uh…" I glanced to the right and left, looking for an escape route, pretty sure there was no right answer here.

"Yes?" I finally decided on.

Mama nodded. "Good. 'Cause one thing about the Ramirez men. They like sex. A lot. You're gonna be busy the first few months."

Oh. God. Kill me now.

"Uh-huh," I mumbled, sure my cheeks were a shade of red to rival the hearts on the front door.

"Now, it might hurt a little at first. That's normal," she said, waving a fat finger at me. "But, let me tell you, it gets better. I didn't have six kids for nothing, if you know what I mean."

She winked at me.

I felt faint, instantly trying to block out unwanted images of her and the dozing cowboy playing the horizontal mambo.

"Here comes our boy," one of the aunts said, rushing into the kitchen.

I could have kissed her.

"Oh, *mijo*, you look so handsome!" Mama clapped her hands together and ran toward Ramirez.

Relief flowing through me, I turned around.

And just that quickly the relief died.

"What is that?" I heard myself ask.

Ramirez was clad in a long, white, billowy shirt with screaming red, green, and turquoise embroidery along the front. It looked like the sort of thing I'd bought on spring break in Tijuana senior year.

"My boy's *guayabera*," Mama said, pride shining in her eyes.

"It's…nice," I lied. "What's a gooberbera?'" I asked, sure I was butchering the word.

"*Guayabera*," BillyJo correct with a smirk. "It's a traditional Mexican wedding shirt."

I glanced at it again. "Wedding shirt?" Holy hell. I was going to be marrying a walking souvenir stand. "What do you mean, wedding shirt?"

"In Mexican culture the groom wears a *guayabera* at his wedding."

"But what about the tux?" I asked, my voice going squeaky. I looked from the billowing tent around his middle to Ramirez's face.

He just shrugged.

Great, lot of help he was.

"I think it's too big," I pointed out.

"No, no, it's supposed to be like that," Mama said, fussing with the hem.

Swoozie nodded. "For the guavas."

"The what?!"

BillyJo piped up. "In Mexican culture the family traditionally puts guavas in the pockets of the groom's *guayabera* for the bride and himself to start their life together."

"We got a whole fridge full of 'em for you," Mama said, patting Ramirez's cheek.

I looked down at his oversized pockets. And did a loud hiccup.

"Sugar," Kiki said. "Eat a spoonful of sugar and those hiccups will disappear."

I nodded. Then hiccupped again.

"Oh, that reminds me," Mama said. "Your cousin Nico, who works at the sugar factory, he called and said he's bringing the whole family up from Mexico City. They'll all be here Wednesday. He can't wait to see his cousin married."

I felt a frown settling between my brows. "Nico? Did we send him an invitation?"

Mama waved that insignificant little detail off. "Don't worry. I invited him. We don't need fancy invitations. It's okay."

I felt a sudden knot of dread ball in my stomach. "Just Nico, right?" I let out another hiccup.

She blinked innocently at me. "And a couple other people."

I felt faint. "How many is a couple?"

"Well…" Mama tapped a finger to her chin, her eyes rolling upward as she mentally counted. "There's Nico and his family, then my cousin Amelia and her son and his two boys, and the girls from Arizona, then your father's aunt Rosa and her kids and…I don't know, maybe a hundred."

I grabbed Ramirez's arm to steady myself. "A hundred?" I choked out.

Mama gave me a blank look. "What? Your mom said the garden seats four hundred."

"But the preparations were made weeks ago! We can't just add a hundred people at the last minute."

BillyJo narrowed her eyes at me. "Oh, so only your family is important enough to attend?"

I shook my head. "No, that's not what I meant. We invited plenty of Jack's friends. And family." Just apparently not all six million of them.

I felt a headache starting to brew between my eyes as I faced the army of aunts all giving me the same stern look. I was severely outnumbered.

I pinched the bridge of my nose. "Okay, it's not that I don't want the whole family there…" Liar. "…it's just that I'm not sure we'll have enough food."

Mama waved me off with a smile. "Oh don't' worry, I'll just make some extra tamales."

"Tam-(hiccup)-ales?"

She nodded.

"No, no, no," I said, feeling my control quickly slipping away. "We have a *caterer* doing the food. We're having Chicken Kiev, baby carrots, and roasted potatoes with cream sauce. Simple, elegant," I said, my voice going up an octave.

"Which will go perfectly with tamales. We've been baking all week. I think we have just under five hundred of them frozen. When do you want me to bring them to the site?"

Panic rising in my throat, I turned to Ramirez for help.

He shrugged. "Mama's right. We need to make sure we have enough food."

Great. He picks now to have input on the wedding.

I looked heavenward. What had I done to deserve this? Was it Bobby Fineman? I remember my Sunday school teacher telling me that holding hands with altar boy Bobby Fineman in the back pew of the church was enough to make me go to hell. So, what had I done? I'd tongue kissed him behind the organ after he'd scored us a couple goblets of sacramental wine. I know, I was a terrible kid. Which was probably why I was in the suburban L.A. version of Hades right now.

"Fine."

What the hell, I was already having an island paradise wedding complete with floating butterflies, crapping doves, seashell bridesmaids, some shirt with fruit in the pockets, and a pair of whacked-out shoes designed by a cop who couldn't tell the difference between a stiletto and a platform if his life depended on it.

What were a few tamales and out of town in-laws added to the mix?

"I'll have Marco come pick them up tomorrow."

Mama clapped her hands. The aunts enveloped me in a group hug. BillyJo actually cracked a smile.

And I did a loud hiccup, wondering what else could go wrong between now and Saturday.

On the other hand, maybe I didn't want to know.

CHAPTER THIRTEEN

———

That damned organ music was playing again. Loudly. Vibrating off the walls, assaulting my poor ears as I walked through a flowered archway to a gazebo across the lawn where Ramirez stood waiting. His back was to me, and he was wearing the big, puffy white shirt. And as I got closer, I could see the pockets were bulging with fruit, guava juice dripping down his thighs.

Then suddenly the organ music turned into a mariachi tune. And all the groomsmen started dancing. And Marco, in his red appliquéd tie, grabbed me by the arm and started swinging me around square-dancer style. I tried to protest, to tell them I wanted the wedding march, not the Mexican Hat Dance. But no one was listening.

"See, isn't this fun, Maddie?" Dana asked, dancing past with Ricky on her arm, her seashell dress clacking like castanets against her ankles.

Suddenly the scene darkened. A shadow fell over the group. I looked up.

Above me was a huge, white dove the size of the Goodyear blimp. People started screaming and running.

"Look out, she's gonna blow!" Marco yelled.

I stood, transfixed to the spot watching the largest glob of bird shit ever fall straight toward me.

* * *

I opened my eyes with a start, dragging in shallow, too-fast breaths. On instinct, I looked above me. No giant dove. Just the blades of my ceiling fan softly twirling above my head.

That's it—this wedding was going to kill me.

I closed my eyes, willing the jackhammer in my chest to slow to a normal heart rate as I listened to the sound of the shower running in the bathroom. Get a grip, girl. The wedding was just one day. No biggie. Just one insignificant little day.

That marked the beginning of the rest of my life.

I heard the shower shut off and a moment later felt Ramirez's hand skim my thigh.

"Hey," he said.

"Hey."

I opened my eyes. God, he looked good. His hair was still wet, curling a little around his ears. His skin shone with steam, a towel wrapped around his waist. A fine sprinkling of dark hairs covered his chest, angling downward in an enticing V that was covered by just enough terry cloth to remain PG, yet low enough to make my mind go straight to what I knew lay beneath.

"You're awake early," he said, pulling open a dresser drawer.

"Bad dream."

He turned around, concern wrinkling his forehead. "You okay?"

"Yeah." No. But it was touching that he asked. "I'm surprised you're not gone already," I said, trying to keep the bitterness out of my voice at waking up with only Mr. Coffee for company the past two days.

"Got a late start," he said, pulling a pair of boxers from another drawer. "I'll be making it up with a late night tonight. Captain wants a status report filed on the Van Doren case."

"Uh-huh," I said. I cocked my head to the side as he leaned over to grab a pair of socks, angling for a better view of his towel clad tush.

"By the way, I opened that box on the counter last night after you went to bed. Your aunt sent us a humidifier." He paused, turning so I got a primo view of his bare pecs. "Does she know you don't have asthma?"

"Uh-huh."

He shook his head, his back muscles flexing as he got up and reached in the closet for a T-shirt.

"Anyway, my brother's picking up the groomsmen's tuxes later today and dropping them off at Mama's."

He picked up the boxers from the bed.

Then dropped the towel.

I sunk my teeth into my lower lip, my eyes riveted to full frontal Ramirez.

Have I mentioned how much I was looking forward to the honeymoon?

"He wanted to know what time the rehearsal is?"

"Uh-huh," I breathed, my cheeks (not to mention certain other parts of my anatomy) filling with heat.

Ramirez slipped his boxers on, then paused, hands on his hips.

"'Uh-huh' what?"

I snapped my eyes up to his. "What?"

"Were you even listening?"

"Yeah. Sure. Your captain. Some asthma. Yada, yada, yada." My eyes strayed down to the front of his boxers again as if I could develop x-ray vision.

He grinned, his eyes crinkling at the corners. "Jesus, I feel like a piece of meat."

"If it's any consolation, you're really yummy meat."

His eyes went dark, and in one quick movement, he was across the room, scooping me into his arms.

I inhaled deeply the scents of clean man and warm steam as his hands buried themselves in my hair, his hips pressing into me, lips hovering over mine.

"You know, you're kinda cute when you're checking out my ass," he whispered. Then before I could respond, he had me in a lip lock I couldn't get out of even if I tried.

Not that I tried.

"Six," I gasped, when he finally let me up for air.

"What?" His eyes were dark, glazed over, full of that there's-no-way-we're-getting-out-of-bed-anytime-soon look.

"Six. The wedding rehearsal is at six."

One corner of his mouth tilted up in a lopsided grin that made my heart slam against my rib cage. Wedding disasters be damned, I was the luckiest girl in the world to be marrying this man.

"Good to know," he murmured, before diving into my lips again, his hands roving slowly down my body, raking down my arms, over my belly, to the tops of my thighs and…

I sighed out loud. He was going to be *very* late for work this morning.

* * *

It was close to ten before Ramirez finally headed out the front door, blowing me a backwards kiss as he left. I staggered out of bed and filled Mr. Coffee, making my own French roast that morning. Not that I was complaining. I grinned at myself in the reflection from my toaster. My lips were red from rubbing against his stubbled cheeks, my hair a crazy I-just-had-mind-blowing-sex bird's nest.

Nope, not complaint number one.

I took a quick shower before attacking my matted air with a leave-in conditioner and doing the blow dry routine. I slipped into a pair of white cargo capris, a stretchy green top, and a pair of cute green kitten heels with little white polka dots all over them. Then I downed a second cup of coffee while I checked my voicemail. One new message. From Dana. I could hear loud rock music in the background, and she was begging me to call her back ASAP as she'd done something "really, really bad."

Uh-oh.

I knew I shouldn't have left miss former groupie alone with a mob of sex-crazed rockers. It was like taking a diabetic into a candy store.

Feeling just the teeniest bit guilty for abandoning her last night, I hit number one on my speed dial. Dana picked up on the first ring.

"Maddie?" she asked, her voice cracking just a little.

"What happened?"

"Oh, God, it was awful! I can't believe this happened. I never meant to do it. Oh, God."

"Slow down," I said, as Dana burst into blubbery sobs on the other end. Geeze, this was worse than I thought. "Honey, tell me what happened."

"Okay, well, I was with the Zebras, right?"

"Right."

"And the bass player, well, he's just got the cutest accent. You know what a sucker I am for a guy with an accent, Maddie…"

"Don't tell me you slept with the bass player."

"No." I heard Dana shake her head, her earrings clanging against the phone. "No, not that. It was when they were called out for an encore."

"Uh-huh," I encouraged.

"Well, the bass player asked if I'd ever done a stage dive before. And I said, no, I'd never even been on stage in a place like this. And he said I had to try it. Well, I'd had a drink or two by then, and I think I was getting a contact high or something, so I said okay. And, well, next thing you know, I'm on the stage, staring down at a mass of people with their arms up to catch me, and the bass player pushes me over the edge of the stage."

"Are you okay? Did you fall?" I asked, trying to get to the root of the sobbing.

"No." Again with the jangling earrings. "They totally caught me. And for a moment, it was the coolest thing ever. It was like riding a wave. But a human one."

"What happened?"

"Well, they kind of rode me over to the side, then put me down at the edge of the crowd next to Smokes Dope All Day Guy."

"Oh, God. You slept with Smokes Dope All Day Guy?"

"No. God, no."

"Okay, so what happened?"

"Well, as the crowd set me down, he was lighting up and, well, smoking dope."

"As he does."

"Right. Then he handed me a bottle of tequila and told me to take a celebratory swig. You have to understand, I was totally hyped from riding the crowd at that point. So I did. And that's when it happened"

I shook my head, not understanding. "So, you're upset because you had a shot of tequila?"

"Some chick from the *Informer* took my picture! Maddie I was standing next to a guy smoking a joint with a bottle of tequila in my hand at a rock concert. It's on the front page. CARTOON FLAMINGO BAD INFLUENCE FOR CHILDREN."

Mental forehead smack.

"Maddie," she sobbed. "I'm a bad influence!"

"Honey, you're not a bad influence. It's just tabloid."

Dana sniffed on the other end. "I don't want kids to drink."

"I know, honey. No kids are going to drink. I mean, kids don't even read tabloids."

She sniffed again. "Yeah. I guess they don't."

"Don't worry. I'll talk to Felix today and see what he can do about getting a retraction printed."

"You think he would?" she asked, hope creeping into her voice.

Honestly? I wasn't sure. If a story moved papers, there wasn't much I could do to persuade Tabloid Boy. But, it was worth a shot.

"I'm sure he will," I said, crossing my fingers it was true.

"Okay," she said. I heard her blow her nose. "Okay, thanks. Yeah, maybe that will work."

But, just in case the rest of the paparazzi had picked up on the story, she said she was laying low today. I agreed that was probably a good idea.

"Hey, since you're hiding out, I have a little phone project for you," I said.

"Yeah?"

"Spike was a little sketchy on when he got back from Topeka. Any way you think you could track down the person in charge of the fundraiser and find out if his alibi is actually solid?"

I heard those earrings clacking again as Dana nodded. "I'm on it," she said, then promised to call as soon as she knew anything.

First crisis of the day dealt with, I keyed in Allie's number hoping to catch the daughter before class. No such luck. My call went straight to voicemail. I left her another message, asking her to call me ASAP.

I hung up, drumming my fingernails on my Motorola. No matter how innocent Allie played, I didn't like the fact she'd left out telling us Gigi was her mother. In my experience, when someone hid something, it was for a reason.

So what reason did she have?

Where she and Gigi on the outs? I thought back, trying to remember how they'd interacted with each other that last time I'd been at L'Amore. I hadn't noticed any sort of animosity between them. But at the time I'd been a little too focused on my own mother and her overzealous invitation frenzy to pay attention. What I needed was someone who knew them both well, knew their history.

And I could think of one guy that fit that bill. Gigi's ex-husband, Summerville.

I grabbed my purse, hopped in my Jeep, and made for downtown. Forty minutes later I was pulling into the parking garage down the block from Summerville's building and clubbing my car. I'd just gotten out and beeped my car locked when a blue Dodge Neon slipped into the spot beside me.

Oh, swell.

Felix hopped out, doing a little wave my direction.

"Good morning, love."

"It was until you showed up," I mumbled.

"What was that?"

"Nothing. What are you doing here? Are you following me again?"

He locked his car, coming around to stand next to me. "Actually, after our little chat last night I thought it might be a good idea to see what Gigi's ex had to say about his stepdaughter. I was just passing by his office when I spotted you. Great minds think alike, eh?"

The day I started thinking like Felix was the day I wanted someone to take me out back and shoot me.

"So, shall we?" he asked, leading the way toward the sidewalk.

Reluctantly, I fell in step beside him. While working hand in hand with Felix wasn't exactly my idea of a good time, it appeared I was fated to be stuck with him. Mrs. Rosenblatt was right. My karma did suck.

Five minutes later we were standing in the lobby of Summerville Development watching Sweater Vest chat into his head set nonstop while his fingers did the mambo across his keyboard.

"I'm aware that the groundbreaking is this weekend. However, Mr. Summerville will be unable to attend.

"Yes, thank you for calling; the Aspen project is still a go, but you'll have to get the particulars from Janet in AP.

"No, we're not hiring at the moment, but thank you for thinking of us.

"Summerville Development, please hold.
"Yes?"

He paused for a breath. Then, "What is it?"

"Oh. Right. You're talking to me."

He gave me his best 'well duh!' face.

"Uh, yeah, hi. I'm Maddie Springer, here to see Mr. Summerville."

"Do you have an appointment?" he asked, his fingers whipping over the keyboard at lightning speed.

"No, not exactly. But I was here before. We spoke about his wife."

Sweater Vest paused mid stroke. "His wife?"

"Uh, ex-wife. Gigi Van Doren. The one that got…well…"

"I'm aware who his ex-wife is," he said, his eyes narrowing. "What I'm not aware of is why he would discuss her with you."

"I was a friend of Gigi's."

"All the more reason he wouldn't want to talk with you," Sweater Vest said. I could feel his finger hovering just above the security button as his eyes narrowed into fine slits.

I was just about to concede defeat when Felix nudged me aside, whipping something shiny and plastic from his back pocket,

"Felix Dunn," he said. "*L.A. Informer*."

"You're a reporter?" Sweater Vest crossed his arms over his chest. "In that case, Mr. Summerville has no comment. Now, good day to you both."

Great. Real helpful, Tabloid Boy.

But, instead of leaving, Felix leaned onto the desk in a way that clearly infringed on Sweater Vest's personal space.

"Summerville owns a lot of properties, doesn't he?" Felix asked.

"Of course."

"Including the Palm nightclub in Hollywood?"

"Yes. That's a matter of public record," Sweater Vest hedged.

I watched the exchange, not sure where Felix was going with this.

"It would be a shame then if word got out that the place was infested with cockroaches."

Sweater Vest and I gasped as one.

"It is not," he replied. "How dare you!"

"I happen to have in my possession a picture of Paris Hilton at the Palm, a roach running over her Jimmy Choos." Felix made little running motions with his two fingers across Sweater Vest's desk.

Sweater Vest blanched.

"Now, I can either run it in tomorrow's edition, or I can speak to Mr. Summerville and see if we can't explain this little incident away. Your choice." Felix leaned back on his heels, a clearly victorious smile playing at his features.

Sweater Vest's beady eyes bounced from Felix to me and back again. Finally, he squared his jaw. "Fine," he said, pressing a few buttons on his keyboard and mumbling into his headset that Mr. Summerville had visitors.

After a moment he turned back to us. "You may see Mr. Summerville now," he conceded.

"Thanks a bunch," Felix said, slapping Sweater Vest on the arm hard enough to make him wince.

I tried not to smirk as we made our way down the hall.

"Do you really have pictures of roaches at the nightclub?" I asked.

Felix grinned. "Hey, if I can put your head on Pamela Anderson's body, I can put a roach on Paris's shoe."

I shook my head as we pushed through Summerville's door, not sure if I should be impressed or disgusted.

Summerville was scrolling his signature across a jumbo sized checkbook as we walked in. As with my last visit to see him, he was dressed impeccably—every scrap of fabric on him tailored exactly to his shape. His shirt was unbuttoned at the top, lending a deceptively casual air to his persona as he held court behind his regal desk.

"Please, sit down," he said, barely glancing up from his task.

We did. And I noticed for the first time that our chairs were lower than his. I wondered if this was done purposely so that his visitors were made to look up to him.

"Summerville," he said by way of greeting, extending a hand toward Felix.

"Felix Dunn, *L.A. Informer*."

Summerville raised an eyebrow. "I see. Though, I can't imagine what the *Informer* wants from me."

"We're looking into Gigi's death," I said.

"Yes, I remember you. But I thought you were working with the police?" He raised an eyebrow, a bit of amusement twinkling in his eyes as if we both knew that was a lie.

"Uh, I switched sides," I mumbled.

"So, what can I do for you, today?" he asked, setting the checkbook aside and clasping his hands together on the desk in front of him.

"I was wondering what you could tell us about Gigi and Allie."

Summerville's forehead wrinkled. "Allie? Her assistant?"

I nodded. "And daughter."

Summerville froze, his entire body going rigid. "Daughter?"

"You didn't know Allie was Gigi's daughter?" Felix asked, slowly leaning forward.

"Hell, I didn't even know she had a daughter!" Summerville got up. Actually, he more exploded up, his chair shoving back into the wall as he shot to his feet and began pacing the room. His body suddenly hummed with the kind of barely restrained anger that made me infinitely glad I didn't have to meet him across a boardroom table.

"So, all the time you were married, she never mentioned Allie to you?" I asked.

"We were only married a couple of years." He shook his head again. "But, no, never." And by the look on his face, I believed him. Even an Oscar winner couldn't fake that kind of surprise.

I had to hand it to Gigi, she got an A plus in keeping secrets.

"Her boyfriend told us that Gigi rarely talked about Allie. That she didn't want people to know she was old enough to have a grown daughter."

Summerville scoffed, a self-deprecating sound, as he stood in front of his giant windows. "I told you she was vain. But, God, hiding a child from me?"

"You never met Allie then?"

He shook his head. "No. Not before she started working for Gigi. I stopped by L'Amore to pick up some personal documents a few months ago. I notice her then, but I never would have guessed…" He trailed off, shaking his head.

"I'm sorry," I said. The man was visibly shaken, something I'd guess didn't happen often to Seth Summerville.

"Well, don't be," he snapped. "Typical Gigi. Appearances were always more important to her than people."

"Um, you didn't happen to see Gigi the afternoon before she died, did you?" I asked, fishing for our mystery cancellation.

He narrowed his eyes at me. "Why do you ask?"

I bit my lip. But I figured I had nothing to lose. If he was innocent, he'd tell me. If not, he'd lie, so what was the difference?

"Gigi cancelled an appointment with a client at the last minute the day before she died to meet with someone."

"And you think it may have something to do with her death."

"It was out of character enough for us to believe it worth pursuing," Felix piped up.

Summerville sat back in his chair, steepling his fingers in front of him. "So, you're hoping I secretly met with my ex-wife then returned the next morning to stab her in the back, is that it?"

I squirmed in my seat, the leather making little squeaking noises. "Well…no…I just…"

Thankfully, Felix jumped in again. "The police are looking at everyone involved as a suspect. If I can print an article stating your side of things, it might divert public opinion away from you. And," he added, "Summerville Development's properties."

Summerville seemed to chew this idea over for a moment before finally answering. "I was in meetings all afternoon with the investors for our Aspen project. After that, I had dinner at my club, met a colleague for drinks, was home in bed by midnight. And, before you ask, yes, I have an alibi and witnesses for the time of Gigi's death. I was conducting a conference call from my office between myself, our head of finance, and our internal auditor all morning. Things got heated, the door was open, anyone on this floor can tell you I was here when my ex-wife was killed. Now, if that's all?" Summerville asked. Though the way he got up from his chair and towered over us, it was clear that was all whether we had more questions or not.

I mumbled a goodbye, and we hightailed it out of the office, scuttling down the hallway.

"Why do I always feel about twelve around that guy?" I asked.

"I'll admit, 'intimidating' is a word that comes to mind," Felix agreed. "So, do we believe him?"

I shrugged. "Well, if he was going to lie, he would have come up with an alibi a lot harder to check up on than that."

"Good point. And he didn't strike me as much of an actor."

"Oh, that reminds me," I said, "I have an actor problem, for you. Or rather, actress." I filled him in on Dana's Flamingo issues.

Once he stopped laughing, he promised to see what he could do.

As we hit the end of the hallway and rounded the reception area, I spotted a familiar face standing at the front desk. Anne Fauston. She was conversing with Sweater Vest, a wicker basket overflowing with chocolate chip cookies in one hand.

"Anne," I said, hailing her as we approached.

She spun around, her eyebrows drawing together in confusion as she recognized us. "Maddie. What are you two doing here?"

"We wanted to offer our condolences to Mr. Summerville," Felix quickly lied.

"Oh," she said, the lines in her expression evening out. "Right."

"You making a delivery?" I asked, gesturing to the basket. Even through the cellophane outer wrap I could smell fresh baked goodness calling out to me.

"Yeah, we deliver cookies every other day for the conference room. My uncle got the account when Gigi was still married to Summerville. I guess good cookies outlast marriage, huh?"

Amen to that, sister.

"Listen, I was wondering if I could ask you something," I said. Garnering a look from Sweater Vest that said we were clearly ruining his carefully plotted schedule.

Anne nodded. "Sure."

"I was wondering what you know about Gigi's relationship with Allie?" I asked.

She shrugged. "Not much. She seemed like a fine receptionist."

"So…you didn't know she was Gigi's daughter, either?"

Anne's eyes got big and round. "Wow. Really? I mean, no. She never mentioned it."

She paused. "But, honestly, most of Gigi's dealings were with my uncle. I was just the delivery girl, you know? She took the pastries, signed the slip, then I was dismissed."

I detected a slight note of bitterness in Anne's voice and jumped on it. "Gigi was rude to you?"

"Oh, no." She shook her head so hard her brown hair followed her like a dark curtain. "Nothing like that. She was just busy, and I wasn't that important. I mean, we didn't like chat about stuff, you know?"

"I see."

"Certainly not about her daughter. I mean, Allie's only worked there since the fall. I don't think I've said more than two words to her."

"They're waiting," Sweater Vest cut in, gesturing to Anne's basket of goodies.

"Right." Anne hauled them off the desk. "See you later," she said, then took off down the hall.

Sweater Vest gave Felix and me a pointed look. I held up my hands in a surrender gesture and made for the door. It was clear we'd gotten all the cooperation we

were going to from Summerville
Development.

CHAPTER FOURTEEN

———

"Well, now what?" I asked once we were outside.

Felix looked down at his watch. "I'd love to continue banging on doors with you, but right now I've got a lunch date."

Right. With Allie.

"Maybe I should come with you," I said. There were more than a couple questions I had for the perky blonde, and I wasn't entirely sure I trusted Felix to ask the right ones. Or, more specifically, pay attention to the answers when faced with her D cups.

"As much as I adore you, three's a crowd, love." He winked at me.

I scoffed. Loudly.

He grinned. "But, I'm glad to see the green-eyed monster is alive and well this morning. Just admit it, Maddie. You want me bad."

I punched him in the arm.

"Ow. Careful, I bruise easily."

I rolled my eyes. "Just call me as soon as she leaves. I want to know everything."

He cocked an eyebrow at me. "*Everything*?"

I made a fist to punch him again, but he scuttled out of reach. "Okay, okay, I'll call you later," he promised, folding himself into his car. Then he pulled out of the garage, making a left at the light.

I stood watching his taillights disappear, a strange nauseated sensation swirling in my stomach. Probably fear he'd botch the interview with Allie. Definitely not jealousy. I mean, she was a college kid, for crying out loud. He couldn't possibly be serious about her. I mean, not that I cared if he was serious with someone. I didn't. Not a bit. He could get serious with whomever he wanted. It didn't matter to me. Because I was not jealous.

Thankfully, before I had to convince myself any further, my cell trilled from my purse.

"Hello?" I answered.

"Maddie!" Mom's voice rang in my ear. "Where are you?"

"Downtown. Why?"

"You didn't forget, did you?"

"Forget?"

"Oh, hell, you did forget. Maddie, I swear to God if you think I'm picking up *that man* from the airport, I'm disowning you."

That man. There was only one person in the world my sweet, loving, even tempered mother would call "that man."

My dad.

My whole life I'd been told the story of how, when I was three years old, my father left Mom and me for Las Vegas and a showgirl named Lola. But recently I'd learned that story was only half true. Dad had left all right, but he hadn't so much *run away* with Lola as *become* Lola—the star of an all-male "showgirl" review.

Yes, my father was a drag queen. (At least now I knew where I got my love for fashion.) So, you can see why my mom might be a little touchy when it came to the subject of *that man.*

After twenty-some odd years being MIA, he'd finally contacted me a couple years ago when he'd gotten mixed up with a ring of Prada smuggling mobsters. Our first face-to-face had been, to say the least, awkward.

Since then Larry (I couldn't yet quite bring myself to call him 'Dad') and I had kept in touch, and I was slowly starting to get to know the man who'd been largely myth my whole childhood. Granted, we weren't in best buds territory yet, but I had asked him if he and Faux Dad would jointly give me away at my wedding. He'd done a giddy squeal of delight and promised he'd be there with bells on. (I only hoped he didn't mean literally.)

"I'm on my way now," I lied, hopping into my Jeep.

"Good." I could hear the relief in Mom's voice. "He said he brought a plus one so look for two of them."

"Got it."

"Oh, and, I talked to the restaurant where we're having the rehearsal dinner. They said they have a big party coming in before us, so they're bumping us back to eight. Which is fine, because we're going to need time for people to get to the rehearsal from work, and you know there'll be traffic."

"Right," I said, making a mental note to give my 'wedding planners' this detail.

"And Molly said Tina's got a cold, but as long as there's no fever, she'll still make flower girl. But, if she gets a fever, she's going to dress Tandy up in Tina's outfit and bump her up to flower girl, so she may have to hem the dress a little."

"Fine. Great." I pulled into traffic, heading toward the 110.

"And your grandmother wants to ride in the limo to the hotel with you. She says she doesn't trust your cousin Shane to pick her up on time."

"Yep. Limo. Got it."

"Oh, and the caterer called and said they weren't sure they have enough chairs for all the *extra* people on the guest list," Mom said, emphasizing the word. Apparently Marco had filled her in on Mama Ramirez's additions to the festivities. "But," she added, "they said if you wanted they could bring in some benches."

"Lovely. Is that all?" I asked.

"For now. I'll call if anything else comes up."

"Super." I hit the end button, suddenly drained.

If this wedding ever went off, it would be a miracle.

*   *   *

If you've never been to LAX, it's an experience everyone should have at least once in their lifetime.

Los Angeles International Airport is *the* West Coast travel hub where you can see anyone from George Clooney to the King of Nigeria (the real one—not the one that keeps sending spam emails about his family's fortune being all yours if you'll just send him all your bank account information) walking through the endless concourses, confused looks on their faces as they try to locate baggage claim. The airport is so big it could actually qualify as its own city, complete with separate police force and fire station. Occupying over five square miles, the place is a maze of ramps running to the domestic and international terminals, arrivals, departures, loading zones, and long-term parking. It's enough to make a person swear off driving forever.

Not to mention the taxis. Maybe in New York taxis are a necessity. But in L.A., where anyone over the age of sixteen owns a convertible, cabs are just an annoyance. One that was currently eliciting a string of curse words I'm sure would make my Irish Catholic grandmother grab her rosary in a two-fisted clutch.

Just as I was really starting to get creative (I swear if one more son-of-a-banana-sucking-ape cuts me off...) I found Larry and his friend at the curb outside domestic baggage claim.

Not that they were hard to spot.

Larry was a six foot two, male, fifty-something version of...well...me. A long blonde wig, red, four-inch heels, and a white minidress bulging slightly around the middle where his corset was losing the battle against his middle-aged spread. He'd donned a wide-brimmed white hat and capped the outfit off with a cropped red leather jacket. All in all, not what you'd call subtle.

Especially considering his traveling companion.

I recognized Larry's friend right away as one of the women (men?) Larry performed with at the Victoria Club in Vegas. Her (his?) specialty? Impersonating Madonna, specifically the "Like a Virgin" years. A role she took very seriously, seldom seen outside of her fluffy black tutus and totally eighties jelly bracelets.

And today was no exception. She was the perfect embodiment of the Material Girl, from her ripped-neck sweatshirt to a little black mole painted on her upper lip, bobbing up and down vigorously as she popped a piece of gum between her teeth.

Between the two of them, they had no fewer than six bags. All in pink leopard print.

"Maddie!" Larry called, waving as I got out of the car and eyed the baggage. Unless we tied Madonna to the roof, I had no idea how we were going to fit all of this.

"Hi, Larry," I said, returning his air kisses.

"You remember Madonna?" he asked, gesturing to his friend.

"Hey, doll," she said, giving me a gloved hand with the finger holes cut out.

I shook it. "Of course, nice to see you again." Madonna had been one of the few innocents at the Victoria Club not involved in a shoe smuggling ring Felix and I had busted a couple years ago. I hadn't spent much time with her then, but I'd gotten the impression she was a nice gal, and, if I remembered correctly, Marco had been more than a little sweet on her.

"I can't believe Larry's little girl is getting married!" She squealed, scrunching up her nose and shrugging her shoulders toward her ears. "It's just so exciting. So romantic."

Romantic was about the only word I *wouldn't* use to describe the wedding so far.

But I nodded and smiled anyway.

"I bought the most beautiful mother of the bride dress," Larry gushed. "Blue chiffon, with little yellow daisies all over. Just darling!"

I tried not to cringe. Partly at the fact that my *father* would be wearing a *mother* of the bride dress. But mostly at the fact that anyone would wear blue chiffon.

While Dad and Madonna peppered me with questions about the band, the hors d'oeuvres, and the flowers, I did a very complicated packing job with the luggage in the back of my Jeep, relying on my years of Tetris training to fit pink leopard print into every inch of available space. When I was done, there was almost enough room for everyone to sit comfortably.

Almost.

We kind of wedged Madonna on top of one case so her head kept bobbing against the rollbar. But she didn't seem to mind, saying it was like she was on an L.A. safari.

"So, tell me what you've been up to lately," Larry said as I navigated my way out of the LAX rat maze.

"Oh, you know. Not much." Ha!

"I, uh, heard there was some difficulty with your wedding planner?"

"Oh. You did, huh?" I asked, biting my lip.

Larry nodded. "You want to tell me about it?"

I could tell by the look on his face, Larry was trying really hard to be "Dad" right now. As if being a sympathetic ear would start to make up for all those trips to the zoo we'd missed out on while he was go-go dancing, and I was day-dreaming about how Ward Cleaver would one day show up at my doorstep calling me his own.

Larry was a far cry from Ward Cleaver. But, in all honesty, the Cleavers were kinda boring.

So, unable to resist his plea for a father-daughter moment, I spilled all, telling Larry and Madonna the whole sordid story as we wound up the 405 to their hotel in Santa Monica. By the time I was done, Larry was doing a concerned, wrinkled forehead face (another eerily "Dad" thing), and Madonna was bouncing up and down on her pink luggage.

"This is so *CSI*!" she said, clapping her hands with glee. "My money is on that Kleinburg girl. Ooo, she's got a temper on her, honey."

"Really?" I asked, perking up. "Do you know her?"

"Well, not me personally," she conceded. "But my roommate used to work at the Rio casino, and Mitsy was there a couple months ago with some of her rich bitch friends."

"What happened?"

"One of the waitresses spilled a cocktail on Mitsy, and Mitsy freaked. Grabbed the gal by the hair, took her down to the floor, and started wailing on her. Turns out, Mitsy's totally into cardio kickboxing and messed that chick up. Security finally broke it up, but my roommate said the waitress was lucky to walk away from it."

I turned off the freeway, mentally digesting this new information. Honestly, all I really had was Mitsy's word she'd fired Gigi. And even if she did, she still might have been upset enough over Gigi's inattention to take it out on the wedding planner. What if Mitsy had come back the next morning and had it out with Gigi? From what I knew of Gigi, she wasn't one to back down. Maybe things escalated and Mitsy had let her temper get the better of her.

I made a mental note to check into Mitsy's alibi for the morning of the murder as I pulled up to Larry's hotel and helped the leopard twins unload their luggage.

Once they were checked in, I left the two girls to unpack and promised I'd call if anything new came up.

As soon as I got back into my Jeep, I dialed Dana's number on my cell.

"Hello?" she asked, picking up on the first ring.

"It's me."

"Oh."

"Gee, don't sound so excited."

"Sorry, I was waiting for a call back about Spike."

"So, no confirmation on the boyfriend's alibi yet?"

"Not yet. But, I did find the car company that drove them to the airport. Just waiting to hear back from the driver what time that was."

"Awesome, Lacey."

"Who?"

"Never mind," I mumbled.

"Listen, did you get a chance to talk to Felix about my, um, problem?"

I nodded as I flipped on the AC. "Yep. He said he'd see what he could do about Flamingogate."

"Oh, thank God," she breathed. "I swear some kid outside the studio even harassed Ricky over it. Can you believe? I tell you, Ricky has been *so* amazingly supportive during all of this, but I've been so worried more photographers were going to show up any second. I wasn't even sure I should go out for the party tonight."

"Party?" I searched my overtaxed brain. "What party?"

"Your bachelorette party."

Oh. No.

"Um, do we really need a party?"

"Oh, come on, Maddie. You didn't think I'd let my best friend get married without one last big hurrah from singlehood?"

I felt myself shaking my head. There was no way this was going to turn out well.

"I'm not sure I really need any hurrahs…"

"Just be at the corner of Sunset and Vine at seven tonight."

"Dana, I don't need…"

"Oh, Ricky just got home. Gotta go. Seven. Don't be late!" she said. Then hung up.

I flipped my phone shut and thunked my head backwards against the headrest. I so needed that vacation when this wedding was over.

I briefly contemplated just driving back to LAX, getting on the first flight to Tahiti and skipping straight to the honeymoon part. But, considering my groom was still currently married to his case, I nixed it. Instead, I glanced at the dash clock. 2:30 p.m. Felix's lunch "date" must be long over by now. I keyed his number into my cell. Straight to voicemail. I left a message asking him to call ASAP. Then I tried Allie's number again.

Again to the voicemail.

I was getting the distinct impression this chick was avoiding my calls.

But, I pulled my Jeep into the right lane, hopping onto the 10 toward her Glendale apartment anyway. As far as I was concerned, Allie definitely had some 'splaining to do. And if no one was taking my calls, I was just going to have to get a straight story out of her in person.

Half an hour later I parked at the curb on Verdugo and walked up the front pathway to unit F.

Only, it appeared someone had beaten me to it.

Felix stood on her doorstep, his usually crumpled khakis looking almost as if they'd seen an iron, his white button-down shirt gleaming with that freshly bleached looked. Even his hair looked like he'd taken the time to comb it since I'd last seen him, instead of just slathering on a handful of Dollar Store gel like he normally did.

"What are you doing here?" I asked, my heels clacking up the front walkway. "Didn't you get enough of her at lunch?"

He spun around, a small frown between his brows. "No, actually, she never showed."

I tried not to smirk. "Ah, stood up?"

"You can wipe the smirk off your face."

Okay, I didn't really try that hard.

"And it wasn't like it was actually a *date*, you know," he said, sulking like a kid who'd missed dessert.

"Right. And you're not actually wearing clean clothes."

"It was wash day," he responded. But the way he shuffled his feet and kicked at a stray rock told me I'd hit a nerve.

"So, is Blondie in?" I asked, gesturing to the door.

"I was just about to ring the bell."

I stepped aside. "By all means, go ahead, Romeo."

He shot me an annoyed look, but pressed the button anyway.

I heard an answering buzz echo inside the small apartment. But instead of footsteps, it was followed by silence.

Felix tried again, leaning into the button.

The door of the unit next to Allie's popped open, an Asian woman with a crying toddler stuck to one hip emerging.

"Can you stop ringing the bell, please? The kid's teething and seriously needs a nap."

From the dark circles under Mom's eyes, I could tell she did, too. Ah, the joys of motherhood.

"Sorry, I thought we were ringing Allie's," I said.

"The walls are thin," she explained. "It echoes. Besides, Allie's not here."

"Did she say where she went?"

The woman gave me a rueful grin. "No. Like I said, the walls are thin. I heard her banging around in there a couple hours ago, then slam the front door on her way out."

I glanced at Felix, wondering where Allie had gone off to, if not to meet him.

"So, can you lay off the bell?" she asked, shifting the baby to the other hip as it continued it's wailing. I didn't know how she didn't go deaf from the racket.

"Yeah, sorry," I said, turning away.

"So much for that," Felix said, falling into step beside me.

I nodded, glancing back at Allie's dark apartment.

"Look, maybe Allie is on the up and up and maybe she isn't. But I've got a bad feeling she's not going to be much help with those phone records."

He nodded. "She didn't exactly come through today. So, what do you suggest?"

"Well, Allie said that Gigi kept copies of her phone bills at the office *and* at home. Maybe we could access her home files?"

He grinned. "By 'access' I'm assuming you mean break into her house?"

"Not break! Maybe, kinda *slip* in. For a minute. For a very good cause."

His smile widened, reminding me of a big hungry crocodile. "Maddie, it's always for a good cause."

"So, you're in?"

"We'll take my car," he said, leading the way to his Neon parked up the block.

"Why?"

Again with the crocodile grin. "Unless you've got a lock-picking kit in the glove box, it's the only way we're getting in."

Right.

I never quite got the full story of how Felix learned to pick locks, but from what little he'd said, it had something to do with a youth spent in a London private boys' school and a young Felix with way too much time on his hands. Honestly, it was probably better I didn't ask too many questions. (Can we say, *accessory after the fact*?) But, I had to admit, his less than completely moral skills had come in handy on occasion. Me, I'd tried to pick a lock once. Just once. (For a good reason, of course!) I'd ended up breaking my Macy's Visa card in half trying to wedge it in the doorframe. Had to wait four weeks for a new one to come in the mail. And trying to explain to the nice customer service rep in India how I'd damaged the first one? So not worth it.

"But we're not really breaking in. Just…"

"*Slipping* in," he finished for me.

"Right," I said, wedging myself into Felix's Neon. I tried not to wrinkle my nose at the pile of newspaper, takeout bags, and computer equipment filling the backseat as we merged into traffic.

"So," Felix said, "any idea where Gigi's house is?"

I shook my head. "We could go back to my place and Google her."

"No need." Felix pulled a phone from his pocket and stabbed at the screen. "I'll do it."

"Geeze, am I the only person left in the world who doesn't have Google in her pocket?"

"I'm fairly certain my mother doesn't," Felix responded, typing Gigi's name into the tiny screen.

Considering his mother was a seventy-year-old widow living in the Cotswolds of England, that didn't make me feel much better.

"Here we are," he said, squinting at the screen. "She's got a white pages listing in Pacific Palisades." He read off the address, getting on the 5 south.

Twenty minutes of gridlock later, we merged onto the 10 west, then snaked up the 1 toward the posh ocean side city of Pacific Palisades. While we were a mere block from the Pacific, the air still smelled more of car exhaust than salty sea water, but the multistory glass homes and funky pink stucco crab shacks were a dead giveaway we'd hit the ocean.

We wound around a golf course, coming up on a neighborhood of towering homes in the eclectic California architecture tradition—imposing faux Tudors next to mock Italian villas next to craftsman style cottages on steroids. The address Felix had pulled up was in the middle of the block, one of the faux Tudors, pale white stucco gleaming against dark woods that crisscrossed like ancient beams along the face. A long expanse of lawn separated the home from the street, edged in a tall hedge along the property giving it the illusion of privacy.

As Felix maneuvered his Neon up the winding drive, I did a slow survey of the place.

"Wow. Nice," I said with a low whistle. "No wonder those place cards cost so much."

"We'll park around the side," Felix suggested, indicating another line of thick hedges.

He pulled around, obscuring the car from the front of the property before we hopped out and made our way to the front door. My kitten heels seemed to clack like cannons on the expertly cobbled drive in the silence. Gingerly looking over my shoulder as if expecting vicious guard dogs to be alerted to our presence, I walked up to the front door and knocked. Since the occupant was currently residing in the L.A. County morgue, predictably there was no answer.

I tried the knob. No such luck. Firmly locked.

I peered in the front windows. Inside I could see the furnishings were every bit as showy as Gigi herself had been. A pair of oversized sofas in gold brocade faced a large marble fireplace with some sort of family crest above the mantel.

"What do you think the chances are that a back door's open somewhere?" I asked.

Felix shot me a look. "Slim."

"Slim as in, let's go check it out?"

"Slim as in Kate Moss after a colon cleanse."

"Damn." I really hated bending the law like this. But...a girl's gotta do what a girl's gotta do.

I stepped aside. "Okay, do it."

Felix sauntered up to the door, "cocky" too mild a word to describe his swagger, and pulled a narrow black case from his jacket pocket. He slowly unzipped it, revealing an array of instruments that all looked vaguely like flat screwdrivers to me. I waited in silence as he slipped one into the keyhole of Gigi's lock. He twisted it back and forth, listening intently for some kind of sign it was working.

I felt distinctly exposed, like at any moment the principal might come by and catch us smoking in the bathroom.

"Can you go any faster?" I prodded, my eyes scanning the empty expanse of lawn for the fiftieth time.

"Not if you want to get in."

I bit my lip, trying to channel patience from somewhere I didn't think I really had.

Finally a small click broke the silence, and Felix pushed the door open.

"Yes," I said, moving to slip inside.

Felix held up a hand to stop me, instead going in ahead. He pulled an electronic device that looked like an overgrown pager from his pocket, then paused inside the door, locating a security panel. Two red lights blinked over a keypad. Felix held the pager thingy up to it. Three seconds later, the lights went from blinking red to steady green.

"Alarm, disabled," Felix said, a distinctly smug smile on his face.

"I'll admit it, you're good," I said, closing the front door behind me.

"That's what all the girls say." Felix winked at me. "So…telephone bill?"

I scanned the entry hall. Marble floors gave way to a sweeping staircase to the right. To the left, open French doors revealed the impressively oversized room I had seen through the windows.

"Upstairs?"

Felix nodded. "All right, let's go see."

I ascended the stairs, Felix a beat behind, our footsteps muffled by the plush white carpeting. I prayed I didn't have any sludge stuck to the bottom of my feet as I gingerly followed the banister upward. It felt eerily quiet in the house, as much due to the tomblike silence as the fact that I knew the inhabitant would never again be back here. But I tried to shake it off, focusing on the task at hand.

At the top of the stairs the landing opened up to three different rooms. Through the open door ahead, I spied a large, canopied bed; the other two doors were closed shut.

"I'll take number one, you take two," Felix offered, heading toward the canopy.

I nodded and opened the door of the first room, pushing into a spare bedroom. A queen-sized bed sat in the middle of the room, adorned with a floral-print bedspread that instantly made me question Gigi's taste. Beside it was a matching nightstand and vanity set. All perfectly accessorized with vases of flowers and pastel candles that had yet to be lit. Your average spare bedroom. No files, no phone records.

"Nothing in here," I called. "You?"

"Not yet," came Felix's voice.

"I'll try number three."

I poked my head in the next room to find a home gym that would have Dana drooling. Dumbbells lined against the wall, floor to ceiling mirrors covered the back of the room, and an array of Nautilus equipment with all kinds of complicated looking pulley systems sat in the center.

No file cabinet.

I closed the door and walked back down the hall to Felix's room.

I found him rifling through a dresser drawer, a pair of pink panties in one hand.

"What are you doing?" I asked, striking a hands-on-hips pose.

Felix spun around, caught panty-handed. "Being thorough."

"In her underwear drawer?"

"No stone unturned."

I rolled my eyes.

"Phone bill," I said, enunciating like I was talking to a child. "Not panties." I crossed the room and grabbed the lingerie from Felix's hand, shoving it back into the dresser drawer with a thud. "The poor woman is dead."

"That poor woman is the most sensational murder since OJ *didn't* slip on a pair of black gloves."

I shot him a look.

"I feel horrible that she's gone," he said, putting one hand over his heart in what I'm sure he thought was a very sympathetic gesture, "but me selling fewer papers isn't going to bring her back now, is it?"

"You are sick."

I tore my gaze from Tabloid Boy and let my eyes scan the room.

The canopy bed took up most of one wall, while framed art pieces filled the others. A long chaise in pale peach sat by the window, positioned to take full advantage of the morning sun. Beside it sat a marble end table and a mahogany file cabinet.

And Bingo was his name-o.

I crossed the room to the cabinet and grabbed the handle on the top drawer, pulling toward me. Only it didn't budge. Locked.

I scanned the room looking for a good place to find a teeny tiny key.

Only, what I saw was Felix at the panty drawer again.

"Jesus, have some decency, will you, Felix?"

He straightened up and turned around. A tiny gold key dangling from his index finger.

"Oh. Right."

He grinned, showing off two rows of white teeth. "Did you really think it was Gigi's knickers I was interested in?"

I gulped down a blush. "No. Of course not."

Neither one of us believed that for a second.

Thankfully, though, he didn't say anything, instead slipping the key neatly into the lock and sliding the file drawer open.

Labeled hanging files indicated this was where Gigi had kept her old credit card receipts, gardener bills, insurance papers, and (I did a silent thank you to the gods of snooping) her phone bills.

I pulled one from its file, handing it to Felix.

"This have what you need on it?"

His eyes roved the page, quickly scanning the account numbers.

But he never got to answer me.

Just as he opened his mouth to speak, the sound of gravel crunching beneath tires made us both freeze.

"Oh, shit."

Instinctively I ducked down behind the chaise, pulling Felix with me, then crab walked over to the window. I lifted my head up, trying to stay hidden behind the thick, damask curtains as I peeked over the sill to see who our unwanted visitor was.

My heart bottomed out my toes as I watched a dark-haired figured emerging from a black SUV just outside the front door.

Ramirez.

CHAPTER FIFTEEN

―――

"Figures," Felix mumbled under his breath as he slipped the phone bill into his pocket

"What do we do?" I asked, watching Ramirez approach the house. Like a deer frozen in headlights, I couldn't move.

"The phrase 'beat a hasty retreat' comes to mind."

Right. Good plan.

We crab walked away from the window until I was sure we were out of Ramirez's line of sight, and then we both bolted for the door. I hit the landing a beat after Felix and almost rammed right into his back as the front door opened and he froze at the top of the stairs.

Too late.

Ramirez was already in the house.

I spun around, retreating back into the cover of the bedroom.

Felix crossed my path, ducking into the home gym instead, shutting the door behind him just as Ramirez's footsteps echoed in the front hall.

My eyes scanned the bedroom for some place to hide. Under the bed? I lifted the duvet.

Crap. Gigi had filled the entire space with back issues of *Modern Bride.*

I stood up and started to panic as I weighed my other options. Behind the curtains? Under the rug? Even on my Dana diet the chaise was too skinny for me to really hide behind.

That left only one place.

The closet.

I threw open the white sliding doors and dove inside, shutting them behind me just as I heard Ramirez ascend the stairs.

I made myself as small as I could beside a hanging shoe caddy (have I mentioned how much I coveted her Prada collection?) and a shelf full of sweaters, praying my bad luck would give me just a one day reprieve.

I held my breath, waiting for any sound to indicate Ramirez's approach. Of course, with Gigis' plush white carpets, I heard nothing. Any footsteps were swallowed up in the mausoleum-like silence.

I did a three count, willing myself to breathe silently as I slowly slid one door open a crack, peeking out into the bedroom.

Nothing.

I opened the door a teeny bit farther.

And saw Ramirez's black boots step into the room.

Yikes! I jumped back, closing the door again ever so stealthily. I hoped.

I watched through the tiny crack between the door and frame as Ramirez did a thorough sweep of the room. His jaw was clenched, his menacing gun pointed straight in front of him. He was no fool. An unlocked front door and a disabled alarm system raised red flags. Especially considering the home's occupant was six feet under.

I breathed low and shallow, an acute sense of déjà vu washing over me as I watched Ramirez look under the bed (good thing I didn't hide there after all!) and behind the curtains (ditto). The first time I'd encountered Ramirez I'd been in exactly this same position—hiding in a closet, watching him and his sleek black gun sweep through a bedroom. Only the last time it had been my ex-boyfriend's bedroom, and I'd been pretty sure it was Ramirez that had been doing the breaking and entering.

Now I was the guilty one.

A thought that made me cower just a little closer to the plastic shoe rack filled with pointy-toed pumps.

Ramirez crossed the room, slowly circling the bed. I could see his entire body tense, on alert, ready to pounce at any second. His trigger finger the only part of him relaxed. Deceptively so, considering I knew he could shoot the balls off a fruit fly at fifty yards. Ramirez was nothing if not good at his job.

Which was why, of course, he turned toward the closet next.

Trying not to crinkle the shoe caddy, I turned to slip behind it, covering my legs with a beige sweater in loose cable knit. I closed my eyes, doing a silent "please, please, please" that he opened the opposite door of the closet, the one not currently hiding a cowering blonde.

The last time we'd played out this scene, Ramirez had taken one look at the closet and found what he wanted, leaving me thankfully obscured.

Apparently I'd used up all my luck then.

He threw open the door right in front of me, thrusting me nose to nose with a threatening black gun barrel.

I'm not sure, but I think I may have peed my pants a little.

Ramirez immediately lowered his weapon to his side, his shoulders slumping, his entire body releasing pent up adrenalin.

"Jesus, Maddie!"

I gave him a half-hearted smile and a one-finger wave. "Hi, honey?"

"What the hell are you doing in there?" he yelled. Then offered a hand, which I gratefully took, as he hauled me out of the clothing and to my feet again.

"Um, well, see…"

He held up his free hand. "Wait. I don't want to know."

"You don't?"

He clenched his teeth together. "No. Because if I do, I'm probably gonna have to handcuff you and take you downtown."

I bit my lip. "Um. Thanks. For not arresting me."

He grunted. Then ran a hand through his hair and let out a few choice curses in Spanish.

"Sorry," I said.

He paused. And shook his head at me. "You always are."

Ouch.

"Yeah, but this time I'm really, *really* sorry."

He narrowed his eyes, that vein in the side of his neck starting to pulsate.

"But," I added, "you did say I could investigate. That was the deal, remember?"

"Without breaking the law."

"Technically, I said I wouldn't impersonate any more officers. I never said anything about not breaking the law."

His vein bulged, his eyes went dark, and a deep growl rose in the back of his throat. I was not making a convincing case.

"Okay, fine." I held up one hand. "I, Maddison Louise Springer, do solemnly swear not to break any more laws during the course of this investigation."

"Turn around."

"Why?"

"I want to make sure your fingers aren't crossed. Turn around."

I rolled my eyes. But did a slow spin for him, holding up both hands, all digits spread wide.

"Satisfied?"

He didn't answer. But he didn't growl again either. Which I took to be a good sign.

I stole a glance at the window as Ramirez holstered his gun   and thought I caught the tail end of a blue Dodge Neon burning rubber down the circular drive. Deserter!

"So, what are you doing here?" I asked.

Ramirez spun around, hitting me with the evil eye.

"What? I'm just asking. You know, if some new lead brought you to Gigi's to look for anything in particular. Just…kind of wondering."

His cop face slowly broke, a wicked smile sliding across his features. "Sorry,

Springer. You don't get any help. That would be cheating now, wouldn't it?"

I narrowed my eyes. Then retaliated with, "And how are the shoes coming along?"

It might have been my imagination, but I swear I saw his smile falter just the slightest bit.

"Fine. They'll be done tomorrow."

"Good."

"How's your *investigation* going?"

"Fine."

"Good."

"Good."

We stood there in a silent standoff. Both of us pretty sure the other was completely full of bullshit.

Finally I was the one to break it, glancing out the window again. "Um, so…would you mind giving me a ride home?"

His eyebrows hunkered down. "How did you get here if… Wait! Never mind. I don't want to know." Ramirez shook his head. "Damn, you're a lot of trouble, girl."

I grinned. "Yeah, but you love me anyway."

"Most days." He shot me a teasing wink. Then he grabbed my hand in his and led me down the stairs. I'd like to think the gesture was a peace offering.

But I was pretty sure it was to make sure I didn't grab any evidence on the way out.

* * *

Forty minutes later I was back at my car and Ramirez's SUV was headed back onto the freeway for parts unknown. At least to me. I still thought it was a little unfair he wasn't sharing *any* information with me. Okay, fine, I hadn't exactly been sharing with him either. What can I say? I *really* wanted to win. Not that I needed him to do that. I had plenty to investigate all on my own.

I grabbed my cell, dialing Felix's number, then waited while it rang twice on the other end.

"Felix Dunn," he answered.

"Hey, it's me."

"Me who?"

"You know who it is!"

"Mum? Is that you, love?"

I gave my phone the finger. "Very funny, Tabloid Boy."

"I do try."

"By the way, thanks for ditching me at Gigi's."

I could almost hear Felix's grin through the phone. "I figured you'd provide a little cover for me."

"So you were banking on me getting caught?" It was official, I hated him.

"Now, don't get all surly on me. If you do, I won't share Gigi's text records with you."

"You're in already?" I asked, trying to keep the admiration out of my voice.

"I know—I'm good."

Apparently I failed.

"Okay, spill it. Who texted her on Friday?"

"She had two outgoing that afternoon. One in the morning to Hollywood Florist saying the tulips should be red. One to an 818 number saying she was terribly sorry, but she'd have to cancel their meeting."

"Mitsy," I interjected. "How about right before that. Any incoming?"

"Five minutes before. From a Kaufman. Said he could meet with her ASAP to draw up the paperwork."

"Paperwork? What kind?"

"Didn't say in the text. But the number it came from is local." He rattled it off.

"I'm on it." I hung up, immediately dialing the number Felix had given me. I waited while it rang on the other end, tapping my fingers on the steering wheel.

Three rings. Four.

Finally a perky voice answered on the other end. "Johnson, Levy, and Kaufman, attorneys at law. How may I direct your call?"

"Uh…Kaufman, please," I answered. Attorneys, huh? My mind whirled at the kind of paperwork an attorney might have ready for Gigi. Lawsuit? Contracts? A will?

"Kaufman." A man's voice came on the line, deep, baritone and gravelly, indicating the owner was no spring chicken.

"Uh, hi. My name's Maddie Springer. Gigi gave me your number," I lied.

"Oh." He paused. "Yes, tragic. I was so sorry to hear about her passing."

"Did you know her well?" I asked.

"We'd been acquainted for some time," he said.

Hmm. Typical lawyer—evade a direct answer at all costs. I tried another angle.

"She was very happy with the work you did for her."

"I only wish I could have done more."

Right. More what?

I bit my lip, trying to figure out what the magic password to this puzzle might be.

"Well, you came highly recommended. Especially regarding the current work you were doing for her," I tried.

"Well, it was long overdue."

"Right."

"So, what can I do for you Ms. Springer?"

"I…" I closed my eyes, taking a stab in the dark. "I wanted to have a will made up?"

"Oh. Well, I'm sorry, but that's not really my area of expertise."

Okay, cross will off the list.

"Oh, right. I mean, I wanted to draw up a will because…I'm suing someone, and I want to make sure my assets are taken care of. But the lawsuit is what I really wanted to talk to you about."

"Oh?" he asked. "Are you suing a former spouse?"

"Spouse? No. Why?"

"Listen, Ms. Springer, I'm sorry if Gigi led you astray, but I'm not really sure I can help you with your problem."

"Wait, you didn't let me finish," I said, wheels clicking into place. "I meant I wanted to talk to you about the lawsuit because it reminded me that I need a…prenup?" I mentally crossed my fingers.

"I see," Kaufman said. "Well, I'd be happy to discuss a prenuptial agreement with you."

Eureka! Divorce attorney.

"What sort of assets are you looking to protect?" he asked.

"Oh, uh…" I racked my brain. Did a plastic ficus tree count as an asset? Then my eyes slid down, settling on my shoes, and I remembered the conversation I'd had with Dana. "My designs! I'm a fashion designer, and I need to protect my work."

"Excellent idea. I highly recommend doing so."

I breathed a sigh of relief.

"Listen, I'm sorry to cut this short," he said, "but I've got a client coming in. However, if you'll make an appointment with my receptionist, I'd be happy to help you with this matter."

"Thanks. That'd be great," I said as Musak came through the receiver, signaling I was being transferred. Once back with the perky voice, I set up an appointment for the next day. (Hey, while I trusted Ramirez completely, protecting my assets might not be such a bad idea after all. I was pretty sure I owned at five figures in shoes alone. I mean, I should at least see what the lawyer had to say, right?)

As soon as I was done, I called Felix back and filled him in on my conversation.

"So, why do we think Gigi was visiting a divorce attorney?"

I mulled that thought over. "Could it be for the same reason I'd pretended to? If she was planning to accept Spike's proposal, it stood to reason that she'd want a prenup."

"That's one scenario," Felix agreed. "On the other hand, maybe it had something to do with her ex. Some alimony she was due?"

I shook my head at my empty Jeep. "Not possible. Summerville said she didn't get a dime from him after they split. They had a prenup, too."

"Alright, let's go with option number one then."

"What if Spike wasn't too happy at the idea of losing his sugar mama? What if he argued the need for a prenup? Maybe it got heated, and he killed her?"

"You're forgetting one thing."

"What?"

"The alibi. Spike was in Topeka."

"Probably," I hedged. "Dana's checking on that."

"Hmm."

"Okay," I conceded, "so let's look at it this way—who doesn't have an alibi for the time of her death?"

Papers rustled on the other end as Felix flipped through his notes. "Summerville was on a conference call. Allie said she had class that morning. Spike was in Kansas."

"What about Fauston?" I asked.

More paper rustling. "No idea where he was."

"He was the last one to see her alive," I pointed out. "And it was his knife used to kill her. What if he lied? What if he really delivered the cake sample to Gigi at 10:32, then offed her before heading back to the bakery?"

"I don't know. What's the motive?"

"I'm not sure. But if Allie was telling the truth, and if he does have some sort of history with Gigi, maybe he still had a thing for her. And if Gigi was going to say yes to Spike, maybe it set him off."

"That's a lot of 'if's."

I countered with the best argument I could come up with. "You have a better idea?"

Felix sighed. "Okay, more cake it is."

*   *   *

Anne was at the bakery case arranging stacks of heart-shaped Valentine's cookies when we walked in. Immediately my stomach growled as if it had some sort of Pavlovian thing going on with this place.

I gave my appetite a mental "down, girl" as Anne looked up.

"Oh, hey." Her forehead puckered. "Is there a problem with the cake?"

"No, I'm sure the wedding cake is perfect." Felix shot her a smile that was all teeth and put his arm around my shoulders.

Oh, brother.

"We actually wanted to speak to your uncle. Is he available?" I asked.

Anne shook her head. "Nope. Sorry. He's doing a wedding in the valley today. What do you need?" she asked again.

Reluctant to totally tip my hand to the girl, I verbally tiptoed around our reason for visiting. "We were just wondering about that morning when Paul dropped the cake off at L'Amore."

"Oh. Right. Well, he'll be back later tonight, I guess."

"He didn't happen to mention what he did after he left Gigi's, did he?" I asked.

She shrugged. "Not specifically. But I know he had deliveries all morning. Three more after Gigi's."

"And he made them all?" I asked, my prime non-alibied suspect quickly slipping away.

She nodded, her eyes serious. "Yep. Every one. I've got the logs right here." She pulled a big black book out from behind the counter, flipping to a page of delivery receipts.

I glanced down, noting the times and signatures on the receipts from the morning Gigi died. At exactly 10:35 an Annabelle Campbell signed for receipt of a chocolate anniversary cake. Damn.

"I know your uncle has been friends with Gigi for some time," Felix jumped in. "In fact, more than friends at one point, yes?"

She gave him a blank look. "I wouldn't know."

From her eavesdropping habit, I clearly doubted that.

"He never mentioned anything about their past relationship?" I probed.

"Not to me," she said. Though I noticed her eyes hit the floor.

Felix must have noticed, too, as he said, "I noticed that your uncle speaks very loudly. You didn't happen to *accidentally* overhear anything of that kind, did you?"

Anne bit the inside of her cheek, looking from Felix to me.

"If you've overheard anything, it would really be helpful," I prodded. "In fact, I'm pretty sure the police are even offering a reward of some kind for *helpful* information." Okay, I had no idea if this was true. But, it could be. I mean, sometimes the police did that, right?

Luckily, Anne didn't know either, and the measly-shop-girl-salary in her won out over the tight-lipped eavesdropper.

"I might have," she admitted.

"Such as?"

"Well…okay last week, I overheard a conversation between my uncle and Gigi. Totally by accident, of course."

"Of course."

"Anyway, Gigi had come by to pick up a cake topper for a client, and she and Uncle Paul were in the back. I walked past the door, you know, to restock the bakery case."

Right. Five-to-one she'd had a glass to the door.

"Uncle Paul was getting really upset. He said he couldn't believe she was even thinking about it again."

"About what?" Felix asked.

She shrugged. "I don't know. But then Gigi said he'd even gotten down on one knee. And then Uncle Paul said something I couldn't hear, and Gigi got real defensive. She said he was not a boy, and he did know what he was doing."

Spike. I chewed my lip. Gigi must have been telling Fauston about the proposal.

"Did she say anything else?" I asked, wondering if Gigi had planned on a 'yes' or a 'no.'

"Well, Uncle Paul said something about it being time she was with a real man. Then she laughed and said, 'What, like you? We've been down that road. No, thanks.'"

"And?"

Anne bit her lip. "That's it. A customer came in, and by the time I was done helping him, Gigi had left."

I mulled this over, feeling Fauston's motive grow stronger by the second. Whatever past relationship he and Gigi had, it sounded like it hadn't been his idea to end it. He'd been resentful of Summerville, and, from what Anne heard, he wasn't all that excited about the prospect of Gigi marrying again. Could we possibly be looking at a case of "if I can't have her, no one can"?

Even if we were, I reminded myself, Fauston had an iron-clad alibi.

"Why do you want to know all this? Even if they argued, my uncle had nothing to do with Gigi's death," Anne said sharply, her eyes narrowing.

"Of course not," Felix said, putting on a reassuring smile. "I'm sure it was just a harmless quarrel between old friends."

"Exactly." Anne crossed her arms over her chest in a defiant gesture.

I was about to ask her more about any other conversations she may have 'not really heard' when the bell over the door chimed again.

I turned around to find myself face to face with bridezilla herself.

Mitsy Kleinburg.

CHAPTER SIXTEEN

———

"You," Mitsy said, zeroing in on me.

I looked left, then right. "Me?"

"Yes, you." She marched across the bakery, advancing on me. "I've been getting calls all week from the florist, the caterer, the reception hall, all hounding me for checks and head counts and a million other little things. I can't take it anymore. I need a new wedding planner. You said you'd find one. Where is she?"

"Oh. Yeah, right…uh, about that…"

"You must be Mitsy Kleinburg," Felix interrupted. "I've heard so many wonderful things about you, I'd know you anywhere."

She gave him her patented blank 'yeah so?' look.

"I'm Felix Dunn," he said, extending a hand her way.

She ignored it.

"With the *L.A. Informer*," he added.

She rolled her eyes. "Ugh. Paparazzi."

My feelings exactly.

"Look, when am I meeting the new planner?" she asked me. "My wedding is only a few months away. There are details to be worked out. Important ones."

"Of course," I said, mentally trying to backpedal my way out of this one. "But, um, I'm having a hard time locating someone…"

She narrowed her eyes. "You said you'd find one, and you'd damn well better. All the good ones fill fast. And I'm not having a second-rate wedding just because some unprofessional old bat decides to up and die on me."

I declined to point out that Gigi likely had very little say in her demise.

"Speaking of Gigi," Felix said, "I heard a nasty rumor that you fired her the day before her death?"

"Yeah. So?" Mitsy asked. "Like I said, she was completely unprofessional."

"You were upset?"

"Of course. No one treats me like that."

"Insulted?"

"Yes."

"Offended?"

"Angry?"

"Yes." She paused, crossing her arms over her chest. "Why?"

"Where were you the morning she died?"

"Oh, hohohono," she said, shaking her head. "No way are you pinning this on me. I had nothing to do with that woman getting herself killed."

"Really?" Felix raised an eyebrow. "Then you won't mind telling me where you were."

"What, so you can print it in that little rag of yours?"

"Precisely. Or, if you prefer, I can run your picture next to the headline 'Bridezilla Kleinburg Prime Suspect in Wedding Planner Slaying.'"

Mitsy's mouth dropped open, her eyes turning into two round saucers. "You wouldn't!"

"Sadly, he would," I said.

Felix shot her a big toothy grin, rocking back on his heels.

Mitsy clamped her mouth shut with a click, clearly not used to being defeated by a guy who thought Bigfoot was front page material. "Fine. You want to know where I was Saturday morning? At the spa."

"All morning?" I asked.

"Yes. My driver dropped me off at eight, and I stayed through lunch."

"Which spa?" Felix prodded.

"Rejuvenation. In Malibu. Satisfied?"

Hardly. As much as Mitsy had been my backburner suspect, the fact that she was miles away from Beverly Hills made my heart sink. My suspect list was slowly shrinking into nothing.

"Now, if you're done torturing me," Mitsy said, "I'm here to pick out my icing rosettes."

Anne (who had been watching the exchange with the vigor of an A-list gossip) snapped to attention. "Right. Um, come on through the back," she said, gesturing to the swinging doors.

Mitsy turned to follow her, then paused and threw a look my way. "I'm serious about that wedding planner, Springer," she said. "I need one *now*. And if you don't deliver I will make sure your designs are blackballed from every red-carpet event in this town for as long as you live. Don't think I won't."

Unfortunately, I had no delusions that Mitsy wouldn't make good on that threat. I made a mental note to call wedding planners about her as soon as possible. God willing, one of them had yet to hear how difficult she was.

"Right," I called to her retreating form. "I'm on it!"

As soon as she was out of sight, I punched Felix in the arm.

"Ow! What was that for?" He rubbed at his bicep.

"That was for pissing Mitsy off so badly she's taking it out on me. Where the hell am I going to find her a wedding planner?"

Felix shrugged. "Want me to Google one?"

I shook my head. "Never mind," I mumbled, pulling him out the door.

"So," Felix said as we stepped back outside into the sunshine. "Mitsy's alibi. Believable?"

I nodded. "Unfortunately, yes. I've been to Rejuvenation. Attendants are in and out of your room constantly. There's no way she could have slipped away unnoticed."

"If she was there."

"Easy enough to find out," I said, grabbing my cell. A 411 and a quick chat with Rejuvenation's receptionist later, we had our answer. Yes, Mitsy had been there. Yes, *all* day. Yes, they were sure it was her—she'd made two attendants cry so hard they'd gone home. And, yes, they did have an opening for me in two weeks. (Hey, I couldn't resist, they had awesome facials!)

"Fine. Mitsy is out," Felix agreed as I hung up.

"So, where does that leave us?"

"Out of suspects," Felix said.

"Well, not completely out."

He looked up, raising one eyebrow in question.

"Don't forget Allie."

Felix frowned as if he would prefer to.

"Right. Allie." He pulled his little notebook from his front pocket. "She had class when Gigi was stabbed."

"Yeah, but has anyone checked if she *actually* went to class that day?"

He shook his head. "Sorry, Maddie, I just can't see her killing her mother."

"But she lied to us."

"She omitted something."

"Something critically important."

He shut his mouth, conceding my point.

"All right. Shall we drive down to UCLA and confirm her alibi?"

Since I was out of any better ideas, I nodded.

"But," I said as we got back into my Jeep, "let's stop at a drive-thru on the way."

Felix shot me a look. "What happened to your wedding-dress diet?"

"I smelled cookies. I'm starving."

I put the car in gear and pulled back out into traffic, making a left at the light and pulling into the first Del Taco I saw.

I ordered a big beefy burrito, large soda, macho fries, and churro sticks. Felix ordered a small soda.

"Don't you ever eat?" I asked, wiping a dribble of Del Scorcho hot sauce from my chin as we sat in the parking lot.

He shrugged. "Lost my appetite at lunch, I guess."

Right. Waiting for Allie.

I swallowed a salty fry, suddenly feeling just the teeniest bit sorry for Felix. Granted, the idea of he and Allie was completely ridiculous. Felix was old enough to be her…well…her very older brother. But no matter how wrong for him she was, it's still never fun to be stood up by a hot young thang. Not to mention the fact that, however murky his feelings for me may have been, I'd not only picked "caveman" Ramirez over him, but I was soon to be Mrs. Caveman.

"Sorry," I said, honestly meaning it.

He gave me a funny look across the console. "For?"

"Allie. Me. Everything."

Something indefinable flitted across his eyes. And the cab of my Jeep suddenly felt way too small, emotion clogging the air. Silence hung between us. I felt myself growing fidgety, wishing he'd say something.

I was just about to bust out with some completely inappropriate joke to break the tension, when Felix finally spoke up.

"Well, don't be, Maddie. I know I'm certainly not," he said, infusing the words with meaning that had nothing to do with one stacked co-ed. And everything to do with us.

Or, what shred of us that could have been.

I nodded, at a loss for words.

Felix cleared his throat loudly. "Uh, you've got a little something…" He gestured to the corner of his mouth.

"What?"

I licked right, coming away with a dab of hot sauce. Great. I grabbed a napkin, self-consciously dabbing at my lips.

"Anyway," he continued, "we better get a move on if we're going to hit the campus before classes end for the day."

"Right." I grabbed another napkin, wiping at my chin for good measure. I shifted my burrito to the other hand and turned the key, roaring my Jeep to life as I pulled out of the lot and pointed it down Santa Monica Blvd.

After wrangling with the parking voucher machine again (This time it took my money, but failed to spit out a slip. I kicked it. Hard. Which did absolutely nothing to help me gain a slip, but at least made me feel a little better.), we made our way to the math department, inquiring who taught Allie's Algebra II class on Monday mornings. We were directed to a Professor Blasberg, a tall woman with dark hair and sharp features, who was just shutting up her office as we approached. Yes, she had Allie in her class; no, she couldn't remember for certain whether she'd actually attended the class on the day in question. Though she did direct us to the tutoring center where Allie's study partner for the class worked, saying maybe she knew.

After traipsing across campus to the student services building, we found the study partner deep in the midst of explaining the quadratic formula to a guy whose eyes were starting to glaze over. Yes, she and Allie took Blasberg's class together; no, she hadn't seen Allie in class that morning.

I almost shouted "Ah ha!" at Felix, until the study partner explained it was because she'd been sick that day and missed class herself. But she said we could check with the computer lab where Allie sometimes did her homework to see if she'd been in that morning.

More traipsing. More vague answers. The small man with thick glasses in charge of the computer lab knew Allie, but couldn't remember for certain if he'd actually seen her that day. But he said we could try the snack shop next door to see if she'd been in for her usual Red Bull breakfast.

One guess what the pimply kid manning the snack shop said?

Apparently everyone on campus knew Allie, but no one could say for certain if she'd been there the day her mother was murdered.

My feet were killing me by the time we finally made our way, defeated, back to the parking lot. To find a ticket plastered to my windshield. I said some really nasty words under my breath.

"You kiss Ramirez with that mouth?" Felix asked.

I sent him a look that clearly said, *Don't mess with the blonde right now.*

"Right." He cleared his throat. "So, where to now, love?"

"I think it's time we talked to Allie," I decided.

Felix opened his mouth to protest, but I ran right over him.

"Look, I know you don't think she did this, but if she is innocent, we might as well rule her out, right?"

He clamped his mouth shut again. "I suppose."

I could tell as he got back into the Jeep he was not all that thrilled at the prospect of seeing the object of his unrequited desire again. Tough nubs. I was tired of talking to her voicemail.

I pulled onto the 405 north, cursing rush hour traffic (i.e. the parking lot that all freeways became between three and seven p.m.) as we threaded our way east via the 101 and 134.

As we hit Verdugo, the sun was just sinking down behind the hillside, the sky a dusky blue, not yet dark, but growing deep shadows along the tree line and softening the edges of the utilitarian architecture. Occupants from the neighboring complexes were trickling home from their day's work, parking suddenly at a premium as I searched the street for an empty spot. Finally Felix spotted a space up the block, and I did the parallel-parking thing, holding my breath as my back bumper inched ever so close to the front of a souped-up Chevy. After a couple of tiny forward then back maneuvers I was pretty sure I was in. Could I get out? Now that was another story. I clubbed my steering wheel and followed Felix down the sidewalk back toward Allie's building.

Again the overpowering smell of curry wafted from unit D, and the poor overtired mother in E was dealing with the cranky toddler, her wails so high-pitched a dog in a neighboring yard yapped in answer. I hoped that kid popped the tooth soon. For everyone's sake.

Felix rang Allie's bell as I stood on the step and waited, listening to the baby/dog duet. And waited. And waited. No answer.

He rapped his knuckles loudly against the door frame. Again nothing.

I tried to get a look in the window, but the room was dark, her renter's blinds shut tight.

"Looks like she isn't home yet," Felix said, stating the obvious.

But I wasn't ready to give up that easily. Allie was the last solid lead we had left. There was less than forty-eight hours until I was supposed to walk down the aisle with Ramirez. That is, if I could even stand living with the man after he won our little bet. Which was debatable.

I stared down at the lock on Allie's door.

"Any chance you've got your trusty picks with you?" I asked Felix.

He frowned. "Yeeees," he slowly admitted. "But, Maddie, it's one thing to slip into a dead woman's house. It's not as if she's going to mind now, is she? But I'm not sure I feel comfortable breaking into Allie's."

I spun around and pinned him with a look. Seriously? He decided to grow a conscience now?

"You're kidding, right?"

"Not really, no."

I narrowed my eyes at him. But this time he didn't budge.

"Fine." I held my hand out, palm up. "I'll do it, then."

"Maddie, I don't think this is such a good idea…"

"I don't care what you think. It's not your future on the line here."

"Maddie…"

"Hand. Over. The. Pick."

The desperation of my situation must have seeped into my voice, as, instead of arguing, Felix sighed loudly, then slid a hand into his pocket and returned with one of his little screwdriver thingies. He slapped it into my outstretched palm.

"Be my guest."

"Thank you."

I turned my back to him, biting my lip as I tried to remember the way I'd seen Felix do this. I put one hand on the knob, and, with the other, slowly inserted the pick into the keyhole. I turned the knob to the right…

…and the door cracked open.

I froze. No way was I that good.

"I think it was already unlocked," I said, looking up at Felix for confirmation.

He frowned. His face mirrored the same apprehension slowly building in my gut. Anyone who has ever lived in L.A. knows better than to leave the front door unlocked. Especially when planning to be gone all day.

I licked my lips, shoving the pick deep into my pocket as I gingerly pushed open the door.

"Hello? Allie?" I called.

The interior was dark, the blinds letting in little of the fading sunlight outside. I ran my hand along the wall beside the door, searching for a light switch. My fingers

collided with one, and I quickly flipped it.
The room instantly flooded with cheap,
buzzing florescent lights.

My eyes roved the room, the
apprehension building. The flowers on the
coffee table had been knocked over, water
from the vase spilling into a dark puddle on
the gray shag. The happy red and yellow
throw pillows were strewn across the floor,
and one of her kitchen chairs had been
knocked over, lying in the middle of the
floor on its side.

But that wasn't the worst of it.

I sucked in a breath, grabbing Felix's arm
for support.

In the middle of the kitchen floor, on the
ugly, nineteen-seventies olive green
linoleum, was a thick puddle of dark red
liquid.

And I'd bet my Manolos it wasn't Kool
Aid.

CHAPTER SEVENTEEN

———

I heard a scream, and it took me a few seconds to realize it was coming from me. I tried to take a deep breath, but it felt like a brick was sitting on my chest.

"Is that…? Is that…? Ohmigod." The room started to spin as I tried to form a coherent sentence.

I went to lean against Felix for support but realized he wasn't there. He'd shaken me off his arm and stepped over me, immediately rushing through each room of the tiny apartment, calling Allie's name. Great, what was I, chopped liver?

Instead, I leaned against her kitchen wall, sliding down until my butt hit the linoleum. I wrapped my arms around my knees, hugging them to my chest, watching Felix duck into the bedroom, the bathroom, check in all the closets.

"She's not here," he said, his face a ghostly shade of white.

I looked back at the puddle. "Do you think she's…dead?" I squeaked out.

Felix didn't answer, his jaw clenched tight, his eyes for once unreadable behind stony features. "Call Ramirez," he said.

Right, Ramirez. Good idea.

I shoved my hand into my bag for my cell. Only my fingers were shaking so badly, I couldn't get a good grip on it. After rifling unproductively through my possessions, I turned my pursed upside down and dumped the entire contents onto the gray shag. Lipstick, compact, credit cards, pens, a little mini calendar from the bank. And my cell. I grabbed it, my clumsy fingers dialing as I watched Felix examine the door frame, suddenly shifting into CSI mode.

Three rings into it Ramirez answered.

"Hey," he said, obviously recognizing my number.

"Youhavetocomerightaway," I slurred, rushing my words together into one sentence.

"Whoa. What happened? You okay?"

"Yes. No. I don't know. But I'm not sure Allie is."

"Allie?"

"The wedding planner's assistant."

"Jesus, don't tell me this is another one of those place card emergencies. Maddie, just pick whichever one you like. I really don't care, okay?"

I tried to swallow down the immediate hurt at the way he said he didn't care about our wedding, telling myself that wherever Allie was, her situation was a whole lot worse.

"Look, I'm at Allie's place. She's bleeding. Or someone was. In her apartment. She's in trouble. You have to come right away."

I think "bleeding" was the magic word, as his tone changed immediately. "What do you mean, bleeding?"

I took a deep breath and closed my eyes, willing my thoughts to settle into an organized pattern. "Her front door was unlocked, there's a puddle of blood on her kitchen floor, and she's not here. It looks like there was a struggle."

"Are you somewhere safe?" he asked, and I could hear the sound of him grabbing his keys.

I nodded at the room. "I think so."

"Don't move, I'll be right there." And he hung up.

I flipped my phone shut, holding it close to my chest. Despite the adrenalin still doing a Daytona 500 thing through my veins, I felt a little better knowing he was on his way.

"It isn't forced."

I pulled myself out of my thoughts and looked up to find Felix still examining the doorjamb.

"There's no sign anyone muscled their way in here. Whoever was in here with her, she must have let them in voluntarily."

I stood up, testing out my shaky legs (which felt like I'd just done an entire Step and Sculpt class with Dana) and joined him. I looked at the bit of wood where the door met the wall. He was right, not even a scratch in the paint.

"So, she knew whoever did this," I said. "Just like with Gigi."

Felix nodded.

He stepped outside, eyes on the ground as he surveyed Allie's porch.

I followed him like a shadow. There was no way I was staying in that apartment alone for even a second. "What are you doing?"

"Looking for signs of a struggle as they left."

I looked to the right. Rows of sickly looking grasses, which might have once been considered decorative, now jutted up from the landscape in rows of untamed tufts. To the left of the pathway a few worse-for-the-wear succulents hovered close to the ground. One near Allie's door had been trampled flat, oozing a green goo. The grasses to the left of the door had a pronounced tilt to one side.

"If she struggled, it means she was alive when she left," I said, hanging on to that little bit of hope.

"Maybe." Felix looked down the drive as if the empty street would somehow tell him where she'd gone. "Or someone struggled hauling her body away."

I winced. As much as I had my doubts about Allie, I didn't want to see the perky blonde six feet under.

Besides, the fact that someone had attacked her made me rethink my whole theory. Generally it was the guilty people who attacked the innocent, not the other way around. If someone had gone after Allie, our killer was still out there somewhere.

I shivered, instant goose bumps forming in the cool evening air as I heard the distant sound of sirens racing up Verdugo.

Half an hour later Felix and I had been corralled out to the street, behind a ream of yellow crime scene tape that ran the length of the apartment complex. The Indian couple from unit D were talking animatedly to a uniformed cop who was struggling to write down their every word. The tired mom from E stood with baby on hip on the sparse lawn, shooting daggers at Felix and me as if it was our fault sirens and plainclothes officers were keeping her baby awake. And Ramirez and his crew of boys in blue were going over Allie's apartment inside and out for any clue to her disappearance.

When he'd first arrived on scene, Ramirez had made a beeline toward me, taking me into a full-bodied hug that threatened to crush my ribs and asked again if I was okay. One quick affirmative was all the invitation he needed to leave me outside and transform into cop mode, his attention immediately drawn to the possible crime scene inside. He'd dropped a rushed kiss on the top of my head, spared a moment to scowl at Felix, then was gone, swallowed up into Allie's apartment. Where he'd yet to appear from.

I sat down on the front bumper of a police cruiser, chewing at my bottom lip as I watched a guy with a metal evidence-collecting kit make his way inside.

"How much longer you think they'll be in there?" Felix asked. I could tell he was itching to get away from the place, partially because Ramirez was in the vicinity but mostly due to his quickly approaching deadline for making the morning edition of the *Informer*.

I shrugged. "I don't know. Depends what they find, I guess."

"Great." He folded his arms over his chest, stealing a glance at his watch.

Luckily, Ramirez emerged minutes later, a frown creasing his brow. He did one quick survey of the scant yard before his eyes landed on us. First me, then Felix, then me again.

Oh, boy.

He stalked toward us with purposeful strides and paused just inches from me.

"What happened?"

I shrugged. Felix did the same.

Ramirez's eyes narrowed.

"Okay. Why are you here?"

"We wanted to talk to Allie," I answered.

"And?"

"And she wasn't here."

"What did you see?"

"Much the same thing you can see now," Felix said. "We're not stupid enough to disrupt a crime scene."

Ramirez shot him a look that clearly said he wasn't convinced that was true.

"What did you want to talk to Allie about?" he asked.

I bit my lip. And looked to Felix. I wasn't sure spilling all to Ramirez now that he was in official cop mode was such a hot idea.

On the other hand, the way that vein in the side of Ramirez's neck was starting to bulge had the words "handcuffs" and "holding cell" ringing in my ears. In the end, the vein won. Hey, I've been in a holding cell before. Hanging out with gang members and hookers and peeing in public is not my idea of a good time.

So, I told him everything. I spilled all about our checking into suspects' alibis and how Allie's hadn't panned out and how, her being Gigi's daughter, we wanted to chat with her, only when we got there she was gone and a puddle of red gooey stuff was in her place instead.

Ramirez listened to it all with his stoic poker face in place, only pausing the narrative to ask the occasional question or clarify an exact time.

By the time I was done, he just looked at me.

"Um, so…we're good?" I asked.

"It's over," he said.

"Excuse me?"

"The bet. We're done."

"Wait," I held up a hand. "What do you mean, 'done'?"

Ramirez ran a hand through his hair. "Maddie, it's too early to say what really went on in there, but I can tell you that's human blood on her kitchen floor. If you had walked in a few minutes earlier…Jesus, I don't want to think what might have happened to you."

While the sentiment was touching, I was still stuck on his first statement. "We shook on it. You can't back out on the bet now."

"Goddamit, Maddie, this is not a game."

"I know it's not!" I shouted. Drawing looks from both the Indian couple and the sleepless mom. Not to mention Felix, who was fidgeting nervously and slowly inching away from us.

"Maddie," Ramirez warned, his voice low and deceptively calm.

But he had me worked up now.

"The fact that my fiancé thinks I'm some helpless, brainless chick is not some game," I spat back.

"Please, you know I don't think that."

"No, Jack. I don't. I know that anytime things get difficult, you try to shut me out, send me home, handcuff me to your car—"

"I only did that once!"

"—and not even one measly time have you ever asked my opinion about a case. Why? Because you think I'm a bimbo." I gulped back the last word as tears started to back up behind my eyes.

"Oh, hell." He ran his hand through his hair again until it stood up in little spikes.

"I don't want to marry someone who thinks I'm a bimbo," I cried.

"Maddie, I don't think you're a bimbo. I just don't want to see my girl hurt."

"Woman. I am not some little *girl*, Jack, I'm a grown woman."

He sighed. Deeply. "Okay. I don't want to see my *woman* get hurt."

He reached a hand out to wipe at my wet cheeks. "Come on," he said, his voice soft. "I hate seeing you cry."

"The bet's still on." I sniffed, crossing my arms over my chest, then narrowed my eyes, squinting through watery tears. "And you better believe I'm going to win."

Ramirez pursed his lips together, letting a long breath out through his nose. "Fine."

I lifted my chin a fraction of an inch in triumph.

"But promise me one thing?" he said.

"What?" I hedged.

"Just quit hanging out with that guy." He gestured toward Felix, now a few feet away, pretending to be really interested in a hangnail on his thumb.

"Felix is a friend."

"He's a sleaze."

"He's a friendly sleaze."

Ramirez narrowed his eyes. "How friendly?" he asked, his stance quickly shifting from loving boyfriend to Caveman.

I threw my hands up in surrender, so not going into that territory again. "Fine. I'll try to ditch Felix."

"Good."

"Emphasis on 'try'. The guy's like a bad fungus you can't get rid of."

He grinned, Caveman retreating.

"I'll take 'try.'"

He took a step closer, dropping a tender kiss on my forehead. "So, stick around, and we'll go to my place tonight?" he whispered.

While part of me would have liked nothing more than to spend the evening curled up in Ramirez's arms, the fact that Allie was missing, my theories were all shot to hell, and Felix was hanging on our every word somehow caused me to shake my head in the negative.

"Can't. I've got a bachelorette party to attend tonight."

He raised one eyebrow. "Bachelorette party?"

I nodded. "Dana's throwing it for me."

"I don't like the sound of that."

That makes two of us, pal.

I looked down at my watch. "I'm late already. I should go."

He frowned. "Okay. But come by my place when you're done."

I nodded. Then planted a quick kiss on his cheek before hiking the block back up the hill to my Jeep. Once inside I quickly turned the key, letting the engine warm up before flipping on the air.

Honestly, the last thing I wanted to do was go to a bachelorette party. The scene I'd just witnessed brought back all too fresh memories of Gigi facedown in my cake sample. Only this was somehow worse. Because Allie was out there somewhere. Maybe alive, maybe not. But definitely in the hands of someone unscrupulous enough to kill.

I thunked my head back against the headrest, closing my eyes.

Think, Maddie, who could it be? I had the nagging feeling I'd missed a vital piece of information somewhere along the way. So far all I had was a handful of unlikely suspects. The only thing they all had in common was that they knew Gigi. And, unfortunately, all had alibis. So, who had stabbed Gigi and possibly kidnapped Allie? There had to be something I'd overlooked.

A knock sounded on my window, and I freaked so badly I nearly peed my pants.

I turned to find Felix rapping on the glass. Trying to still the jackhammer in my chest, I rolled down the window.

"What?"

"Any chance I can catch a lift with you?"

I rolled my eyes. "Where are you going?"

"*Informer* office. Hollywood. Near your bachelorette party by any chance?"

I opened my mouth to tell him that I honestly had no intention of going through with the party now. But, quite frankly, I figured the easiest way to "ditch Felix" was to drop him off somewhere myself. At least then, instead of looking over my shoulder for a Neon tag-along, I'd know for sure which rock he was under.

"Fine, get in," I said, putting the car in gear as Felix climbed into the passenger side.

I made a semi-legal U-turn and headed back toward the freeway.

*   *   *

The *Informer* offices were housed in a nondescript white(ish) building in Hollywood, smack in the center of tourist heaven. I counted no fewer than four souvenir shops on the same block, all four sporting life-sized cutouts of Marilyn Monroe. I dropped Felix off out front, each of us promising to call the other if we heard anything from Allie.

I looked down at my dash clock. Seven fifteen. I could go back to my apartment. But somehow the idea of being alone right now was less than appealing. Despite my bravado in front of Ramirez, I was more than a little creeped out by the site of all that blood in Allie's kitchen. Option number two was to go to Ramirez's place and wait for him to get home. But somehow, the idea of being alone in Ramirez's place was even more depressing than being alone in my own.

And then there was option three.

With a resigned sigh, I pulled out onto Hollywood Boulevard and made for Vine. And did a double take as I pulled up to the address Dana had given me. The Garden of Eden. And I wasn't talking Bible study here. The place had those kind of blacked out windows and neon signs with lots of Xs in them. A neon eye above the door alternated between doe-eyed wide and winking seductively as I locked my car and steeled myself, hitting the front door.

Loud music emanated from speakers hidden in the ceiling, pounding out a rendition of "Cat Scratch Fever" that made me want to scratch out my own eardrums. A stage to one side held three stripper poles, all being made love to by women wearing teeny tiny G-strings and strategically placed tassels. On the floor of the Garden sat rows of tables, most occupied by Asian businessmen and groups of rowdy frat boys with Sierra Nevada bottles in hand.

I glanced back at the door. Did I have the right place?

A waitress in a pink bikini who obviously believed in the "more is more" credo of silicone cup sizes approached carrying a tray.

"Can I help you, honey?" she asked.

"Uh…I'm here for a bachelorette party?"

"Oh, right!" She nodded.

And any hope that I'd been mistaken in writing down the directions vanished. (As did stripper number one's tassels, I noticed. Yikes!)

"In the back," she said, indicating a pair of doors to the far right of the place. "Your friends are already here."

"Thanks," I mumbled, trying not to look at the wiggling boobies on stage as I made my way through the club.

"And, hey, congratulations!" Miss Double D called after me with a wink.

I waved feebly. Then pushed my way through the back doors.

The backroom wasn't as large as the main area, obviously reserved for private parties. A smaller stage was constructed here, though a trio of silver poles was still the highlight. Luckily, they were empty. (For now.)

Three tables were set up in front of the stage. At one sat my mom, Mrs. Rosenblatt, Marco, Dana, and Molly. All four sipped from some kind of fruity drink with pineapple slices floating on top.

Dana jumped up, grabbing me in a hug.

"Maddie, I'm so glad you made it." She pulled back. "You're late, you know."

"Long story. Tell you later." I looked up at the stripper poles again. "Um, please tell me we're not here to see strippers?"

Dana laughed, propelling me over to the table where Marco shoved a fruity drink into my hand.

"No, silly, we're not watching strippers."

Oh, thank God.

"We're being the strippers!"

The fruity drink froze midway to my mouth.

O-kay. Much worse.

"Say what?" I looked around the room, a sudden vision of Mrs. Rosenblatt going full monty triggering a gag reflex in the back of my throat.

"We're getting a pole-dancing lesson from Eden. She's like the best exotic dancer in all of Hollywood. She's totally going to teach us how to work the pole. You know, so you can make the honeymoon extra special," Dana said, waggling her eyebrows up and down.

"Plus, it's great for your glutes," Molly added. "I joined a pole-dancing class after Connor was born. Worked off the baby fat in six months flat."

"Huh." I took a big gulp of my drink, hoping that whatever it was there was lots of alcohol in it.

"Is this the bride-to-be?" A tall woman with a thick wave of shiny brunette hair emerged from behind a curtain to the left. She wore a black latex bikini and six-inch black leather boots that came all the way up to midthigh over a pair of fishnet stockings. "Hi, I'm Eden," she purred, holding a hand out to me.

I shook it. But didn't get a chance to respond as a loud hiccup erupted from me.

Eden giggled. "Woo, looks like someone's enjoying the drinks already. Okay, are we ready?" she asked, turning to my assembled group of friends.

"Doll, I was born ready," Mrs. Rosenblatt said.

Oh lord. I took another sip of my drink. A really big one.

"Great, you can go first. Maddie?" Eden asked, gesturing to an empty pole.

I shook my head. "Can't. Hic-(hiccup)-ups." For once those buggers came in handy.

"You got them things again?" Mrs. Rosenblatt asked. "You gotta get rid of them. *Bubbee*, what you need is a good scare."

I was pretty sure if she got on that pole, I was going to get one.

"Okay then, anyone else want to try?" Eden asked.

"Oh, I'll do it!" Marco said, raising his hand and bouncing up and down in his seat.

"Great, let's get started." Eden crossed to a stereo system in the corner and pushed a few buttons. Immediately the room filled with the sound of the Pussycat Dolls wondering if we wished our girlfriends were hot like them.

"Our first move is the butterfly twist," Eden yelled over the beat, jumping up onstage and claiming the pole between Marco and Mrs. R. "You start with an extended right arm, swing your body, then crook your right leg around the pole and ride it down." She demonstrated, her legs wrapping around the pole as she swung in an arcing circle. With her long, lean form and hair flowing behind her, I had to admit, the move was fluid and almost elegant. Maybe this pole dancing thing wasn't so bad.

I took another sip of my fruity concoction and even found myself bobbing my head to the music a little as Double D walked in carrying a tray of fresh drinks.

"Once you master that one, we'll add a twist to it where you arch your body back, then release, engaging your abdominals," Eden instructed. "Why don't you both give it a try?"

"This is so fun!" Marco grabbed the pole in both hands, swinging his weight around it. But, since Marco weighed about as much as a mayfly, he didn't so much slide seductively down its length as look like a kid flipping around the monkey bars. Or maybe I just got the jungle gym image from the way he shouted out, "Weee, look at me!"

"My turn," Mrs. Rosenblatt announced.

Then I watched in horror as she kicked off her Birkenstocks and grabbed onto the pole with both hands, grunting as she tried to hoist her weight off the ground. Which, since *she* weighed more than half the linebackers in the NFL, was completely futile. But that didn't stop her from continuing to try. She pulled with all her might, lifted one leg and wrapped it around the pole, arching her back until her muumuu rode up her leg exposing a roadmap of varicose veins.

"Am I doing it?" she asked, her cheeks turning pink as the blood rushed to her head

"Um, maybe a more stationery move might be—" Eden started.

But she didn't get to finish.

An ominous cracking sound interrupted the Pussycat Dolls, and Mrs. Rosenblatt flew backwards onto her derrière as the base of her metal pole ripped away from the stage, taking a plank of hardwood flooring with it. The pole toppled to the right, hitting Marco with a thud and taking him down to the floor as little white chunks of ceiling fluttered down on them both.

"Did I do it?" Mrs. Rosenblatt asked, coughing up ceiling dust.

Eden screamed, Mom gasped, Dana laughed, Double D's mouth hung open like a fish, and I grabbed another fruity drink from her tray of cocktails and downed it in one big gulp.

Hurrah to singlehood.

CHAPTER EIGHTEEN

———

By the time I left Eden's Garden I'm pretty sure I'd heard enough Pussycat Dolls to last a lifetime and had decided that those women in the tiny tassels were way underpaid for the skills it took to do their jobs. And I was drunk. After seeing Mom give the pole a go—really, really drunk. I called a cab and had the driver take me to Ramirez's place. I only vaguely remembered slipping my little pink key into the lock and collapsing on his bed before going into a fruity drink coma.

I awoke with the distinct taste of gym socks in my mouth and a ringing in my ears that sounded like a thousand fire alarms all going off at once. I groaned, rolling over and glancing at the clock. 6:00 a.m. Way too early to be awake. I moaned, sinking into my pillow and putting my hands over my ears to the stop the ringing. Only it didn't help as I realized the sound was actually coming from my phone. I twisted left, cracking one eye open as I fumbled for my cell on the nightstand.

"Hello?" I croaked out.

"Hey, it's me," Felix yelled.

"Shhh. Hangover."

"Oh no, don't tell me Dana got you drunk last night?

"Worse. She made me pole dance."

There was a pause. Then, "How come you never invite me to these things?"

"It's six a.m. What do you want?"

"Any word from Allie?" he asked.

I shook my head. Ouch. Bad idea. An instant migraine erupted behind my eyes. "Unh-uh."

"The police have any leads?"

I rubbed at my temple. "None that they've shared with me." I looked at the empty half of the bed beside me, noticed the distinct lack of percolating coffee scent in the air. "Ramirez didn't come home last night."

"He didn't?"

"He was out looking for Allie!" I said. A little more defensively than necessary perhaps.

"Right."

"I take it you haven't heard from her either?" I asked.

"No." His voice was rough and tense as if he hadn't gotten a whole heck of a lot of sleep either. "Listen, I think we need to talk with the attorney again."

"The attorney? Why?" I asked, propping myself up on one elbow.

"Gigi died the day after visiting her attorney. I find it hard to believe that's just coincidence. Whatever they discussed is likely what got her killed."

"And will lead us to Allie," I finished for him.

"Right."

"Well, we're in luck then," I said.

"How's that?"

"I've got an appointment with him this afternoon to draw up a prenup."

"A prenup? Ramirez is really making you get a prenup?"

"No!" Again with the overly defensive thing. I blamed the hangover induced migraine. "No, he would never do that. *I'm* having *him* sign one."

"Ah. Trust issues."

"Ramirez and I do not have trust issues!" Much. "It's just…I mean…I have to protect my shoes."

"What?"

"Nothing," I mumbled. "Look, my appointment's at two. Are you in or not?"

"I'll meet you there." And he hung up.

I flipped my phone shut and stumbled into the bathroom, immediately rifling through Ramirez's cabinets for an aspirin. Never mind that they were soon to be *our* cabinets, I still thought of everything at his place as his. I wondered how long it would be before I got over that. Would I ever get over it?

I tried to shake that thought—it was way too deep for a hung over chick—instead locating the magic pills and popping a pair into my mouth.

Trying not to feel too sorry for myself, I hopped into the shower, changed into a fresh pair of cropped jeans, a stretchy pink shirt, and white peep-toe pumps. (Because the pink ones that matched my shirt were still at my place. Dammit.)

I was almost beginning to feel human when my cell rang out, clanging those fire alarms again. Did Felix just love torturing me? I dove for it to cease the nausea producing noise.

"What, now?" I yelled.

"Wow, someone is little Miss Sunshine this morning," Larry said.

"Oh. Sorry. I thought you were someone else."

"Not Ramirez, I hope? You two are okay, right?" he asked.

"Yes, we're fine. Why does everyone think we're not fine?"

"Is this a bad time?"

I paused, counted to two Mississippi. It was totally unfair to take my hangover and Felix annoyance out on Larry. "No, Larry. It's fine. Sorry, it's been a long…" Night? Week? Six months? "What's up?" I asked instead.

"I just called to let you know I'm running a little late, but I'll meet you at Fernando's for our mani-pedi appointments in an hour, okay?"

Right. Manicures.

Three months ago when I'd first asked Larry to walk me down the aisle, he'd squealed like a tween at a Hannah Montana concert thing, then promptly made an appointment for us to get father and daughter matching manicures and pedicures for the wedding. I had to admit, it was my favorite way to bond.

I glanced at the clock. "Um, right. Okay, manicures. Sure. Two hours?"

"One!" Larry said.

"Right. I'll be there."

"Oh, and, Maddie? I'm bringing you your somethings," he sing-songed.

"My what?"

"You know, your somethings. Something old, something new, something borrowed, something blue. Well, I've got something for you that fits all four."

I had a sudden vision of walking down the aisle in drag queen chic. "Uh, Larry…"

"No, I'm not giving any hints, don't even ask. It's a surprise. See you in an hour!" And he hung up.

After retrieving my Jeep from Eden's, exactly one hour and seven minutes later I was pushing through the glass front doors of Fernando's, the doo-wop strains of Ricky Nelson hitting me full force as I entered the salon.

"Hey, blushing bride," Marco greeted me, roller skating out from behind his desk to give me a pair of air kisses. "Was last night fun, or was that fun?"

"Uh-huh," I gave a noncommittal nod. "Is Larry here yet?"

Marco gestured toward a pair of pedicure chairs near a cardboard cutout of James Dean. Larry, dressed in a lacy white sundress and red wig today, and Madonna sat side by side, debating between pink or raspberry polish. Larry looked up and gave me a little wave. Madonna nodded my way, then blew Marco an air kiss. I swear I think I saw Marco blush.

"They just started soaking," he assured me, grabbing me by the arm and steering me toward the duo. "Come on, let's get you in a tub."

Ten minutes later I was soaking my toes and filling Larry and Madonna in on the latest developments in the murder turned kidnapping.

"That's awful!" Madonna said, lifting a lace-gloved hand to her ruby painted mouth. "That poor girl."

I nodded.

"Do you have any clues who did it?" Larry asked, his bushy eyebrows puckering in concern.

I shook my head. "We have lots of theories, but that's about it. We've weeded out Mitsy. Dana's checking on Spike's alibi in Topeka. The ex was on conference calls the whole time. Fauston was making deliveries."

"So, no one did it," Marco said, skating up behind us with a tray of different colored nail polishes. "Pick."

I checked out Larry's color and selected a matching shade from the tray. "Well, Gigi is dead, and Allie is missing, so someone has to be lying. The question is: who?"

"My money's still on Mitsy," Madonna said. "Oh, I know! Maybe she has a secret twin who she forced into giving her an alibi while she killed the wedding planner!"

The three of us turned and gave her a look.

"What? It could happen…"

"What about this," Larry said. "What if Allie staged her own disappearance to throw you off track? What if she did kill her mother, thought you were getting too close to the truth, and decided to leave town?"

I pursed my lips together. I'll admit, I hadn't thought of that. "It's possible I suppose."

"It's brilliant!" Marco said, skating in a neat little circle. "This is better than a telenovela."

"Unfortunately, if it's true, she's probably skipped to Mexico by now," I pointed out. A thought so depressing I could hardly voice it.

"Okay, enough murder talk," Larry said, sensing my mood. He clapped his hands together. "I've got something important to show you!"

He reached into his oversized handbag, and I took a deep breath, steeling my self against the worst.

"Ta da!" He drew his hand out and held up a big white hair scrunchie with little blue plastic butterfly charms sewn onto it.

"Um…what's that?" I asked, terrified of the answer.

"Your somethings to wear to the wedding."

I did a loud hiccup.

"It's from an act I used to do in the '80s to Billy Idol's 'White Wedding,'" Larry said. "It's real silk made from your grandmother's wedding dress—very old. I sewed on the butterfly charms which are, obviously, blue and also new—"

"—I helped picked them out," Madonna chimed in.

"—and since it's mine and I'm letting you wear it, it's also borrowed." Larry beamed. "Here, try it on."

Before I could stop him, he had my hair fisted into a ponytail and was wrapping the scrunchie around it like a butterfly-clad tourniquet.

"Ohmigod, she looks just like you, Larry!" Madonna squealed.

I did another hiccup.

"Geeze, you've got those bad, Maddie," Marco said. "You know, my mama always used to feed us a spoonful of sugar to get rid of the hiccups."

"Oh, I've got some Sweet 'N' Low," Larry exclaimed, digging into his handbag again.

"No, I'm fine re-(hiccup)-ally," I protested.

But, of course, no one listened. Larry found a pink packet, Madonna tore it open, and Marco dumped the entire contents down my throat as my mouth opened in another involuntary hiccup.

I clamped my lips together, feeling my face scrunch tighter than the hideous band in my hair as sacchariney sweet stuff melted down my throat.

"Better?" Larry asked.

"Oh yeah," I shuddered. "Peachy keen." I gave him a feeble thumbs-up.

Madonna tilted her head to the side. "You know, that scrunchie needs something."

A butane lighter and blow torch?

"Earrings!" Marco exclaimed.

"Oh, I have the perfect pair," Larry said. "Big white hoops, I wore them in my salute to Bette Midler last year. What do you think, Mads?"

I think my migraine was back.

* * *

By the time my nails were dry, I'd convinced Larry I already had a perfectly good pair of diamond earrings to wear to the wedding (not that they were fancy Bette Midler style or anything), and I'd slipped my freshly pedicured toes back into my peep-toe heels, I had just enough time to hop on the freeway and make it to Kaufman's office before my appointment.

That is, if traffic weren't backed up all the way to the 110 because of an overturned ice cream truck. I kid you not, there was mint chocolate chip all over the freeway. It would have been hilarious had I not been stuck in it for over an hour.

As I sat idling behind a pickup with a decal of a Calvin and Hobbs character peeing on the back window, my cell rang, displaying Dana's number.

"Hey," I said.

"It's me. Listen, I got through to the driver who took Spike to the airport."

I sat up straighter in my seat. "And?"

"And, he said he dropped them off at seven a.m. the day Gigi was killed. Which means their flight didn't arrive at LAX until eleven."

"Which means Spike is in the clear." As much as I'd genuinely felt sorry for his grief, I was a little disappointed at crossing yet another name off my mental suspect list. At this rate, I was starting to wonder whether it wasn't just a case of random wedding planner stabbing.

"Sorry," Dana said.

"Thanks for checking."

"No prob," she asked. "Oh hey, did you see the front page of the *Informer* this morning?"

Uh-oh. "No. What did Felix do this time?"

"He totally pasted my head on Hilary Clinton's body."

"Oh, shit."

"No, it was brilliant! He found this picture of her reading to underprivileged kids, and now it totally looks like I was reading to them. I'm not a bad influence anymore!"

"Oh. Good." I think.

"That's not the best part," she continued. "After it hit the stand this morning, my agent got a call from CBS. They want me to do a bunch of public service announcements during Saturday morning cartoons about how drinking is bad. Is that cool or what? I always wanted to do PSAs! Of course, they want me to do them in the Flamingo outfit, but it's still pretty cool."

Huh. Who knew Felix could use his Photoshop skills for good instead of evil?

"That's great, Dana."

"Thanks. Oh, and I confirmed with the makeup artist for tomorrow. He says he'll be at your place at ten."

"Cool."

"And the hairdresser will be there at eleven."

"Okay."

"And the limo is picking you up at one."

"Do I have to remember all this?"

"Nope, that's what you have me for."

For once, I was grateful Dana had taken over planning.

"Thanks."

"Anytime. Oh, hey, Ricky just walked in." I heard her giggle, then a low male voice and a half-hearted "Stop it, you," on Dana's part. Followed by more giggling.

"Well, I guess I'll leave you two lovebirds alone…" I trailed off as a couple growls came through the other end. "See you tonight," I said. Then quickly hit the off button before I was ear witness to sex Flamingo style.

Miraculously, only twenty minutes later, a giant tow truck with a crane came and cleared the ice cream truck off to the side of the road, allowing traffic to crawl past, and I pulled up in front of the shining chrome and glass office building that housed Johnson, Levy, and Kaufman only marginally late.

As I huffed through the front doors, a receptionist with springing auburn curls looked up with a placid expression. "May I help you?"

"Maddie Springer. Here to see Kaufman."

"Oh, right," she said, smiling. "Just down the hall and through the door on your left," she said, indicating behind her. "Your fiancé is already here."

I paused and for a moment insanely wondered how Ramirez knew where I was before I realized who she was talking about. Felix.

"Thanks," I called, making my way down the hall as I concentrated on bringing my breathing back to normal.

I pushed open a door marked *A. Kaufman* to find my *fiancé* lounging in a leather chair across a sleek mahogany conference table from a large, barrel-chested man with a graying crew cut on a head at least a size too big for his body. They both rose as I entered the room.

"Maddie, what took you so long, darling?" Felix asked, planting a kiss on my cheek.

"Traffic. *Darling*," I answered, wiping it off with the back of my hand.

"Lovely to meet you, Ms. Springer," Kaufman said, offering a large, beefy hand. "Your fiancé here is quite a character. I can see what drew you to him."

"Hmm." I made a noncommittal sound as I gave Felix a sidelong glance, wondering just what he and Kaufman had been chatting about while I suffered through mint chip traffic.

"So," Kaufman said, as we all took our seats, "you'd like me to draw up a prenuptial agreement?"

"The little woman here has some silly notion that I'm only after her money," Felix said, sending me a wink.

I think I showed great restraint in not hopping over the table to strangle him.

"Well, I have to say, she's right," Kaufman said, nodding. "I recommend them to anyone. Divorce is a terrible thing for newlyweds to contemplate, but it happens all the time. Fifty-two percent of the time to be exact. And it's better to be safe than sorry, isn't it?"

I shot Felix an I-told-you-so look, before I remembered he wasn't actually my fiancé.

"I've got a couple of forms here," Kaufman said, sliding a pile of papers across the table to me.

I looked over them as he explained the main points, the legalese wording, and how exactly we should customize our agreement. Then he had his assistant type it all up, and in record time I had a prenup sitting in front of me with Ramirez's and my names on it, just ready for signatures.

I stared at it. The entirety of "mine," "his," and "ours" spelled out in black and white suddenly making me nervous. I tried to tell myself it was just your average case of pre-wedding cold feet. But as I shoved it into my purse I feared frost bite.

"Would you like to sign it now?" Kaufman asked, slipping a pen across the table toward Felix.

"Oh, uh, maybe we can do it later?" I said.

Kaufman raised an eyebrow.

"Well, I just want to sleep on it and make sure we're not missing anything."

Felix nodded. "Excellent idea, snookums."

I rolled my eyes.

"Of course," Kaufman replied. "I completely understand." He started tidying up papers and putting his pens into a briefcase.

Felix gave me a kick under the table, inkling his head toward Kaufman.

"Uh, I wanted to thank you again for fitting me in on such short notice," I said. "Gigi was right, you are wonderful."

At the mention of Gigi's name, Kaufman faltered, clearing his throat. "Yes, well, I'm glad we could fit you in, as well."

"Gigi came to see you the day before she died, didn't she?" Felix asked.

Kaufman frowned.

"Uh, I was having lunch with her that day, and she mentioned it," I quickly covered. Which was almost true. I'd seen her, then had lunch. It was close.

But it seemed to satisfy him as he nodded his oversized head. "Yes. Yes, she did."

"She told me you had something to discuss?"

He frowned again.

"I'm sorry, but I can't discuss that."

I felt the desperation of another dead end bubbling up in my throat.

Felix leaned forward, "Listen, I understand that you can't tell us what went on between you because of confidentiality. But Gigi was a good friend of ours, she's dead, and the police have no idea who her killer may have been. I find it an awful coincidence that she was killed the day after an emergency meeting with her attorney."

Kaufman's face blanched, his shoulders slumping as he leaned back in his chair. Apparently he hadn't thought of it that way.

He shook his head. "I'm sure that what Gigi and I discussed had no bearing on her death."

"Is there anything you *can* tell us?" I asked, stopping myself just short of adding "pretty please with sugar on top."

Kaufman ran his tongue over his teeth, his gaze ping-ponging from Felix to me. Finally he made a decision.

"Look, I can't go into what was discussed at our meeting. But, I can tell you that Gigi was anxious to have the matter resolved as soon as possible. I had a client cancel and could fit her in at the last minute. We discussed her…needs, and I promised I'd have the necessary papers drawn up for her to sign by the following evening."

But someone got to Gigi before he could. Right at that moment I would have given anything I had to know what Gigi had come to Kaufman for.

But it was obvious from the way he stood and cleared his throat that wasn't going to happen.

"Listen, I am sorry about what happened to Gigi. But I can assure you that it had nothing to do with why she saw me. Now, if you'll excuse me, I'm already running behind." And with that he ushered us out of the conference room and back out into the lobby where a perky receptionist said she'd send me a bill.

Once outside I threw my hands up.

"Well, great. We're no closer than we were before."

Felix shoved his hands in his pockets, staring back at Kaufman's building. I could see him mentally calculating just how difficult it would be to break in and peek at Kaufman's files. But, I had a feeling the security in the lawyer's office was a bit much even for a pro lock picker like Felix.

"So what now?" I asked.

"I'm going back to Allie's. Maybe there's something there the police missed."

I raised an eyebrow.

Felix let out a long sigh. "Yes, I'm aware it's a long shot. But I can't just do nothing."

I nodded. I knew the feeling. "You know, there is another possibility," I hedged. Then told him about Larry's theory that Allie had staged her own disappearance.

Felix's face grew stony, his eyes narrowing as he shook his head. "No way. Not possible."

"Why not?"

"What about the blood on her floor?"

"She could have put it there on purpose."

"What about the trampled leaves?"

"She has feet, Felix. She could have done that, too."

He shook his head again. "I don't believe it."

"Look, I'm not saying I totally believe it either, but just that…well…we should keep an open mind."

But I could tell by the set of his jaw, his mind was sealed shut. Amazing how a pair of big boobs did that to a guy.

"I'm going to Allie's," he said again, his resolve picking up steam. "You coming or not?"

I did an internal shudder, the image of all that blood—staged or not—way too fresh. "No thanks. I've got…wedding stuff to do," I lied. Hey, it sounded a lot better than "I'm a big fat chicken."

Felix nodded, then shuffled off to his Neon parked three cars down.

I got into my Jeep and cranked on the air, pulling back around toward the 101.

The truth was, all the wedding stuff was done. The last thing on my checklist had been to get my nails done. Today was the day I was supposed to be relaxing, going to a spa, recharging for the chaos that would undoubtedly ensue tomorrow.

Instead, I was worried about one stacked blonde gone MIA, one wedding planner six feet under, a stupid bet with my soon-to-be husband over just how much of a bimbo I might be, and last but not least, a prenup just in case I was one of the not-so-lucky 52%. All of which added up to an anxious churning feeling in the pit of my stomach.

Honestly, there was only one thing to do at a time like this.

Eat chocolate.

Which is probably why my car exited the freeway at the 2 and snaked west into Beverly Hills until it hit Fauston's bakery.

I parked my Jeep at the curb and pushed through the front door, the bell jangling to signal my arrival. Immediately Anne came out from the back, carrying a fresh tray of peanut butter cookies. I inhaled deeply, wondering why no one has bottled that scent.

"Hi, Maddie," she said, then frowned. "Don't tell me there's a problem with your order?"

"Actually, I'm having a major chocolate craving." I eyed the offerings in her bakery case. "Are those chocolate turtles?"

Anne nodded. "Uh-huh. Pecans, caramel, and dark chocolate."

I think I drooled a little on the counter.

"Wow. I'll take four. No, wait. Better make that six."

I salivated in anticipation as she bagged them up for me, not even waiting until I was out of the store before biting into one ooey, gooey piece of heaven. Caramel exploded onto my tongue as I bit into it, and I swear I had a near orgasmic experience.

"My God, these are good, aren't they?"

Anne shrugged. "Haven't tried them. I don't really like chocolate."

I froze. "Seriously?" What, was she from Mars?

She just shrugged her slim shoulders. "Not much of a sweet tooth, I guess."

No wonder she was a stick figure. I shoved the rest of the turtle into my mouth and paid for my chocolate, giving her a wave as I left.

I made it all the way to my Jeep before indulging in another piece. Okay, so maybe my life was still in turmoil, but at least with a piece of chocolate in my mouth I didn't care about the turmoil quite so much. I leaned my head back on the headrest and let my thoughts wander as I rolled the dark chocolate over my tongue.

The problem with this whole case was that there was motive galore. Too much motive. If Gigi was getting her own prenup drawn up, there went Spike's gravy train. Mitsy was known for her temper, and the way she'd threatened me, I could easily see her snapping at Gigi. Summerville, well, who knew what kind of hostility existed between a man and his ex.

And then there was Fauston.

I watched Anne carefully loading her cookies into a pink bakery box through the window.

Fauston had been sketchy about his and Gigi's relationship. But if he'd resented Summerville, it was likely he'd resent Gigi marrying a hot young rock star even more. Had he resented it enough to kill her to prevent it from happening?

Anne taped the box shut, then took her empty tray back into the kitchen.

As much as I liked the Fauston theory, it had one fatal flaw. He had an airtight alibi. The delivery log showed him across town at the time Gigi was killed. There was just no getting around that.

I sighed, popping another turtle in my mouth as Anne swung through the kitchen doors again. She took off her apron, hanging it on a hook near the door and switched the sign from "please come in" to "sorry we're closed".

Lucky me, I'd gotten my turtle fix just in time. And it's a good thing I did. Never again will I underestimate the powers of chocolate on an overtaxed mind. Because as I sat there watching Fauston's niece grab the pink box and disappear into the back of the shop again, it hit me.

Anne didn't have an alibi.

CHAPTER NINETEEN

———

I felt little cogs clicking into place as I stared at the empty window of Fauston's bakery. When I'd asked about the day of the murder, Anne had said her uncle was out on deliveries. But I'd never thought to ask about where she'd been. It would have been the easiest thing in the world for her to switch the little sign to closed, drive the three blocks to Gigi's, off her, then slip back to the shop with no one the wiser. I'd never thought of her before because she had no motive. But her uncle did. I wasn't sure how, but I *knew* Fauston had connived his niece to off Gigi for him while he went on deliveries, providing him with the perfect alibi.

I shoved my hand into my purse, grabbed my cell, and, with shaky fingers, dialed Felix's number.

"Hello?"

"Felix, it's me."

"Me who?"

"Can it, this is serious. I know who killed Gigi!"

Felix was silent for a moment on the other end. Then, "Alright, let's hear it."

So, I told him my theory, about how we'd completely overlooked Anne even though she was right under our noses the whole time. By the time I was done, I could hear him breathing hard.

"I hate to admit it, but you may be right. Where are you now?" he asked.

"Outside Fauston's...oh shit."

"What?"

I watched as a big white van with the words "Fauston's Bakery" pulled out from behind the building, Anne at the wheel.

"She's leaving."

"Where's she going?" I could hear the sound of Felix grabbing his keys in the background.

"I don't know. She's in the bakery van."

"Well, follow her. Don't let her out of your sight. If you're right about Fauston, she may lead us to Allie."

"Right."

I flipped my phone shut and gunned the engine, pulling out into traffic half a block behind Anne. Luckily, her big bakery van stood out like a white elephant among the subdued Bimmers and Jags, and I had no trouble keeping an eye on her as she wound through the rush-hour crowd, finally stopping outside a large office building on Wilshire. She parked at the curb, and I pulled into a loading zone four car lengths behind her, watching as she hopped out of the van with a big pink box in hand. She disappeared into the building, then fifteen minutes later emerged empty handed and got back into the driver's seat.

Back into traffic, this time hopping onto Santa Monica Blvd. east toward Hollywood. I followed her through the bumper-to-bumper maze of cars, only losing her once at a red light, before I caught up two blocks later at La Brea. When we hit the 101, she got on going south and didn't exit until we were near the civic center. I followed her through the downtown streets until the impressive outline of the Summerville building came into view.

Again Anne parked at the curb, this time grabbing a basket of muffins before slipping inside the building. I waited, watching out my window, tapping my fingers on the steering wheel. Twelve minutes later she finally she emerged, then jumped back into her van again, this time heading north toward the Echo Park area. I was beginning to wonder how many deliveries she had to make when my cell chirped to life on the seat beside me. I flipped it open.

"Yeah?"

"Where are you?" Felix asked.

I looked up at a passing street sign. "Sunset and Elysian."

"Good, stay on the line and don't lose her. I'm on my way."

"While I appreciate the help, I don't really think two cars trailing her would be less conspicuous, do you?"

Felix made a funny sound in the back of his throat. "I'm not coming to join you, I'm taking over."

I scoffed. "Felix, I've been tailed by you. You suck at it. I'm doing fine thanks."

"You have somewhere else to be."

I made a hard right, trying to concentrate on the road. "Oh, I do, do I?"

"Your wedding rehearsal? I do believe it starts in half an hour?"

I looked at my dash clock. Dammit, I hated it when Felix was right.

"Shit. I totally forgot."

"You've been doing that a lot lately. It'll be a wonder if you remember the actual wedding."

I did a double take at his words, remembering how that had been my exact sentiment about Ramirez when we'd originally found Gigi. Now who was the one so wrapped up in a case that she forgot her own wedding rehearsal? And Felix was right. It wasn't the first item I'd forgotten in the past few days. If it wasn't for my friends and family, I'd have missed half the wedding-related stuff I was supposed to be doing. I made a mental note to cut Ramirez a little slack the next time a homicide ruined our dinner plans.

Anne pulled into a small strip mall, driving around to the receiving bay of a mini mart. I followed, pulling the opposite direction and parking near a Subway Sandwiches.

"Hey, I'm at the mini mart on Silver Lake," I relayed into the phone. "Anne's making a delivery."

"Keep an eye on her. I'll be there in three minutes," Felix promised.

I waited on the line listening to the sound of his little Neon being pushed to its limits as Felix shouted a string of curses at the other drivers. I kept my eyes glued to the back bay of the mini mart, counting the seconds as they ticked by. I bit my lip as one minute turned into two, then five. Come on, Felix, where are you?

Finally six minutes and thirty two seconds later, his little Neon flew into the parking lot, bottoming out on a speed bump as he took it at forty miles per hour.

Just as Anne returned empty handed to the bakery truck.

Instinctively, I ducked down, even though I was pretty sure there was no way she could see me at this angle. Not that it seemed she was looking. For a guilty person, she seemed pretty carefree, whistling as she made her way to the driver's side and slipped behind the wheel again.

"She's leaving," I whispered into the phone. Then realized how ridiculous I was being. If she couldn't see me, she certainly couldn't hear me either.

"I'm on her," Felix assured me. Two beats later he pulled out of the lot, following Anne's van west on Silver Lake. "Go to your rehearsal. I'll call you when I get something."

And with that, he clicked off.

I sat staring down at my silent phone, feeling rather anticlimactic. I just hoped Felix did a better job of tailing Anne than he did me.

In the meantime…I had a wedding to rehearse. Taking a quick stock of my location, I pulled out of the parking lot, pointing my Jeep toward Beverly Hills and praying traffic was light.

*   *   *

Only forty minutes later, I pulled into the lot of the Beverly Garden Hotel and raced through the lobby to the back gardens where

Ramirez and I were scheduled to walk down the aisle in less than twenty-four hours. Then came to a screeching halt as I rounded the corner and saw the scene that Marco and Dana had set for me.

Palm trees lined the yard, strung with hundreds of tiny white lights. In the center, two men in coveralls were setting up rows of pristine white folding chairs next to a long red carpeted aisle. Leafy green vines intertwined with delicate little white flowers lined the pathway, leading up to a large, white latticework gazebo, strung with more tropical flowers and tiny white lights. Beyond the altar I could see tents and clusters of tables and chairs being set out for the reception. The air was so fragrant with the scent of blooming foliage, I'd swear I'd just stepped into Tahiti and not Beverly Hills. Despite all my misgivings about putting the tacky twins in charge, it was beautiful. Tears sprang to my eyes.

(Okay, maybe the two giant wooden tiki heads leading toward the reception area were a little over the top, but I could overlook those.)

"Maddie's here," I heard a child's voice call. I wiped at my eyes to see Molly's middle child, Tina, bouncing up and down on the toes of her little pink Mary Janes. "We can start wehearsing now!" she lisped.

Mom, Faux Dad, Larry, Molly, Dana, and the entire Ramirez clan all emerged from one of the big white tents, Marco bringing up the rear with a clipboard in hand.

"Okay, people, we're already behind, and we have a schedule to keep if we want this thing to go off. So, places. Chop, chop!"

I couldn't help laughing. If Gucci ever decided to take over the world, they had a readymade dictator right here.

And suddenly I had a brilliant idea.

"Marco," I grabbed him by the arm, pulling him aside. "You have been the best wedding planner ever," I said. And, right at that moment, I can honestly say I meant it.

Marco blushed. "Well, it's been a labor of love."

"How would you like to plan another one?"

He cocked his head to the side. "How many times are you and Ramirez getting married?"

"Not mine. Mitsy Kleinberg's."

His eyes went round, his mouth dropping into a perfect "O". "*The* Mitsy Kleinberg?" he squeaked out.

I nodded. "Yep. I think you'd be *perfect* for her." Marco was the one person I knew woman enough to handle Mitsy's tantrums and actually enjoy the drama.

Marco nodded, his little face bobbing up and down so fast it was almost a blur. "Yes, yes yes! Ohmigod, yes!"

I put a hand on his arm, trying to calm him down lest the hotel patrons think he was having an orgasm on the spot. (Honestly, I wasn't entirely sure he wasn't.)

"Great, I'll give her your number."

"Ohmigod, Mitsy Kleinberg," he walked away, fanning himself with his clipboard as he ordered the bridesmaids into position.

After we were all lined up, Marco ran us through the paces of "elegantly" walking down the long aisle. He then paired up my bridesmaids with Ramirez's groomsmen by height. (Conveniently matching himself with

Ramirez's cousin, Alfonso, who starred in a Latin soap.) Finally he cleared his throat and hummed a little "Dum, dum de dum," tune, signaling my cue. With Tina pretending to make a rose petal trail in front of me ("I get weal ones tomowow!" she gleefully told me.) I did the slow feet together, step, feet together, step thing as I'd been instructed until I made my way toward Ramirez, waiting for me beneath the flowering archway.

I've always thought there was supposed to be something magical about walking down the aisle. Like that slow journey toward the love of your life, watching you with adoring eyes, was supposed to make something click inside. Some sort of feeling that you were walking toward your destiny. Or at least an evening of really great sex ahead.

But I didn't. Instead, I was mostly trying not to trip over Tina. And Ramirez wasn't so much adoring as laughing at some joke Alfonso told him that included some hand gestures I was pretty sure the flower girl wasn't old enough to witness. For all the magic I felt, I could have been walking an aisle at the supermarket. It was mildly depressing.

I swallowed down a tiny prickle of panic, telling myself it was just because I was preoccupied by my very silent cell in my pocket and the fact Felix had yet to call in with any news.

I finally made it to the altar to stand between Ramirez and Dana, my maid of honor, then turned to face the person presiding over the ceremony.

Mrs. Rosenblatt.

"Wait, where's Father Mahoney?" I asked, turning on Marco.

"Uh well, he wasn't feeling well..." He looked to Dana for help.

"Something about a bad clam sauce last night," she filled in.

"But he promised he'd be here tomorrow."

Dana nodded. "Absolutely. I mean, they pumped his stomach for a full twenty minutes last night, so he's totally emptied out by now."

"In the meantime," Marco said, "Mrs. Rosenblatt is our stand in."

"Yeah," Mrs. R piped up. "And if he don't show, I do a pretty snazzy Kabbalah ceremony you'd love."

A loud hiccup erupted from me.

"Maddie, you better take care of those before the ceremony," Mom said, a frown of concern settling between her brows.

Yeah, 'cause it was *hiccups* that were gonna ruin this wedding. Trust me—this wedding never had a chance.

Marco walked us through the rest of the paces without incident, (unless you called Dana choosing a Don Ho version of "All You Need is Love" as our first dance an incident—which, in an effort to stave off further hiccups, I didn't), and we all made our way back to our cars to caravan to the rehearsal dinner.

I lingered behind, checking my cell readout for the fiftieth time that night. Nothing.

I slipped behind a palm tree and dialed Felix's number. Luckily, he picked up on the third ring.

"Felix Dunn."

"It's me. Maddie me," I clarified before he could ask. "Where are you?"

"I'm watching Fauston have dinner at a Taco Bell."

I frowned. "Fauston? What happened to Anne?"

"She went back to the bakery. She and Fauston had a conversation. Then he took off, and she stayed behind. I thought he'd be the better bet to lead us to Allie."

"And you just left Anne there?" I hissed. While I agreed with his logic, the idea that Anne could at this very minute be carrying out some orders from Fauston to axe Allie made anxiety curl around my stomach.

"I can't very well be in two places at once, now can I?" he said. Though I could hear the same anxious thoughts swirling through his voice.

"Look, I'll…" I bit my lip, watching my wedding party trail down the street. "I'll go follow Anne."

"What about your rehearsal dinner?" he asked.

"This is more important." Something I never thought I would have said even a few weeks ago. "I'll be there in fifteen minutes," I promised, then flipped my phone shut.

"Be where?"

I squeaked out a yelp as I spun around to find Ramirez standing behind me, a frown puckering his brow.

"Nowhere," I said.

He gestured to the phone in my hand. "Who was that?"

"No one."

His eyes narrowed. "A blond British tabloid reporter no one?"

I bit my lip again. "Maybe."

I didn't think it was possible, but his eyes narrowed even further, into dangerous cat-like slits.

"Look, I…something came up," I said lamely.

Here's the deal—as much as I was sure Anne and her uncle were the ones who'd offed Gigi, I had zero proof. Basically, it was just a really, really good hunch. And, as Ramirez had pointed out to me numerous times, hunches didn't stand up in court. If I wanted to help Allie, following Anne was my best bet.

"'Came up'?" Ramirez asked.

"Yeah."

"Hmph." He crossed his arms over his chest. "Everything okay?"

I nodded vigorously.

"You sure?" he probed.

"Yeppers," I yelled. Geeze, when did I turn into a Disney character? Tone down the perky a bit, girl. "Yeah, everything's fine. I just…I kinda have to leave a little early."

"How early?"

"Now."

He clenched his jaw shut. "Wanna tell me why?"

I shook my head. "Nope."

"Maddie…" he said, his voice a warning growl low in his throat.

"Look, you just have to…trust me," I said, slipping around him. "I'll call you later. Tell Mom I'm sorry."

For half a second I thought he might chase after me. But apparently he thought better of it, instead, calling after me, "Just be careful. And don't get into any trouble, okay?"

"Who me?" I asked, blinking innocently as I walked backwards toward the parking lot. "Never."

* * *

Three minutes later I was in my Jeep heading toward Fauston's. I felt just the teeniest bit guilty at abandoning Ramirez with *both* our families, but I shoved it down. If we ever did make it to that honeymoon, I promised myself I'd make it up to him. Instead, I concentrated on driving as I sped down the surface streets at speeds that would make a CHP officer's head spin, weaving through Beverly Hills and pulling up to Fauston's Bakery again just as the white van rounded the corner, Anne at the wheel. Talk about timing. I gave myself a mental pat on the back. Was I good, or was I good?

I followed her east on Wilshire, wondering if we were on one last late night delivery or if Anne actually drove the van home. She made a right on Dayton, then a left on Palm, and I suddenly realized I was retracing my Speed Racer moves from just a few moments ago. My suspicion was confirmed when she pulled up to the back of the Beverly Garden Hotel ten minutes later. Mental forehead smack. She was delivering *my* wedding cake.

I parked in an empty spot behind a Dumpster (lest Ramirez wander back and spot my Jeep), then hoofed it around the corner of the receiving bay just in time to see Anne wheeling a huge box toward the prep kitchen on a metal dolly. I ducked behind a bush, out of sight from the back of the hotel, where a couple of waiters stood smoking cigarettes.

I looked to the right, my rows of chairs and flowered archway sat in the dark, mocking me as I started to wonder if I wasn't on some wild goose chase. Here I was crouched in the shrubbery while half a mile away my entire wedding party was dining on veal piccata and toasting my happiness. And the truth was, I really didn't have any evidence that Anne was involved outside of a non-alibi.

I glanced back at the bakery van sitting in the lot a few yards away. What do you think the chances were there was any evidence of her crime in there?

I stole a glance at the kitchen door, still closed. Then, not even really sure what I might be looking for, made a dash for the van.

I dove behind it, first trying the driver's side door. Locked. As was the passenger side. With one last glance at the kitchen door—still shut tight as a drum—I tippy-toed around to the other side and jiggled the silver handle at the back of the van.

Ah ha! Apparently it was a little hard to lock a door while juggling a metal dolly and a three tiered wedding cake.

Feeling rather proud of my self, I turned the handle.

But I never got a chance to see what was inside.

Before I even realized what was happening, pain exploded at the side of my head, a loud crack echoing through the air as the landscape danced in nauseating circles before my eyes.

CHAPTER TWENTY

———

My head instantly throbbed as I struggled to keep the black fuzzing at the corners of my vision from taking over.

I spun around to find Anne standing behind me, something flat, dark, and menacing looking in her hands. What the hell was that thing? I squinted, trying to blink away the pain gnawing at my every nerve ending as I focused on it. Had she hit me with a cookie sheet?

I didn't have time to find out as she swung the heavy metal square at me again. This time I ducked, instinctively diving to the right, and took off at a sprint in the other direction.

Anne dropped the pan to the ground with a clang and took off after me. Luckily, thanks to Dana's gym regimen, I had a good head start, diving into the first white tent I saw.

Which was apparently set for my reception dinner as empty chafing dishes and piles of silverware graced the linen clad tables. Red linen. With a big white hibiscus print on it. Then again, what did I expect hiring a flamboyant hairdresser as a wedding coordinator?

But I didn't have time to linger on Marco's tropical travesty décor further, as footsteps pounded behind me.

"There's nowhere to run," Anne yelled, pushing the flap back on the tent. "I know you're in here."

I grabbed the nearest thing I could find— a shiny silver chaffing dish—and spun around, whacking her square in the face.

I heard a crunch and a grunting sound as she staggered backward.

"Bitch! My nose!" she yelled, hands going to her face where I could see red liquid gushing between her fingers.

I fought back a wave of nausea and turned to run.

Unfortunately, Anne recovered quickly. I only got a couple of steps away before I felt her grab a handful of hair, yanking sharply.

"Uhn." I cried out as my body followed my hair, stumbling backward on my heels. She whipped me around, throwing me toward a group of tables and chairs, where I landed with a thud, taking three place settings down to the ground with me.

I shook the stars out of my eyes to see her lunging again. I rolled to the right, quickly scrambling onto my hands and knees, crawling out of her reach.

Well, almost out of her reach. Damn those long willowy arms of hers.

A hand shot out and locked onto my ankle. I twisted right then left, kicking at her with my free leg as my eyes scanned the ground for a possible weapon. Spoon, napkin, butter knife. Shit, I knew we should have ordered steak.

Then I spied an orange plastic cooler with an Anaheim Angels sticker on the side stuck under the buffet table a foot away.

I clawed my way forward, my fingers digging into the soft grass. A couple more inches, one more…finally my fingers connected and I ripped the lid off the cooler, tossing it backward. It collided with Anne's forehead with a satisfying thud.

"Ow! Bitch," she spat out.

But she didn't let go. I leaned forward, shoving my hand in the cooler and coming out with...a frozen tamale?

Without thinking, I threw it behind me too, hearing another thunk answer back. I grabbed another and another, chucking them behind me rapid fire.

"What the hell are you throwing at me? Burritos?" she screamed. Her grip loosened on my ankle just enough for me to wiggled free.

I leapt to my feet (Wow, those step classes were *really* working. I'd never leapt to anything before.) and took off at a dead run for the back of the tent. I heard Anne following suit a step behind me. As I burst through the flaps I paused only a second to get my bearings. The hotel was dead ahead of me. But, since Mom had booked the largest garden in L.A. County for my "small and intimate" wedding, it was a full football field away. Or at least it seemed that far as I ran for my life toward the safety of lights, people, and snooty concierges.

I got as far as my tropical-flower laden altar when I felt a sharp shove between my shoulder blades, propelling me forward with a jerk. My arms flailed as I went down, grasping for anything to hold on to. I caught a vine. A big one. Only, as I hit the ground, it came with me, pulling the entire altar to the right. I watched in slow motion horror as the white lattice gazebo tilted, then creaked, then fell forward, collapsing down on both Anne and me as she struggled to get a hold on my hair again.

Luckily, Anne took the brunt of it, her eyes rolling up into her head, momentarily stunned. I wriggled out from underneath her as she struggled to lift the heavy beams off her legs. I rolled to the left, just as she freed herself and rolled right. Both of us coming up on opposite sides of the mangled structure. Only her side was closer to the hotel. Damn.

We stood there in a sort of standoff, our breath coming hard, knees bent, ready to bolt either way should the other lunge first.

"You killed Gigi," I said, trying to distract her. If I could inch to the right just a couple steps, I thought I could make a break for it.

Anne grinned, showing off a row of white teeth that looked eerily like the Cheshire cat in the sparse moonlight. "And here I thought you were just some dumb blonde."

I narrowed my eyes. "No, you're just some psycho brunette."

She laughed, a high-pitched kind of cackle that held more menace than humor. And I realized my insult wasn't too far off the mark. There really was something seriously wrong with this chick. I should have known. I mean, really, what normal person doesn't like chocolate?

"Where is Allie?" I asked, watching her eyes dart to the left, then right, as if looking for a way to get the jump on me.

"Wouldn't you like to know, Miss Nosey? You know, everything was going fine until you showed up."

"Yeah, I get that a lot," I mumbled. "Does he have her?" I asked.

Anne's eyes clouded for a moment, then narrowed. "Oh, you know about him, then, do you?"

I nodded. "No way did I think you were smart enough to pull this off on your own."

I know, maybe not the brightest plan to piss off the psycho. But the longer I could keep her talking, the greater the chance some hotel employee would see the standoff in the wedding garden.

"Shows how much you know!" she shouted. I glanced toward the hotel. Sadly, we were too far away for anyone to hear us.

"How so?" I stalled.

"Allie was my idea!"

Aha. Now we were getting somewhere.

"So, you did kidnap her?"

"Of course."

"And kill Gigi."

"That old cow. She looked right through me. I was happy to see her gone. It was so simple. I just showed up at her studio, told her that my uncle had forgotten something for the samples and, when her back was turned, hit her with a cake knife."

I fought down a wave of sickness, remembering the scene. "But it wasn't your idea to kill her, was it?" I asked, treading carefully.

Anne faltered. Then shook her head. "No. I did it for him. I love him. I'd do anything for him."

Geeze, I loved my family too, but no way was I offing my Uncle Mickey's ex-girlfriend in Boca.

"But why Allie?" I asked. I glanced back toward the hotel, again. I could see a group of businessmen in suits drinking scotch on the back patio. Could they see us in the dark out here?

"Because he found out she was Gigi's daughter!" Anne shouted. "Duh!"

And I'd been the one to give Anne this bit of information. I mentally kicked myself. I so owed Allie after this. If there *was* an after this, I decided, seeing the way Anne's eyes had taken on a crazed look talking about her beloved uncle.

"And now your uncle has her?" I asked.

Anne cocked her head to the side. But instead of answering right away, a crooked smile took over her face. There went that Cheshire cat look again. "You really have no idea where she is, do you?" she asked.

I paused. "Uh, sure I do."

But, as Ramirez had pointed out many a time, I was a terrible liar. And Anne didn't buy that for a minute. Instead, she jumped right at me, lunging over the altar debris and hitting me square in the chest, knocking us both backwards into a row of folding chairs. They toppled over with a domino effect that rippled on for three whole rows, taking the delicate ribbon and floral edging with it.

Her hands went around my throat, instantly cutting off my air supply. I clawed at her fingers, kicking my knee upward to catch her in the gut. Her grip loosened as the wind went out of her. I rolled sharply to the left, knocking into the little white table that held the guest book. It went flying, landing in the flowerbeds. Anne grabbed a handful of my hair and thunked my head against the hard earth.

"Uhn." I tried to ignore the lump I was sure I'd have tomorrow, clawing at her face with my free hand.

She jerked out of the way, rolling us to the left, knocking into a glass terrarium full of monarch butterflies. I grabbed a handful of her hair, and we went right, taking down a table full of wine bottles and little bubble blowers. I winced. Marco was going to kill me.

That is, if I ever got out alive.

Anne's hands went around my throat again as she rolled me up against a palm tree, the little white lights hot against my back. I felt her fingers squeeze until gurgling sounds erupted from the back of my throat. I twisted right and left, turning my head side to side, but it was no use. For a stick figure, she was freakishly strong. And she had me completely pinned. I felt my limbs going heavy, fog starting to fill my head, my vision fuzzing at the edges.

This was it. And my first irrational thought as the wave of unending dizziness swept over me was that I never got to be a wife. Ever since we'd gotten engaged, all this wedding stuff had taken on a life of its own. I'd forgotten that it was really all just the means to an end. An end where I'd fall asleep in Ramirez's arms every night. Where I'd wake up every morning to the sound of his shower and the smell of freshly brewed coffee. Where we'd sit on the sofa and watch movies without worrying about which one of us had to drive home in an hour for an early morning. Where I knew that no matter how horrible my bed-head was in the morning, he'd still love me anyway. Where no matter how many cases took him away in the middle of the night, I knew he'd always come home to me. Our home. Where one day we'd start a family, watch it grow, and hold hands on the front porch as we turned into old, wrinkly, prunes who only had eyes for each other.

That was the part I wanted. That was the part I'd said yes to in Paris. And I was damned if some skinny homicidal freak was going to rob me of it.

As I felt my vision fade, my fingers grasped along the ground for anything I could use as a weapon. Just as my head felt like it was about to explode, my fingers wrapped around something long and smooth. I swung wildly in front of me, and felt the pressure on my throat release as a wine bottle collided with the side of Anne's head.

She fell off me, rolling to her hands and knees as I dragged in deep, painful breaths of air. But I didn't care—nothing had ever felt so good.

Anne stood up, shaking bits of green glass from her hair. And grabbed another discarded bottle, swinging it my way. "Bitch!" she yelled.

I ducked just in time, scrambling up off the ground and diving behind one of the giant tiki heads. She was a step behind me, the wine bottle slicing menacingly through the air.

I ducked down and shoved at the tiki head with all my might. It wiggled a little. I threw my shoulder into it, and shoved like my life depended on it. Which, if the crazed look in Anne's eyes was any indication, it did.

The tiki head tilted forward, slowly leaning on one edge. I shoved one more time and felt it tip forward. I heard Anne scream, and then the sickening crunch of the tiki landing on top of her, pinning her body to the ground.

And apparently Anne wasn't the only thing it hit. Because within seconds, hundreds of tiny, winged butterflies filled the air, fluttering up into the night sky.

I watched them, panting as I crumpled to the ground, my legs giving out entirely. Marco was right. They really were kind of spectacular.

* * *

Fifteen minutes later the air was filled with the sound of sirens, my perfect shambles of a wedding site bathed in flashing blue and red lights, crime scene tape holding back a mob of curious hotel patrons that *now* couldn't seem to keep their eyes off the garden. (Where had they been half an hour ago?)

I was seated in the last row of what was supposed to be my wedding venue watching paramedics try to pry Anne's screaming, swearing form from beneath a giant tiki head as I fielded questions from a very confused rookie cop in a starched blue uniform.

"So, you followed your caterer here?"

"Yes."

"And she attacked you?"

"Yes."

"Because she killed your wedding planner?"

"Yes."

"And you pinned her with a giant tiki head."

"That about sums it up."

He gave me a funny look, then jotted something down in his notebook. Probably a note to self never to get married.

"Maddie!"

I looked up to find my entire wedding party running toward me. Mom, Faux Dad, Larry, the Ramirezes and everyone else, all jogged across the lawn toward the flashing lights. (Well, most of them jogged. Mrs. Rosenblatt mostly waddled.) But the man leading the pack was the only one I noticed. Ramirez.

Shoving the uniformed cop aside, I fairly leapt into his arms as he ducked through the crime scene tape.

"Are you okay?" he asked, his arms instantly around me.

For a moment I couldn't respond, my throat clogged with emotion. "Yeah," I finally squeezed out.

He pulled back, running an assessing look over my person. A few cuts, bumps, a nasty bruise forming on my neck. And I could feel a hell of a headache brewing. But I was essentially okay.

Once he finished looking me over, he glanced around the scene I'd created. "Wow, when you stay out of trouble, you really do it with style."

I couldn't help a smile. "Thanks."

"I'm not sure that was a compliment."

"I know."

He grinned down at me. Then he gestured to Anne. "So, she killed Gigi?" he asked.

I felt the corners of my mouth heading north, my spine straightening. "Yes. I got a full confession. She also kidnapped Allie."

"Wow."

"Guess this means I win, huh?"

Ramirez looked down at what I was sure was the biggest shit eating grin ever pasted on my face. His eyes crinkled at the corner, his own lips twitching.

"Damn. I guess it does. All right, you win, Springer. You're a kickass detective."

Have I mentioned how much I love this man?

I wrapped my arms around his neck, kissing him square on the lips. I might have even used a little tongue had the entire L.A.P.D. not been watching (not to mention my mother), but as it was, I restrained myself.

"Maddie, honey!" Mom and the gang finally broke through the police barrier, enveloping me in a series of group hugs that I was sure were going to leave bruises tomorrow. Everyone was talking at once, Mom alternating between jaw-dropping awe and tears, Dana doing a series of "ohmigod"s and Marco eyeing the cute paramedic with an earring. Finally Ramirez corralled them all into one of the reception tents and sat me down alone.

"So," he said, going into cop mode, "tell me exactly what Anne said to you."

So, I did, relaying the entire story. "She said she did it because she loved him," I finished.

"That makes sense," he said, his eyes doing a slow survey of the scene. "My captain picked him up an hour ago."

I froze. "He did?"

Ramirez nodded. "We suspected him from the beginning. When we learned why Gigi visited her attorney, it sealed it. Only problem was, with the airtight alibi, we knew he must be working with an accomplice."

"Her attorney talked to you?" I asked, dismayed. And here I thought we got on so well with Kaufman.

Ramirez grinned at me. "A warrant helps. Hey, you wouldn't happen to know anything about a blonde in heels who had him draw up a prenup, would you?"

Guilt heated my cheeks. "Nope."

"Hmm," he said. "Yeah, I didn't think so."

"So, uh, anyway," I said, clearing my throat. "After you arrested him, did he tell you where Allie was?"

He shook his head. "No. He swore he didn't know. But I have a feeling Anne may be a little more forthcoming." He gestured to the woman, still squirming and shouting curses as the tiki was lifted from her right leg. I winced, looking away. The way that leg was bent was definitely not natural.

"I don't know," I said. "I'm not sure she'll talk. She seems pretty devoted to her uncle."

"Her uncle?" Ramirez gave me a funny look.

I nodded. "Yeah, Fauston. He's the one who told her to kill Gigi."

Suddenly the mammoth grin that I'd been doing ever since Ramirez conceded defeat was on the other face. His eyes twinkled down at me. "Honey," he started.

Uh-oh. I'd gone from crack detective to honey. This did not sound good.

"We didn't pick up Fauston," he continued. "We arrested Gigi's ex. Seth Summerville."

"Summerville?" I felt my jaw drop open. So much for my big gloating win.

Ramirez nodded. "After talking with her attorney, we learned that Summerville and Gigi had never actually finalized their divorce. Gigi was still hung up on him and had stalled the proceedings. That is, until Spike proposed to her. She called her attorney to have papers drawn up to dissolve the marriage with Summerville right away."

"So she was going to say yes to Spike?" I made a mental note to tell him. While nothing would bring his girlfriend back, I had a feeling it would help.

"It would seem," Ramirez went on. "Only Summerville wasn't happy about it. See, his company was in trouble. Big time. He'd over-invested, and with the real estate market in a slump, he'd gotten in over his head. He was on the verge of bankruptcy and losing everything. But, as long as he was married to Gigi, he could still borrow against her business."

"Which was thriving. Only once they divorced, there went his cash cow," I added.

Ramirez nodded. "Exactly. So, he came up with an even more lucrative idea. Kill Gigi and inherit her entire estate. He'd been carrying on an affair with Anne ever since she'd started delivering cookies to his building, back when he and Gigi were still together. He promised Anne he'd finally be free to marry her if she killed Gigi for him."

The puzzle pieces were rapidly falling into place. "Only he wasn't the one to inherit. Her daughter was. He really hadn't known about Allie."

"No. Not until you told him."

I winced. Geeze, had I tipped everyone off? That was it, I owed Allie free pedicures for life.

"So, they kidnapped her?"

Ramirez nodded. "When Summerville found out he wasn't inheriting, he said he couldn't marry Anne after all. She got desperate. The plan was to force Allie to sign a will leaving everything to Summerville, then kill her."

I bit my lip. "Did she?"

Ramirez shrugged. "Like I said, Summerville swore he didn't know where she was. The kidnapping was all Anne's doing."

I looked over at Anne, resisting the urge to go kick her broken leg until she gave it up.

Beyond her, I saw a figure in khakis and a white button-down jogging toward us from the parking lot, his mussed hair floating around his flushed ears.

Ramirez followed my line of vision. "Is that who I think it is?" he asked, his eyes narrowing.

I punched him in the arm. "Don't start."

Considering I'd already crushed one person that night, he complied. Smart man.

Completely ignoring the crime scene tape, Felix came at us, almost as out of breath as I'd been a few minutes ago.

"Maddie, you okay?"

"She's fine," Ramirez answered for me, wrapping a possessive arm around my shoulders.

Oh, brother.

Luckily Felix either didn't notice or had perfected his ignoring Ramirez technique. "Any sign of Allie?" he breathed.

I shook my head.

His entire body immediately went slack, the hope draining out of him as he slumped into a wooden chair. "What happened here?"

I took a deep breath, trying to rewind to the beginning of the evening again.

"Well, after I went back to the bakery, I saw Anne leaving. I followed her from the bakery to here, where she put my wedding cake in the kitchen. Then I had the idea to check out her van. Only I didn't get a chance because just as I was opening the door she whacked me on the back of the head with a cookie sheet…"

I trailed off. And felt my eyes grow big as it hit me.

It must have occurred to Felix at the same time as he sat bolt upright. "The van!"

He jumped from his seat, toppling over the chair, and took off for the bakery van at a full-on sprint. Ramirez and I followed a step behind, covering the expanse of lawn to the back parking lot.

Fauston's van was still in the same place it had been, sitting three spaces from the front of the building. Felix hit it first (who knew Tabloid Boy could run so fast?) and fairly ripped the back door off in his vigor to open it. I closed in a few steps behind Ramirez, my right side cramped from way too much exertion in way too short a time span. That's it, after this I was permanently off exercise.

I strained to see around Ramirez's broad shoulders, pushing in front of him.

Then froze.

There, sitting in the back of the van, amongst pink boxes of peanut butter cookies and chocolate fudge squares, her feet bound, her mouth covered with duct tape, sat Allie.

CHAPTER TWENTY-ONE

———

Felix jumped into the van and started tearing at her bindings before Ramirez could stop him. Not that I'm entirely sure anything could have stopped him at that point. I'd never seen cool, collected Felix so frantic before. Allie winced as he ripped the duct tape off her mouth in one Band-Aid-like motion, but as soon as her hands were free, she threw both arms around his neck and buried her face in his shoulder, tears flowing like they'd never stop.

Felix carried her out of the van as Ramirez hailed a paramedic team over. After a thorough head to toe, they said she was a little dehydrated, and the cut on her head where Anne had knocked her out in her apartment needed a couple stitches, but she was basically okay. Physically, that was. Mentally, I had a feeling it would be awhile before Allie looked at cookies the same way again.

It was a good two hours later before the last of our wedding party was bundled into their cars and the police officers had finished their interviews, clearing Allie and me to go home. Felix insisted on taking Allie home with him so he could keep an eye on her overnight.

"But," he assured me as he bundled her into his Neon, "she can sleep in the guest room. No funny business, I swear."

I grinned. "Hey, your funny business is your business, Felix."

He nodded, that odd emotion flitting behind his eyes again. "Yes, I suppose it is."

I gave him a wave and turned to go.

"Maddie?" he called.

"Yeah?" I spun back around to face him again.

"Happy Valentine's Day."

I looked down at my watch. 12:03. I guess it was technically Valentine's Day, wasn't it?

"Thanks," I said. Then looked over his shoulder to where Allie sat waiting for him. "Happy Valentine's Day to you, too, Felix."

"Thanks. Oh, and by the way," he said, a mischievous grin spreading across his face. "She's twenty-*five*."

I couldn't help the answering tug at my lips. "Well, I guess that makes it all okay then."

He didn't answer right away, instead giving me a long look that I wouldn't dare to try to interpret. Then finally just said, "Goodbye, Maddie," and walked away. He slid into the driver's seat of his car, pulling out of the parking lot.

I watched his taillights disappear around the corner, trying to ignore the little empty spot in the pit of my stomach.

"Hey." I felt Ramirez's warm hands rest on my shoulders.

"Hey." I leaned back against his chest. It was warm and solid, and I suddenly realized how exhausted I was.

His arms went around me. "You ready to go home?"

I nodded, then turned around and looked into his face. It was the first time I'd really stopped to get a good look at him in days. His eyes were tired, drooping a little at the corners, their tiny laugh lines more pronounced. His jaw was dusted with a fine sprinkling of stubble, and I wondered when the last time was that he'd actually slept.

"Happy Valentine's Day," I said.

He smiled down at me. "Happy *wedding* day."

Oh, hell.

With all that had happened, I'd almost forgotten that we were supposed to be man and wife in just hours. I waited for those pesky panic hiccups to hit at the thought. Oddly enough, in Ramirez's warm grasp, they didn't. Huh. I guess maybe being chased around by a homicidal maniac had scared them out of me for good. Go figure.

Though, as I looked around at my shambles of a wedding site, I felt my heart sink.

"There's no way we can get married here today," I said.

Ramirez frowned. "It is kind of a crime scene now, isn't it?"

I shook my head, watching uniformed officers tromp up and down my red, carpeted aisle. "The tamales are melting all over the reception tent, the guest book's in the mud, the flowers are trampled, the altar's wrecked, the butterflies are gone and the tiki head has blood on it!"

Ramirez chuckled. Actually chuckled.

I narrowed my eyes at him. "You find our ruined wedding funny?"

"Who me?" Though he valued his life enough to stop laughing. "No way."

"Everything is wrecked."

He wrapped his arms around me again. "Well, not everything."

I cocked my head at him. "Meaning?"

"I wanna show you something." He took my hand and led me out into the parking lot where he opened the back of his SUV. He pulled out a plain brown shoebox and handed it to me.

"Your shoes."

I hesitated. On top of the day I'd just had, I wasn't sure I could take another disaster. Especially if I had to wear it.

But the way he was watching me, like a little kid waiting for Christmas, I sucked it up and opened the lid anyway.

"Eeeeeeee!"

I'm not certain, but I'm pretty sure that girly squeal came from me. Because inside, nestled between folds of delicate white tissue paper, were the most beautiful pair of shoes I had ever laid eyes on in my life. They were white satin with a two-inch heel that did a delicate inward curve to a perfect point. Tiny white beads had been sewn along the edge in an intricate pattern, trailing down the back of the shoe like a cascading waterfall. They were my dream shoes to a tee. I slipped one on. It fit perfectly, like it had been molded exactly to my foot.

I felt tears back up behind my eyes, and I threw my arms round Ramirez's neck.

"How did you…?"

He grinned. "Okay, I'll admit, I cheated a little."

"Well, duh!"

His smile widened. "You were right. Designing shoes is not easy. My attempt looked like they belonged on an elf. A deformed one. So, I found an old sketchbook of yours and kinda stole one of your designs."

"Thief. I thought they looked familiar."

"Forgive me?"

I looked down at my feet. "Are you kidding? How could I not?"

I reached up and planted a kiss on his lips. Which he heartily returned, his hands gliding down to my hips, pulling my body tight against his until I feared someone might shout, "Get a room!"

When we finally came up for air, Ramirez pulled back and looked me in the eyes. "I promise that as soon as we can get this whole mess cleaned up, we'll try again. We'll plan the most beautiful wedding you ever saw. Together. I promise you'll get your perfect day."

I loved the man, no doubt about it.

And I realized as I melted into his arms that I couldn't wait for the perfect day. Any day that we were together would be perfect in my book.

"I have an even better idea," I said.

He raised an eyebrow.

"How would you feel about a little trip to Vegas?"

He grinned. All the way from his crooked smile to his wicked chocolate eyes.

"Honey, anything that gets us to that honeymoon sooner works for me."

* * *

The first thing I did was call Dana and tell her to cancel the makeup and hair appointments. The wedding was off. To which she wailed out a long, "Noooooo!" before I could tell her the marriage was definitely still on, we were just eloping. Then she did a squeal so high pitched I was pretty sure she woke up every dog in L.A. County. Of course I should have known that she'd immediately call Marco, who called Faux Dad, who told Mom, who called Mrs. Rosenblatt and Larry, who then called Mama Ramirez who probably put an ad out in the *Times* because by the time Ramirez and I made it to the gate at LAX for our 3 a.m. flight to Vegas we were eloping with a party of twenty.

I shrugged. At least it was a "small, intimate" elopement.

Two hours, one flight, and seven hotel rooms later, we were all crammed into the Little Chapel of Love on Las Vegas Blvd. waiting for the Elvis-impersonating minister to make it official.

I'd changed into my wedding dress (hey, just because I was eloping didn't mean I couldn't do it in style) and Ramirez was wearing the billowy white *guayabera* over his tuxedo pants. Which, actually now that I saw the whole effect, was kind of nice. Casual chic even. I had to admit, it suited him a lot better than formal tux tails would have anyway.

As Elvis asked if we promised to "love each other tender" and "don't be cruel" to one another, my eyes swept over our little wedding party. Mom and Faux Dad sat in the first row of the chapel, holding hands, both of them getting a little misty-eyed. Though I had a feeling part of that was due to the fact that Larry and Mom had shown up in the exact same chiffon mother of the bride dresses. Sadly enough, Larry had accessorized it better.

Madonna sat next to Larry, Marco on her other side giving her the moon eyes. Behind him, Dana had her head on Ricky's shoulder, mumbling the words, "So romantic," every few seconds. Mama Ramirez, the aunts, and BillyJo sat beside her, all dabbing at their eyes with handkerchiefs. Mrs. Rosenblatt was blowing her nose loudly into hers.

"Do you, Maddison Louise Springer, take this man as your hunka hunka burning love, to hold tight and be true until you both go to that big 'ol heartbreak hotel in the sky?" Elvis asked me.

I looked up at Ramirez. I could tell he was trying really hard not to laugh. His dark eyes crinkled just a little at the corners, his lips twisting upward. But as I stared up into his eyes, I could see something else there, too. Something that promised years of laughter. Of friendship and respect, of being challenged at every turn and growing into a better person for it. Of hot stolen moments in the dark, and long, lazy mornings in bed. Of always knowing someone's got your back no matter what kind of trouble finds you.

And I'd never been so sure of any answer in my life.

"I do."

ABOUT THE AUTHOR

Gemma Halliday is the *New York Times* and *USA Today* bestselling author of the *High Heels Mysteries*, the *Hollywood Headlines Mysteries,* and the *Deadly Cool* series of young adult books. Gemma's books have received numerous awards, including a Golden Heart, a National Reader's Choice award, and three RITA nominations. She currently lives in the San Francisco Bay Area where she is hard at work on several new projects.

To learn more about Gemma, visit her online at www.GemmaHalliday.com

Made in the USA
San Bernardino, CA
13 March 2017